MW01265643

To Steve -

Ken Oca

Chalk

by

Kenneth Orr

Bloomington, IN Milton Keynes, UK

authorHOUSE

AuthorHouse™
1663 Liberty Drive, Suite 200
Bloomington, IN 47403
www.authorhouse.com
Phone: 1-800-839-8640

AuthorHouse™ UK Ltd.
500 Avebury Boulevard
Central Milton Keynes, MK9 2BE
www.authorhouse.co.uk
Phone: 08001974150

First published by AuthorHouse 11/9/2006

ISBN: 1-4259-3434-X (sc)

Printed in the United States of America
Bloomington, Indiana

This book is printed on acid-free paper.

INTRODUCTION

Chalk Goodwin is a fictional character. But really, he did exist in many forms and in the times and places outlined in this book. In the years after the American Civil War people everywhere were struggling to find a better life and to change the economy to a better level for everyone.

Slavery was now illegal, but it was still everyday reality with the everyday life of the poor and minority population. People who had any means were anxious to move forward with their lives and they formed the mass migration that surged westward. The plentiful and rich land west of the Mississippi river was calling and those that listened could not refuse the invitation.

Chalk and many more like were the typical Americans who moved to the west and helped build the images we all hear so much about today. America was growing and the visions formed in the dreams and hopes of many were fulfilled beyond their wildest expectations. Horses, wagons, dirt roads and human muscle power fueled this migration. Life was not easy but it was still better than what they came from.

This story is divided into four parts. Each part is concerned with a major segment of Chalk's life and how he met his everyday activities head on. The first part describes his home and life in Kentucky and how he grew into a young man. The second part outlines his life in rural Texas and what happened to get him from a young man into the ranks of a full adult and family man. Part three covers his business and growing family. Part four outlines how he and a lot more like him served out country. Each part is distinctive yet they all are one continuous story.

I know for certain that many of the events included actually happened. My father grew up in this era and he told me about many of the conditions and problems that everyone experienced. He was a blacksmith and his daily contact with reality was both interesting and accurate. I hope you enjoy this book.

Ken Orr

In A Time Before Ours

A Western Novel that tells it
Like it was,
And more

Book 1 of 4

Kenneth Orr

CHAPTER 1
The Beginning Experience

Chalk Goodwin was born in 1863 in rural Harlan County Kentucky. His family was living in an Appalachian coal mining community where everything was structured around coal and the supporting operations for mines. They were as poor as sick sin.

Chalk's mom, Irene, was a full-blooded Cherokee Indian and his father, Jacob, was an unskilled Englishman. He had come to America as a young boy to find a better life. Jacob met Irene in a coal mining camp. She was the cook and after a short and tedious engagement, they were married. Irene had come to Kentucky from North Carolina looking for a better opportunity in life. The Indian community was looked down on in North Carolina, as they were never given any work or considerations beyond being servants.

Jacob was a part time coal miner, part time carpenter and a part time moon shiner. He was from somewhere in England and was part of a group that had originated in the town of Birmingham. Jacob had worked in a small steel mill there and was never happy with his job. His family had fallen apart when he was a young boy and America seemed like a better place to find a good job.

Irene was a typical homemaker of the era and spent most of her time making clothes, cooking, raising a garden, canning, keeping health matters attended to and most of all, trying to keep peace in the family. She suffered the abuses of a husband who was once a calm man but over time became abusive, violent, and unpredictable. Making whiskey became his main goal in life and he drank about as much as he made.

Their house was a small mountainside shack built on the side of a wagon road. It was so poorly built that keeping it warm in the winter was near impossible. The only good thing about the living situation was the fact that the land and shack were paid for.

Chalk was born about three years after Jacob and Irene were married. His birth was attended by a neighbor lady who was known to be the only local mid-wife. Chalk was an only child and was a great joy to his mother. Jacob was never home enough to become close to Chalk and his mother gave him what little education he received.

When Chalk was born his Dad gave him his name, Chalk. He named him after the hard white limestone he had to dig in the mine to get to the coal vein. He always said that the white limestone was tough and he wanted his son to be just like a hard rock. Chalk was dark skinned from his Mother's side of the family and his hair grew in as black as coal. His facial features were more like his mother than his dad.

Irene was experienced in many of the life supporting skills and handicrafts associated with the native Indians. She could clean and cook wild game, make clothes from animal skins and perform simple medical tasks to heal common wounds. She was often called upon to come to some miner's home and take care of sick people.

She also, on occasion, would wear her Indian style clothing and show the personal pride she always maintained in being from an Cherokee Indian background. Chalk saw her as both a mom and a lady that stood for something. He really never saw his dad as being of much value as he was drunk a lot and when he was sober, he was never home.

Irene made clothing for Chalk to wear that was fashioned in the Indian traditions and he often would wear them with pride. She also made more traditional Kentucky schoolboy clothes that he wore everyday.

On Saturdays Chalk and his Mom would often put on their Indian style clothing and go to town for supplies. That is when there was money. The local people all knew them as good people and Chalk was popular with the local children.

He was never bashful and easily made friends. The local women liked his mother and often asked her for cooking tips and Indian food recipes. She was always a sharing Lady and everyone was always glad to see her.

Her husband, Jacob, was not liked, but he was a good local source for whiskey. His sidekick, "Panther Maggard" had a whiskey still hid in an old coalmine. The smell of cooking corn mash was disguised by a cattle barn's smell. The barnyard was next to the old mine entrance. Panther was a skinny man and had a lot of people willing to shoot him. He was crooked and everybody knew it.

Whiskey was considered as the cause of many family problems and the local minister often called it a tool of the Devil. He would scream and yell as he gave his Sunday sermons and tell everyone they were not going to go to heaven if they drank whiskey. Hell, he screamed, was a horrible place and fire and brimstone would be everywhere. His congregation was often scolded and told they were not paying enough attention to the Lord.

Every Sunday was an experience unlike the last. The local social circle revolved around the church. The Preacher's weekly stories and topics were frequently discussed, especially by the women, for the next week.

Jacob had never attended church but his name was known to all of the wives who had husbands that drank. Jacob had his own crowd of friends, mostly coal mining men, and they would play cards, drink, and in general, just raise hell on the weekends. Panther was Jacob's best buddy.

In 1870 Jacob was arrested for being involved in a bar room fight where several men were killed. Panther had a brother who was the local Peace Officer. His name was Harlan Maggard. Harlan never liked Jacob because they had fought him a few years earlier and broke his nose. Harlan's nose never grew back straight and he always said he would get even some day.

It was a common practice for all of the men to carry guns and to gather at local hangouts after working in the mines. They would drink and visit and when they were done, go home. On one such evening a fight broke out and a man was killed. No one person was ever given the specific blame for the killings but Jacob and three others were sent to prison. Jacob never returned or was never heard from again. Panther was not in the group when the fight happened. He was in jail for something else, probably sobering up. Chalk and Irene were for all purposes, left on their own.

Chalk was eager to learn. There was little to do in the eastern Kentucky hills except to work in the mines or cut timber. He became interested in the work at the coalmines and started hanging around in the same mine where his Dad had worked. He was too young to go into the mines and dig but the owner of the mine took him to heart. He gave Chalk the task of handling the mules and horses that were used to pull the wagons and coal carts into and out of the mine. The work was hard at first as Chalk was still a small young man and big horses were strong and often hard to manage. Over time he learned what to do and the best way to do it and the work became easier. For Chalk, it was actually a lot of fun.

Mules were commonly used for many tasks. They were strong and would make the job of mining easier on the men. Mules were also known to be stubborn and independent. To handle a mule one had to understand their stubborn ways and keep the animal aware that **you**, not them were the real boss. Chalk mastered this skill and the mules that were assigned to him were normally good working animals. He had a big 2 X 4 club that he would lay across their rear-end when they got out of line. They all feared this piece of lumber.

The mine owner, Mr. Clay, had a son who was about the same age as Chalk. They became close buddies. They both worked with the mine animals and ran around together. His name was Bill. He was thin, had black hair and a lot of bad teeth. His clothes were always dirty from coal dust but he was still Chalk's friend.

Bill also had a lot of skill in the outdoors. Bill owned a single shot rifle and together, he and Chalk would hunt small game in the woods. They would share the same gun. Over time both became excellent shots and could regularly hit a small target at a long distance.

Chalk wanted to buy a similar rifle but had so little money that it just was not going to happen. What little money he made was always taken home and turned over to Irene. She needed it to keep food on the table and the bills paid.

After about a year, at the Christmas season, Bill's Dad recognized the fun the two boys were having in hunting and knew that they were very close friends. He called Bill aside one day and told him he had a surprise. When Bill asked, what is it, he showed him two new 22 rifles. There were two boxes of shells next to the rifles. He told him one was for Bill and the other one was for Chalk. He wanted the gift to Chalk to come from Bill, not himself.

They carefully wrapped the new rifle in a blanket and put it next to where Bill normally kept his old rifle. The next time the boys came to get the rifle and go hunting, Bill surprised Chalk. He showed him his new rifle. He saw the joy in Chalk's smile and knew he was feeling a little left out. Bill then gave Chalk the second rifle just like his. The boxes of 22 bullets made the gift complete.

Bill's Dad saw the boys enjoying the new rifles as he came into the room. He had several additional boxes of ammunition and shared it equally with each. Chalk knew that Bill's Dad was behind the whole deal and he gave him a big hug. Chalk told him this was the nicest that anyone had ever been to him. He thanked both Bill and Mr. Clay and the boys went to try out the new guns. He never forgot that experience and often brought it up as he grew into being a young man.

After the hunting and trying out the new rifles was over Chalk went home and showed his Mom the new gun. She was happy for Chalk and told him that he should always remember that guns were dangerous and should never be used to harm people. He had seen the pain that his Dad had suffered from being in a bad situation with a gun and he understood exactly what his Mother was saying.

Mules are easy to spook. They have little tolerance for strange surroundings, loud noise and other nearby animals. When they were often led into a mine with a sack over their head. Once inside the sack would be removed and the mule would be hooked up to the load they were to pull. Coming out of the mine was not a big problem. The younger mules were not always predictable and would often bolt up and try to run to the light. As they grew older they slowly calmed down and were much more manageable.

Another problem always happened when the men used dynamite to blast a vein of coal. The noise was always loud and it would make the mules nervous and upset. When a blast was being planned, Chalk would take all of the mules to a place outside the mine where the noise was not so loud. That was sometimes two or three times a week. Horses were not as sensitive but they had to be managed the same way. Often a horse would help calm down the mules just by being in their area. Chalk understood animals and some people called it his sixth sense. It was also common to have a couple of dogs in the area. Mules and dogs were always careful about watching each other. This kept their attention on something other than the noises.

The mine owner gave Chalk a newborn colt that was out of one of the mine horses. The colt soon became the center of his focus and the horse was his pride and joy. He swapped work at a local pawnshop for a used saddle and when the horse was grown Chalk had a well-mannered, fine riding animal.

When Chalk's Dad was sent to prison, the Sheriff had given Jacob's pistol to Chalk. He never wore the gun and it was put into a small box with Jacob's other personal items. Everything was put away. Over time it became lost and the gun was never seen again. Irene had sold the gun to a man who worked with Jacob but never told Chalk. Chalk never missed this gun. However, he was happy to have the rifle that Mr. Clay and his friend Bill had given him at Christmas. Guns were to respect and the danger of any gun was always a concern to Chalk.

His mother was pleased to see him doing something that was meaningful and encouraged him to learn everything he could about the care and use of animals. He was paid a very small wage but without it, he and his mother would have been penniless. There were few schools in rural Kentucky and the education a youngster could receive was what was handed down from the people that he was around.

With some difficulty, Chalk learned to read and to do simple arithmetic calculations. He also learned that you had to have some money in your pocket to be respected and how you got it was as important as how much you had.

The black families in the area had no schools and in many ways were still being treated like slaves. Several black men were laborers in the mines and were paid very little. White men always controlled these people sometimes using force. It was not important how hard a black man worked he was always given low pay. This amount of money did little to provide for them or their families. Most families had gardens to raise food. The women would can and dry vegetables to keep food on the table the year round. They also would have a few hogs and a cow to provide milk and butter. The women were almost all good cooks. A meal at any of their tables was always delicious and you never would leave hungry.

The local culture was still had a lot of similarity to the years before when all black people were considered as slaves. Little had changed. Kentucky had been a border state and not everyone practiced slavery. The big towns up along the

Ohio River were less involved but the hills and hollers of Appalachia were a lot more prone to have slaves.

Indians in the area were giving some broader level of respect, but not much. Life was hard and the only thing to look forward to was making it to the next day. Being that Chalk's mother was an Indian a few of the local boys called him a half-breed. His public stature was never given the same respect as a white man. He never let it get to him. He loved his Mother and that meant much more to him that a boy calling him a name.

He began working with the mine's blacksmith who taught him how to make horseshoes and mount them on the mules and horses. By the time he was 12 years old he had learned a trade and had become aware of the hardships associated with hard work and rural mountain life. Irene was his best supporter and encouraged him to look beyond the mines and the mountains to improve himself.

Irene had grown up in a culture where medical services were based completely on the Indian culture. She knew what natural materials such as roots and special tree leaves were a medical help in healing sickness and injuries. She passed a great deal of her knowledge on to Chalk and he learned to use these practices to keep himself, the horses and some of his friends healthy.

On the negative side, he learned that whiskey would relax a person when minor surgery or tooth extraction was required. Sometimes a person wanted a drink and used the excuse that it was to help with a "pain". Chalk sometimes had "pains" and had to resort to the medicine. He also learned that natural honey applied to a burn or to an open wound would help the healing process and would slow infections. The only negative was that the bees and flies would sometimes come to reclaim the honey.

When Chalk turned 13 his mother came down with a sudden sickness and within two weeks she died. Chalk was now on his own. He went to see Panther Maggard, his Dad's old running buddy. One of his brothers had a funeral parlor. His name was "Digger".

Chalk asked if he could get a coffin and bury his Mother out behind the family home. He worked out the cost and got a pine casket for Irene. "Digger" buried Chalk's Mother in a grave he and his helper dug behind their shack. Chalk put a wooden cross with her name on it on her grave.

He went to a local headstone cutter and gave him $20 to make a headstone for his Mom. He promised to make it with her name and the dates she was born and died. He would deliver it and install it as soon as the fresh dirt had settled.

Chalk was more than ready to get away from Hazard, Kentucky and his not so wholesome childhood. Chalk found a buyer for the old house, got the money, paid Digger for his services and put the rest in a small sack. He kept the money on his person as he had learned that money sometimes wipes out old friendships.

Chapter 2
Becoming a Man

Harlan County Kentucky had little to encourage Chalk to stay. He took what few dollars he had gathered and put them in his pocket. He saddled the horse he had raised from birth. He had a set of leather saddlebags in which he put some dried apples and other simple food. He also took his rifle and his homemade clothes his mother had made and started the trip to Lexington. Before he left he went to say good-by to Bill and Mr. Clay. They were his true friends and were the last people in the community to ever see him.

The trip was a whole new experience for Chalk and he enjoyed meeting new people and seeing more of the country. This was the first time in his life that he had been outside of the Hazard, Kentucky area. The trip, on horseback, took about two weeks. He made frequent stops to just see the countryside and often slept in covered areas under a tree.

Lexington, Kentucky was a lot bigger community than where he had grown up. His first feelings were of fear and of the overwhelming size of the town. His first days were spent in a small barn where a friendly horse farm owner told him he could sleep. He saw a lot of big houses. Most of the people who lived in them could read and write. There were also several factories where people worked everyday. Factories were places where there were opportunities to learn and to make money. Most factories had a lot of people working but they were paying really low wages. Most factories were all known to have serious safety problems and for having people hurt while working. The community was growing but was still downtrodden from the aftermath of the recent Civil War years.

There were many small businesses there that had moved there from Cincinnati, Ohio to use the available low cost labor to build farming machinery, wagons and other metal products. The railroad had just come to town and the support required to get it woven into the economy was present in every area of the business community.

There were several small whiskey distilleries located south of Lexington. They where making corn whiskey. Corn whiskey was a standard, in high demand, Kentucky product. All of these businesses used horses and mules to carry the required materials needed to make and market the products.

There were many small farms in the area where corn was a cash crop. The farmers could make more money selling it to the distilleries than they could in feeding hogs. Chalk went to several distilling companies and asked for work in the care and outfitting of their animals.

A 14-year-old boy was not well received, as there was a great surplus in people who had similar skills. This did not discourage Chalk and he soon found a horse farm that gave him a temporary job. He soon ended up at a racehorse farm as a stall cleaner and part time groom. Within a very short time his skills were recognized and he became a valued employee. He also had a good place to sleep in a room at the end of a horse barn, a place to keep his horse and a place at the servant's table to make sure he was getting good food. He loved the work and over a couple of years he became highly respected by the owner. Chalk was soon given additional responsibilities.

The horse farm was breeding and supplying top of the line racehorses to several wealthy farms. They raced them in Lexington and Louisville, Kentucky. Keenland Racetrack was only a few miles away and the horses from this farm's horses were regular winners.

It was 1877 and the railroad had come to much of northern Kentucky. However, rail travel was still not dependable. The farm owner did not trust the railroad for carrying horses to Louisville. The trains were not dependable and the safety of rail travel was still a concern. Engines were blowing up when they were pulling long grades and the brakes were so marginal that run away trains were common.

The racehorse industry was concerned and as a result only used rail services to move horses as a last resort. Good racehorses were just too valuable to risk in a train wreck. Chalk was given the opportunity, several times, to take high valued horses, over land, to Louisville and deliver them to the new owners. He enjoyed the work and did this job often. He used a small covered wagon that was specially built to allow one horse to stand inside. A team of work grade horses was used to pull the wagon. On some occasions the farm would tie a second group of horses to the back of the trailer. The extra horses were used as spares. They often were also sold in Louisville.

He always took his horse with him. On one such trip he had tied his horse up while he was doing business with the people who were buying the horses. When he was done he went to get his horse and it was gone. Someone had stolen his horse, saddle and all. He went back to the people who he had sold the horses to and told them what had happened. They told him this was common and horses were valuable and they were hard to trace. They gave him an old horse they had with them and a used saddle.

On one trip he delivered a horse to an owner in Louisville who was shipping the horse up the Ohio River to his farm in southern Ohio. Riverboat transporting of horses was considered as a safe and common method for the farms that lived near the river.

Most of the developing cities and towns along the major rivers had docks that could be used by riverboats and the local services and facilities were reasonable.

The new racehorse owner approached Chalk and asked him to work as a groom and deliver the high dollar horse. Chalk would need to go on the riverboat and to make sure that the horse was delivered in good shape. This riverboat trip changed Chalk's life forever.

The trip took two days each way. Chalk took his delivery trailer to a local livery stable and asked them to keep it until he returned. He sold them the two spare houses. The horse farm owner back in Lexington was sent a telegraph that the racehorse was being given additional service and all was well. Chalk knew that his employer would approve of this additional service. This gentleman was an important and frequent customer.

When the horse was delivered the owner was very pleased with the condition that he was being maintained and gave Chalk a nice $20 gold coin tip. Chalk got back on the riverboat to make the return trip to Louisville. The Captain of the riverboat noticed how well Chalk had managed the animal and asked him to come to his cabin. Chalk had no idea as to why.

The Captain sat Chalk down, poured himself a stiff drink. He invited Chalk to join him in the refreshments. After a few minutes and some idle talk the Boat Captain told Chalk he wanted to hire him to come aboard as a crewmember. He needed a man to manage the animals he was almost always transporting and to do other work.

The American economy was growing rapidly. The movement of people from the northern communities to the west was creating a massive stream of people traveling to the west. Everyone was anxious to find a new place to live and to find new opportunities that were available out where land was free and the stigma of the Civil War was not a concern.

The riverboat system was a major element in the movement for people to reach destinations where they could go further west. Thousands of people became unhappy with life in the war zone areas where the Civil War had been fought and were heading west to find a new life.

The civil war had made many people loose their fortunes and they were unhappy the life they were being forced to live. This was true in both the North and South. The urges to move west became common in many communities east of the Mississippi River and the stories from the first settlers were a magnet drawing people of all occupations.

The riverboat system had become a favorite approach for moving horses, wagons, tools and emigrants to cities like St. Louis, Memphis, Natchez and other dropping off places where wagon trains were forming and heading to the new western frontiers. This particular riverboat was always busy and the pay was good.

Chalk never went back to Lexington, Kentucky. Upon arrival in Louisville He found a man to drive the horse trailer home and sent his employer's wagon back to Lexington. He also sent a note and thanked his boss for the experience he had allowed him to gain. Chalk told him he had found a new life on the river. He asked him to give his personal belongings to a fellow employee who not well off. He knew he would appreciate these few small things.

Kentucky was a place where people expected to come to town, make enough money to move on and then go to the next part of life. This was an expected part of hiring people. Chalk had gone as far as he wanted working on the horse farm and knew it was the right time move to his next challenge.

Chapter 3
Life as A Young Man

The riverboat was setup to carry cargo, animals and passengers. There were a lot of riverboats running the bigger rivers. All of them used steam power for propulsion and to run other support equipment that some boats carried. Most were set up to have paying passengers and to carry freight. They provided a means of transportation to places where the railroads were not yet serving. The cost on the riverboat was less. River trips were never predictable. The cargo on board might be more people or more freight. Every stop along the river was handled as a new opportunity to make money. People were allowed to board by the room available and cargo was either accepted or rejected by room available and where it was going to be unloaded.

The mixed load of passengers congregated many cross sections of people. Everyone on the boat had just become mobile. River travel was a preferred form of mass transportation. Steam powered boats was still a new innovation on the rivers. The business of river travel was also the beginning of a new adventure for people who were considering moving west. It was the best and least expensive method to carry heavy freight to the growing river cities in the new west.

Older riverboats were used primarily as freight hauling vessels. Newer boats were much more fancy with special, well decorated cabins for the wealthy. There were planned programs for the passengers to attend while in transit. They also had food facilities and liquor for the thirsty.

The riverboat that Chalk had signed on with was somewhere in between being the worst and the best and was generally a dependable vessel. Her name was "The Orleans Belle".

The Captain had been on board the same ship since it was new. He was known to be a good river pilot and had never been involved in any accidents. His boat was predictably dependable.

There were always horses, cows and even pigs being carried as freight. Everyday they require feeding, attention to keep them calm and then every stall had to be cleaned to keep the foul odors and generally undesirable odors down. The animal stalls were located in the rear area and their odors were hopefully behind the boat.

When there was a full load, this job of tending animals was seemingly endless. When there were storms the thunder would spook the animals, the job of keeping them calm was endless. On trips where the load was not so large, Chalk would have free time to do other things and to sleep a little more.

Keeping the feed clean and the rats off the boat was another part of the job. When buying hay at local docks the rats would attempt to come on board. The best cure was a pair of big black tomcats that made quick work of any undesirable creature hiding in the hay or trying to scale the port ladders and mooring ropes.

One of Chalk's favorite pass times during travel was to gamble. The boat was always full of people who were carrying large amounts of money and the thrill of a poker game was always a temptation for many people. The result was an endless collection of professional gamblers who would ride the boats and seek to encourage the other passengers to gamble. This was a common situation and the result was a group of crooks that preyed on everyone, even sometimes, on each other.

Chalk would stand back and watch the poker games in progress. He saw all kinds of tricks and underhanded approaches to cheating. On one night in a small poker game he saw that a player he was standing behind was holding a pair of aces. He drew three cards and got a second pair. They were 6's. The other card was a 5.

Another player on the other side of the table stayed in the game, called the opening pot and drew three cards. The first player made a substantial bet. The second player called his bet. He also raised the bet. He was showing confidence that his hand was a winner.

The first player called his raise. The pot was reasonably large and both players were sure they were winning. The second player laid down his cards and he had three aces and a 4 and a 6. Chalk knew immediately that the second player was cheating. Five aces in one deck…….. no way!

The first player saw the other player's hand and knew that there was a crooked player betting into him. He left his cards face down, stood up, drew his gun and shot him, point- blank, in the chest. The table and the room cleared immediately. The first player calmly picked up all of the money, turned his cards over and walked away. When calm was restored the Captain saw the cards and told Chalk and another crewmember to take the dead man to the livery stalls. When they examined his coat sleeve there was a smooth wristband discovered that was still holding another ace?

It was determined that this man had been cheating for several days and he had taken a lot of money from several other gamblers. They took his money, watch, diamond ring and fancy pistol. The crew then took his body to the rear area of the riverboat. When it got dark the crew threw his body overboard. The Captain put the money and other valuables in a strongbox in his cabin. He had a habit of claiming any item that was involved in crooked gambling.

Navigation on the big rivers was never easy. Going upstream was always more difficult that going downstream. Storms would cause the river to change course and the constant threat of floods and droughts made travel treacherous. In the spring the river flooded regularly and the river traffic had to stop until the water was safe to travel. When the river was flooded the riverboat captains always tried to find a safe mooring place and in a place where the river was calm and anchor before it got dark. The best place to dock was near a town but this was not always possible.

Another part of the trips that made them dangerous was the river pirates. They would wait in safe places along the shore and watch for the boats to pass. They would wait until darkness and then attempt to board the boat. Boats that were moored in less than obvious places were always pirate targets. The Captains knew that these situations were the most dangerous

When it was too dark or too dangerous to travel at night being too far away from a big town was not a good. The Captain would look for a place at the river's edge and out of the main navigation channel and drop anchor. It was a standard practice to place armed guards on watch to prevent boarding from all unwanted people.

This worked most of the time. On two occasions the pirates snuck aboard at mid ship and headed for the gambling room. There, they burst into the area, took all the money, jewelry and whiskey and the traveler's guns. Then they would disappear as quickly as the appeared. On one invasion the three men who had boarded were killed and their bodies were dumped overboard. There with no remorse. The river was an easy way to bury undesirables. The river critters and swift flow always made the body disappear.

Another part of working on the riverboat was the variety of tasks that would be assigned to everyone. The people who cleaned the cabins in the daytime became card dealers, waiters, cooks and bartenders at night. The few crewmembers that had musical talent were often playing the piano and singing in the bar room during the dinner hour.

Chalk was good with simple medicine and would tend sick folks, often using the same approaches that he used with animals. Chalk never claimed to be a Doctor, or a Veterinarian, he just helped sick people and animals. He only did this when there was not a regular doctor on board as a passenger. One such event required that he pull a passenger's tooth. The passenger was given a good dose of whiskey and Chalk got the pliers out. The result was swift, but painful.

Sleep was never a planned time event. Riverboat work required everyone to be available as required. The riverboat schedule always took top priority.

Trips could take a month or more and there was plenty of time to meet other travelers on the boat and to build relationships. Upstream travel was normally slower than going downstream. There were normally fewer people on these trips. Freight was almost always a more common cargo when going upstream.

Many of the travelers, especially on the longer down river trips, were going west and wanted to leave the riverboat at St. Louis. There were regular stops all the way up to Pittsburgh, Pennsylvania and as far south as New Orleans They were local stores in the cities along the Mississippi river where settlers could buy wagons and other travel essentials. It was vital that the wagons had sufficient supplies to make the trip to the far west. Many settlers brought horses and cattle on the riverboat. These animals were to be used in their westward trip and to swap for other items they were going to need. A good milk cow was always in demand. Settlers with young children wanted cows to take with them on the trail.

River boat trips served to bring people together that had common objectives. The relationships formed on the riverboats often led to becoming members of the same wagon trains. In many respects the best parts and traits of everyone were on display when they boarded the boat. Their past, no matter how good or bad and terrible was never discussed. Chalk knew that most of the passengers were not rich but were going somewhere new to find a better life and to start over from failed first life experiences. There was an unwritten code of silence about such discussions.

Chalk was always aware of the great differences in the people on board. Most were traveling as families and these people were always easy to identify. Businessmen were also east to spot. They were more formal to be around and always wanted the best in service. There were also gamblers, saloon women and on some trips, there would be stowaways. The stowaways would come aboard posing as dockhands and merchants who were loading cargo and hide until the boat was underway.

On one trip the boat was docked in Memphis and the cook was loading food and liquor for the next leg of a trip to New Orleans. The loading was complicated as ice and perishable food was being loaded into a locker down in the same area as the livestock stable. The loading was completed and the boat set out for the next leg of the trip. It was near evening and the river was stable and easy to navigate. Chalk went to his small room next to the livestock stable and when he went in there was a young lady setting on the floor trying to hide. He saw her at once and asked her what she was doing there? She was frightened and asked Chalk not to report her, as she was desperate to get away from Memphis. Chalk sat down on the edge of his bunk and asked her to tell him what was going on.

She told him her name was Hilda. She was a white girl and told Chalk that her Uncle was trying to catch her and send her up to Kentucky where her Father was living. She did not want to go as she had run away to escape his beatings and constant stress. She told Chalk that she would do anything he wanted just to stay on board. Chalk told her to calm down and asked her if she was hungry. She thanked him and asked if there was any food in his cabin. Chalk had some fruit and he gave her an apple.

Chalk told her to stay in the cabin and not make any noise. He had to do his chores with the horses and cattle that were in the stable. He went back to the stable and was gone about an hour. After he was done he went to the kitchen and made a couple of sandwiches to take back to him cabin. When he returned Hilda was still hiding behind the bunk and was still very nervous. Chalk gave her a sandwich and a glass of water. She ate the sandwich quickly and thanked him for the food. It was now about 11:00PM and it was bedtime. Chalk told Hilda to sleep in the bunk and he would sleep on the floor. Hilda lay down on the bunk and told Chalk he could sleep there with her if he wanted. Chalk looked at the situation and told her to have a good nights sleep, he would be glad to sleep on the floor.

Chalk got a spare pillow and a blanket and layer down on the floor. He was uneasy as to the fact that Hilda was there but he knew she was in trouble in Memphis and understood her emotions. At about 2:00 AM Chalk woke up when a horse started acting up in the stable. He went out to calm the animal down and went back to the cabin. When he entered he saw that Hilda was awake and she told him she was cold. Chalk got a blanket and gave it to her.

She took the blanket and stood up and grabbed Chalk and kissed him. Chalk sensed that she was wanting more than a blanket. He kissed her back and soon the bunk was holding both of them.

The next morning came quickly and Chalk was not sure as to what to do. He told Hilda that she could stay on the boat until the reached Natchez but he would not be able to keep her hidden any longer than that port. He also told her he had to tell the captain about her or he could loose his job. She thanked him and said she would leave the boat when it docked.

Chalk went to the Captain and told him about her. The Captain just laughed and told Chalk that he was glad that he had enjoyed some "sporting fun" in his cabin. He told Chalk that she could stay onboard until they reached New Orleans if she wanted. Chalk was relieved to see that he was not in trouble. He went to this cabin and told Hilda about his conversation with the Captain. She thanked him and gave him a big kiss. She spent seven more nights in Chalk's cabin and left the boat when it docked in New Orleans. Chalk was getting attached to Hilda and she was really not wanting to leave, but. Everybody knew that this was not a good situation.

Everybody was full of the thrill of becoming a pioneer and the efforts they were putting forth were reflections of their pride and hope they had for the future.

There were people on board who had been involved in every walk of life before the left their past. Now, all of that life was behind them and this was a real new, fresh start. This was a common expression for everyone as they left the riverboat and went on to the next part of their trip to a new home.

Another common outcome was the pairing up of the single people. A common event was for a couple to get engaged and have the Captain marry them. Everyone needed to have a partner to face the upcoming pioneering adventure. On several occasions there were group weddings on the riverboat.

The Captain took a lot of pleasure in doing the honors. He even had a standard marriage certificate printed up to supply to newly married couples. He never charged a fee but expected to have an open tab at the boat's bar.

There were always a lot of ministers, shoemakers, carpenters, blacksmiths and many other tradesmen on the same boat. They saw the need to bond together to help reach all of their goals. For the most part, the trips down river from Ohio and Kentucky were like giant conventions where everyone was looking to see what they could do to make this trip and their future work better.

For the next 8 years Chalk managed the animal cargo on the riverboat. He soon had accumulated a small bankroll from salaries, tips, gambling winnings and other riverboat activities. Chalk learned how to play poker and blackjack. He studied the card sharks who rode the boat, learned their skills, especially of poker, and he made a substantial side income from this source. He had a self-imposed rule to never take money from a person who was drunk or just plain stupid. His greatest delight was to beat the sharks and send them home as losers.

On several trips there were often "old-timer" wagon train organizers who were collecting settlers who were going to western destinations. There were also many people from other countries, especially Germany, England, and Russia and sometimes from the country of India. The Indians were often servants for the English and they were considered as being in bondage for several years. This was a common way to pay their sponsors for the trip.

Many foreign languages were common on deck and the lady folks were never the focus of attention. This was a man's world. Their husbands were often the eager members of the family to go west. The ladies were going because they were married to their husbands. They had the opportunity to gather and talk in their own groups. Most of these discussions were small talk and the desires of the men were never questioned.

Men were always seen as the ultimate family member of authority and their wives were not at liberty to challenge this person. Every wife and child knew that this was rule of authority was the only rule that really mattered.

There were many groups of people who were following a trip established by "trip organizers". These key people were always in a high focus position as they were responsible for outfitting and leading the group until they were successful in reaching some predetermined destination. On the trail there were often referred to as "Wagon-masters". This occupation was common for young men who had made the trip before and supposedly were capable of leading others on the same trails.

The west was being settled quickly and there were many trails that were considered as safe and easier to travel. Small towns were growing up on the trails and each had a unique offering to cause it to survive. The most common resources were available water and good farmland.

Trips to the west were never planned, undertaken and ended without a lot of changes. There were many opportunities for s person to change their mind as a trip progressed. Many pioneering families changed their destination plans several times before they reached their original goal. A lot of this changing happened while the people were still on the riverboat.

The people who managed wagon trips knew this was reality and to protect them financially, always required up-front payment from trip members before they started west. Guiding wagon trips to the west was a business, not a pastime. The wagon masters knew the best places to buy wagons, provisions and all of the other basic necessities for a wagon trip in the river port where they were starting. This service plus the opportunity to be part of a "train" of wagons was a magnet to draw people into groups that had common objectives and destinations.

By the time a riverboat reached a major river port everything had to be settled and the wagon train leader would immediately become the new point of focus.

The railroads were also going west. Many of the original wagon trails were the basic paths that were chosen to build track. Wagon trains were becoming less common on many western trails in the northern areas and trains were becoming the best way to go west.

In many of the southwest areas new railroad tracks were coming, but with much less speed. The railroad race was to connect the eastern coastal cities with the big settlements in California, especially in the areas north for San Francisco. The resulting result was changing the way people and freight traveled. Wagon trains were still the best way to get to the places where rail travel was not available.

The Mississippi River was a major problem for the expansion of rail lines to the west. The river was wide and bridges were not cheap. The further south the river flowed, the wider it became.

Several major cities in the north had built simple bridges at narrow crossings. Bridges were more common on smaller rivers.

Some cities had also developed train barges to move a few railroad cars at a time over rivers. On the opposite side the cars were joined back together into a train. One of the first cities to use this approach was Cincinnati, Ohio on the Ohio River.

Everyone who was going into the relatively unsettled west knew that they would be challenged in many ways. Survival and travel into a still wild portion of the country would bring hardships and many years of hard physical work. There were still a few remaining hostile Indian bands, bandits and a continual influx of crooks. Security was never "for sure" or predictable. On some riverboat trips there were scouts, looking for work. They had often just returned from a trip to the west and had the latest information on conditions on a particular trail or area. They would get in touch with the wagon masters who were on board and looked for work. They had helped lead wagon trains west and knew the utmost about the trails. Every scout was a great source of information and high interest for Chalk.

Over time and with a lot of homework, Chalk recognized that the job on the riverboat was not what he wanted to do for the rest of his life. He was now 23 years old and was full of the thrill that comes from doing something for the first time. The pioneering spirit had got to him.

The thrill he saw in the pioneer's faces and their voices were infectious and he started to ask a lot of question from everyone he could find. His skills in managing livestock and in planning the trips on the riverboat were matured. There was no real future in this job and he knew he needed a change.

The summers were spent working on the river every day and the winters, when the rivers were not very busy were spent fixing the boat and getting ready to go again as soon as the ice and spring flooding was gone. The boat spent the winter months in Memphis and Chalk had developed several good friends, especially in the gambling joints. When springtime came the days got longer and the rivers were once again safe to navigate. Chalk was always ready to get back on the river and to meet all of the people who were traveling. Each one of them was interesting and had a story to tell.

On his 24th birthday a wagon master, who was heading west to Texas noticed Chalk and made friends with him. He was named Carl Harmony. Carl was a relatively old man at 45 and already had several westward trips under his belt. His reputation as a wagon master and former scout were well known to all. To be in one of his trains was considered to be riding with the best. He and Chalk talked about what they were doing and soon Carl saw that Chalk was a young man that was made up of solid, honest and great values. He also noticed that he needed some roots and would probably be a good man to have on a wagon train. Chalk had learned how to plan out activities and what working with people was all about. Carl saw these skills and was impresses with Chalk's style.

In about a week Carl offered Chalk a partnership for a trip he was forming to go to south Texas. To get him to sign up he promised him a tract of land in southwest Texas if he would join up with him. Carl already had a family in Bandera, Texas and was considering making this his last trip. He wanted to stay home and be with his family for a few years and enjoy a little life before he died. Life expectancy for a man in that time was not much over 60.

The temptation was great and Chalk said he would consider it overnight. That night was a completely new experience for Chalk and he had to consider a lot of things.

The risk of getting to Texas was not high but his future from there on was not clear. Texas had not been a state for very long and the frictions between the Mexican State and the local citizens in south Texas was not always comfortable.

Clay had an old map that showed the lands west of the Mississippi River. Mexico was shown as a large country. Texas, he explained, had been cut away and several other states had also been formed. He also explained that there was still much open land and the opportunities were everywhere.

The next morning Carl came down to the animal area and told Chalk that he would form a wagon train company called "Harmony and Goodwin" and set it up completely out of his pocket if Chalk would join with him. He took out some old maps, spread them out on a bale of hay and showed him what was happening. Carl told him about the open fields, clear night skies and all of the places that were there in Texas.

The temptation was to great to refuse so Chalk said, OK. They went back to Mr. Harmony's room, opened a bottle of good whiskey and had a healthy drank to the deal.

Chapter 4
A Young Man's Ambition

When the riverboat reached Memphis, Tennessee, it was early August and the hot summer was driving the afternoon temperature up near 100 degrees. Chalk went to talk to the riverboat Captain and told him of his decision. He was happy for Chalk but told him that if it didn't work out, his old job was always open. They were great friends and the Captain gave him a nice bonus to show him how much he appreciated his loyalty and years of help.

The two old friends parted company. When the riverboat pulled away from the dock without him on board Chalk felt like he had just become an American pioneer and leaving his past was not that difficult. The next month was spent with Carl in planning and organizing the wagon train. The route was to go across the Arkansas wetland, into Texas at a good crossing on the Red River in central Texas. From there it would travel on west to the hill country area and into southwest Texas.

There were initially about 30 families and several merchants who wanted to be included in the train. Some wanted to go all of the way to Texas and some were looking to go part way and then on to other places.

Each wagon owner or group would pay the wagon-master a fee to be in the train and in return they were promised a guaranteed place in the train. All fees were clearly identified as not refundable. This allowed Carl's money to be spent on supplies and the many necessities that were going to be needed to make the trip.

An Army Lieutenant named Charles Ramsey showed up at their hotel and approached Carl. He asked if his troop could accompany the wagon train. His Commander in Memphis was anxious to send additional troops and supplies to a small outpost Army Fort near Brackettsville, Texas, Fort Clark.

Traveling with wagons and depending on them to not breakdown was risky. He told Carl the wagons were carrying guns and ammunition. The Military wanted to do everything they could to assure that these items did not fall into the wrong hands. The answer was an immediate and automatic yes. The military was always a good deterrent to bandits and outlaw Indian raiders along the trails. Having the Army as a part of the wagon train was not a problem, it was a big plus.

There was also a special heavy-duty military wagon set up to haul freight. The cargo was not discussed among others but the U.S. Army was shipping several cases of a new model Springfield rifles and a large supply of ammunition to the west Texas Army post.

This cargo was so important that the wagon train had a detachment of 30 Calvary riders assigned to it for security. Many of the soldiers were black men and were commonly called "Buffalo Soldiers". They were also being assigned to the western Texas Fort and were being used as escorts for the supply wagon.

To the settlers, this was a real positive event and this gave everyone a high sense of feeling safe. The route had been crossed by many wagon trains before. There were known bands of bandits and renegade Indians along the route, especially after entering Texas.

The first portion of the route was to cross Arkansas territory and to make several river crossing at shallow places The area just west of Memphis was a large delta area. The river had formed countless pattern-less marshes and wet zones. Over time the drainage to many of these areas was often slowed or stopped completely. The rainy season had passed and the stream levels, by late summer, were supposed to be low. It would be foolish to take a wagon train into such country with mud and flooding conditions.

This also was a consideration as to the availability of wildlife. It was considered better to kill wildlife for food than to try to carry large supplied of preserved foods. The cows in the train would provide fresh milk and the flour; sugar, coffee, cornmeal and other foods in the wagons were all standard staples. Any game and fish the men could kill in route would supply fresh meat for the settlers.

From there, the route was to go south to a town called Little Rock. From there they would go through the piney woods area. The trail would be going more to the south until they reached a settlement on the Texas border. In route they would travel to a known low water crossing of the Red River.

There was also a ferry down stream if the water was too high. To everyone's delight, there was also a group of stores in the border town that could buy additional supplies that would be needed to finish the trip.

There was also a good blacksmith shop and a qualified veterinarian. The town was small but was growing and reaching there would provide a break from trail time and a chance for everyone to refresh.

When the trip was finally organized there were 23 settlers wagons and enough horses to pull ever wagon with every wagon having one spare horse. The Army detachment had two additional wagons and a small cannon mounted on a special trailer. There were 112 people 67 men, 45 females, 31 horseback Soldiers and 24 cattle. The wagons all had families or young couples on board. Most had young children, some several, and the mix was from Kentucky, Ohio, Pennsylvania and there were two German immigrant families. Most of the cattle were milk cows. There was one young Jersey bull and two whiteface Hereford bulls.

The bulls were going to Texas to be used to start a herd of beef cattle. Texas was known to have longhorn cattle as a native animal. They were supposedly not the best beef and never were used as milk cows.

The settlers wanted this to change. They wanted to have beef and milk cattle all on one ranch. Many of the settlers had purchased chickens and small pigs to take with them. Several of the wagons were headed in the San Antonio direction but they all were free to drop off at any location they saw as the right place to call home. The "move out" date was September 6th.

Chalk and Carl had also had bought a wagon and were using it to carry tools and materials that were going to be needed by everyone during the trip. This list included spare harness parts, axle grease and rope. There was also spare canvas and chain to be used in to repair broken wagons. The wagon also had simple medicines and other first aid type equipment to be used as needed.

Carl added three casks of whiskey for good luck but marked the boxes as nails so nobody would want to get into it. Out of pride, Chalk bought a small can of green paint and inscribed the name, "Harmony and Goodwin" on both sides and back of the wagon.

They hired two local men who wanted to go west to drive the wagon and gave them enough front money to buy personal supplies to make the trip. These men were from Mississippi and said they had just got out of jail. They claimed they were accused of being in several fights but claimed this was not true. They wanted to get away from the area quickly and were anxious to sign on.

Carl knew that ammunition was always a good thing to have. He went to a local gun store and bought several cases. He loaded the boxes into his wagon and kept the knowledge of what was in this cargo to just he and Chalk. You could never have too much ammunition. It was needed to hunt, if attacked, it was a vital supply in Texas and in many places it was a good bartering commodity.

Carl also knew that several of the wagons would drop off as soon as they got to a growing small town. He had seen it happen before and he knew it would happen this trip. He also knew that there would also be new wagons joining the train as it went west. Many of the earlier settlers had heard even more stories of the vast open lands further west and had made up their minds to sell out and go even further.

This practice was common in western Arkansas and eastern Texas as the new influx of settlers always created a great market of buyers for a ranch that was already established.

Another serious concern was carrying money on the wagon train. In the 1870's the U S Government had not begun using any form of paper money. All of the Government backed money that was in circulation was in the form of coins. There were several Banks who were also circulating money they were issuing. In some rural areas, Confederate money was still being used. Other money was not yet available or popular. The best money was silver and gold coins.

Chalk did not carry a pistol. Carl told him to get one before they left Memphis. Chalk told Carl about his Dad's problem with a pistol and how much he wanted to never have a similar problem. After a lot of discussion Chalk saw the need and bought a chrome plated six shot Colt revolver.

Large amounts of high valued coins were heavy and they were easy for bandits to steal. The answer was that each wagon had a metal strongbox that often had several locks. The hinges were on the inside and the hasps were welded in place. They had few handles and were by design hard to handle. Every wagon had at least one and it was always out of fashion to discuss the contents or the amount of money anyone was carrying.

The week before departure Carl and Chalk held several group meetings with everyone that was going on the train. The soldiers attended these meetings. It became clear that the young Lieutenant, 2nd Lt. Charles Ramsey, wanted to get going soon.

He was very cocky and kept repeating that all communications between the train and his platoon was to be directed through him and him only. Carl listened, smiled and said that's fine, just keep you soldiers away from the young women on the wagon train. There were several Black Soldiers in the troop and they automatically knew their place. They were never an issue to Carl or the other people.

Carl had a lot of past experience with southerners in the wagon train. Many still had memories from the civil war days and held grudges. Some were members of the klu klux klan. Carl told everyone that any problem between people that was based on racial problems would not be tolerated. If it happened, the people involved would be left by the side of the trail to fend for themselves. There was no doubt in his voice that this was a hard and fast rule.

The group was instructed to assemble their wagons in a large open field near the Mississippi River two days before departure. There, an inspection of each wagon and wagon train line up would be determined. All last minute details would be checked off.

Everything went according to plan with the exception of a few women who had last minute jitters. A large campfire cookout was held the last two nights and the weak-minded travelers were reinforced as best as possible.

Carl held a short but strong toned meeting to inform the wagon train members that his word was the final word and anyone that was unwilling to live with this had better not cross the Mississippi the next morning.

He put Chalk in the second position of command and told the settlers to have hope, overcome fear and work together. Everyone listened and agreed to become one body of people to make this trip as easy and safely as they could. The Lieutenant also spoke and told the people his men were there for any emergency and that they were being protected by the military of the United States of America.

The next morning was discussed in detail. Every wagon was to line up in a designated order then, as a lined up group they would all go to the edge of the river. A steam powered river ferry would then carry two wagons at a time over to a landing site in the Arkansas territory.

The departure date arrived. The sun was coming up at about 5:00 AM and the men and women all were up attaching the horses and mules to their wagons. The first wagon in the train lined up and all of the following wagons followed in a well-controlled pattern. The last wagon was the one marked. "Harmony and Goodwin". The military troop and their cannons and now three military supply wagons were then added at the rear.

Carl gave the command to "Roll Out". The train reached the ferry landing. The first two wagons were loaded. The trip to cross the river was about a half-hour, there and back, and by late afternoon all of the wagon train was across and had reassembled on the other side. Carl went to the lead wagon and per prior instructions, they started to roll.

The first day was about over and at a wide spot in the trail, about 10 miles from the dock, he circled the wagons and sat up camp for the day he called "crossing the river". This was the first time the wagons went into a circle and it was a lot of learning for every driver. The circle was sloppy and the routine was still not understood. Everyone had made the crossing with no incidents and the group moral was high. Chalk called all of the wagon drivers to the center of the circle and told them where they could improve. He said tomorrow evening will be better and after a full day of travel everyone would be better at driving their wagons.

This was really a practice day for everyone. It was a good way to get ready for all that was ahead and everyone was showing what they had learned. In some instances, it was not much! After a dinner meal, each wagon bedded down for the night. Guards were posted and the new group of pioneers went to bed in the wagons. In the morning, the Army bugler sounded a wake up muster.

Chapter 5

The Trail West From Memphis

The new dawn was brilliant and the sky was clear, cloudless and blue. The air was fresh and humid and the smell of jasmine was strong in the breeze. Everyone was on an emotional high and in spite of a lot of eagerness, a lot of things just did not seem to go completely right. The wagon train got off to a slow start. The original plan was to start out as soon as the sun was above the horizon. This happened but there were still wagons with unfinished travel preparations.

The biggest problem was that many of the men had little experience with horses and the teams were not ready to be hooked up on time. The harness and hitching equipment were new items to most of the men. Carl rode up and down the train adding his help where he saw problems and slowly each wagon was able to roll. In about an hour the train was underway and seemingly organized.

This trail was well marked and the ruts in the road allowed the lead wagon to follow a path that was obvious. Most of the wagons were being pulled by a two-horse hitch. One wagon was obviously loaded with more weight and they had four horses. Several wagons had a couple of mules attached to the rear. They wanted to use then for pulling stuck wagons if the road got muddy. Clay had placed this wagon at the tail of the train and the rest of the train to be a final check that everyone ahead was moving ok. The Soldiers wagons were the last wagons in the train and were followed by the soldiers on horseback. Each of the settler's wagons had at least one spare horse or mule tied to the back. Often a cow was also tied to the back of the same wagon. The whole procession was slow moving but that was to be expected for this type of wagon train.

Carl knew that the settlers needed cattle, especially the milk cows, to make the trip. Need was a fact but so was speed. Cows walk slow and have a low level of stamina in long travel. Bulls do a little better but they also are slow moving animals.

Several wagons had brought dogs. Most were large dogs, shepherds, collies and mixed breeds called cow dogs. They were running along side the wagons.

Dogs were actually good travelers. They were desirable to have along as they were scaring snakes and other small critters away from the trail. This lowered the risk for a horse or mule to get spooked by a pesky trail animal. Occasionally a dog would get bit by a snake. This was tragic but it was a normal part of the hazards on a trail.

Chickens and one cage of small white ducks on one of the wagons were also a concern. The fox were always looking for a good meal and these birds would be a great prize meal if they could get to them. The kids on the wagons were always aware of the danger and fed the chickens with corn and other grain at the evening campsites. The birds were never let out of their cages. This was Carl's personal order. Keeping chickens safe was always a clear responsibility for the wagon that had them, no body else.

Carl and Chalk took turns riding up front. Their horses were nimble and each had a shared responsibility to keep the train moving. They also had concerns to keep everyone safe and all of the wagons on the proper trail. On several occasions there were side trails that had been established to allow local wagon traffic to travel to small settlements off the main trail. Often the trail markings were vague.

The decision to follow the right trail was always made by Carl. He knew the route and also knew the differences in main trail and side trails.

The experience of wagon travel was new to most of the people in the train. This was to be expected. A rest stop was made about every hour to help the people become trail hardy. This would allow the people to get down from the wagons, go into the woods, and stretch themselves.

Carl had seen many similar groups and he knew that over a relatively short time the folks would toughen up. On the first few days, they were still learning to be trail tough. There was always a small patch of grass nearby at every stop and the horses were allowed to drink and sometimes eat when a long stop was undertaken. The hot temperatures were demanding but the wind always seemed to add a little coolness. The air was always filled with sweet aromas of nature and the scenery along the trail was a joy in the daytime hours.

The first real night campground was an experience for everyone. The train had traveled about 20 miles and the trail had been level and easy to travel. The campsite for the first night was a small meadow where a stream flowed on the north side.

When they reached the site Carl led the lead wagon into a path that caused all of the wagons to park in a big circle. This time the wagons were all spaced out a lot better and the circle looked better that the one they had made the last evening. This allowed the center area to be open and soon a small campfire was started. The sun was about to go down and the entire group of people was ready to stop and were tired.

After the wagons were parked the men took the animals away from the wagons and allowed them to eat grass, drink water and in general, just rest. The women took to cooking and caring for the small children. The entire community was busy for about an hour and a slowdown started to fall over everyone. The first night on the trail was going by quickly. Carl knew that there was a new, more difficult, day just a few hours ahead.

As soon as everyone finished supper the pace of activity was slowing. Carl called everyone into the circle and held his first regular trail meeting. First, he made comments about how things had gone on the first day. There was good news but there was also bad news. The good news was that everyone was learning and becoming trail smart. The bad news was that there were hills ahead that would be steep and the trail was narrow and full of sharp turns. He gave them a lot of verbal information about pulling wagons on this kind of trail but he knew that there could always be trouble.

Everyone was tired and the thought of sleep was on everyone's mind. Carl and Chalk told the group about having to guard the campsite at night. This duty was to be shared by every man on the train and the first night was no exception. They asked for volunteers for 4-hour shifts of two men each. Several men came forth.

Carl also told them what to watch and listen for. The area they were in was not considered as dangerous but there was never a certain situation on campground safety. The night passed and there were no problems.

Carl had arranged with the Soldiers to sound revelry at about an hour before sun up. This would allow time for the people to eat, tend to personal matters and to get the animals in place for an early start. Per the plan, the bugle sounded. Everyone responded and the second day was much better planned than the first.

This area along the trail had been settled for a long time and prior to the Civil war. There were many big cotton plantations everywhere the trail went. There were still many black people living and working in the fields. They were still growing cotton much like they had for many years before. According to the law, they were free to leave. The Federal Government granted them this freedom. In reality, leaving the old plantations would have been the poorest choice for them. Where would they go? This too, was still the old South.

The Civil War had been lost but the social movement required granting a complete freedom to former slaves was not strong. The landowners grip and hold on Black people was still firm. Many of the social and economic practices of the white people in every location only allowed a minimum freedom. This was characteristic of every community in the entire south. Arkansas was not any different.

Black People were uneducated, had no money and were still very much controlled by the wealthy landowners. Working for pay was not much different than being a slave. They were still whipped and abused in many ways.

The biggest real difference after slavery was ended was that the "Master" could not sell you away from your family. You were not his property any longer and he had no legal rights to hold you or sell you as an owner. But, what he wanted you to do was controlled by how you were treated.

The same shacks that they had lived in for years were still home and the way of life was not changed. The passing wagons were an interesting sight to see but they were too busy doing their work to do much more than look and occasionally wave.

The train traveled south. The lead wagon reached was a long ridge of hills that seemed to just stick up from the flat delta area. Carl had the train stop to rest the horses.

Carl knew the upcoming trail was gradual in grade but was a long pull to the top. When they reached the base of the trail everyone was stopped and a short rest was given to the horses.

While stopped, Carl gave all of the drivers a speech of confidence and instructions about how to go up hill and then to go down hill. The biggest problem on the "down" hillside would be in keeping the heavy wagons from pushing the horses.

The speed had to be slow enough to allow them to keep the wagon on the trail. This could be minimized by the proper use of the wagon brake. So far, the brake had not been a concern. Flat land pulling had been hard work but it was simple. Carl suggested that a second person might be added to the drivers seat. The driver would control the horses and the second person could work the brake lever. This suggestion was taken to heart by most. Several of the women got their first experiences in driving the wagon as a result.

The trip up the ridge took about an hour and went smoothly. The horses were strong and the trail was not really as bad as Carl had made it seem. Everyone who reached the top of the ridge enjoyed this feeling of success. At the top there was a small flat area where everyone took a rest.

The downhill trip was equally smooth and without incident. This experience was a training lesson for the much bigger challenges that were still ahead. The women quickly became partners with their men in running the wagon. The young boys were also becoming equally involved with trail education.

The other side of the ridge was less flat than the delta country but the trail was still not hard to pull. This area was full of marshes and ponds and wild rice was growing everywhere. The train had to cross a few small drainage streams but they were not deep.

The river channel bottoms at the crossing points were rocky. This allowed the wagons to roll freely and the thrill of seeing clean water around the wagon was both exciting and refreshing. There were also some new challenges in the area. The weather was dry but the wet areas were magnets for wild game. The cattle were potential targets for bands of coyotes. Chickens, even though they were in cages, were a target for foxes. The dogs were a good deterrent.

The trail had a couple of optional routes to get to the Arkansas River. The northern route was about 30 miles longer but avoided several water crossings that were often deep and dangerous. Carl selected the longer route, as his drivers were still green and not up to such a series of challenges.

Water snakes and coyotes were commonly seen. There were also abundant fish in almost every water area. Deer were seen on rare occasions. Another potential danger for the cattle was the attack of a wild hog pack. Mosquitoes were everywhere and they were a real problem at night. The wagons would attempt to close the ends of the covers and keep the insects out. This was an honorable effort, but it seldom worked well .All of these animals had positives and minuses. The positives were the availability of fresh meat. An occasional skunk would spray a dog and the odor was everywhere. The negatives were obvious.

The women and some men were skittish when snakes were discussed. They soon learned that they were not as bad as the stories they had heard. Most of them would crawl away rather that fight if they were not frightened. The biggest concern was the nighttime. Snakes could travel into the campsite at night and when the sun came up in the morning, they become a problem.

The women would keep the children in the wagons when there was water anywhere close by. They also watched as they were exiting the wagons in the early morning.

At the second day stopping point there was a small clearing and there was also a small up-start town trying to happen. This settlement was a welcome site to everyone. The nightly routine of supper, wagon driver's meeting and make preparations to rest went well. Some of the men, mostly the ones who were single, went into the town. They visited a local saloon that was selling whiskey and homemade beer. The owner was a salty old Frenchman who had been there for about 10 years. He had started his bar when he saw the traffic level on the westward trail pick up. He also had a small general store where basic supplies were sometimes available. He also had a brothel located next to the bar.

When a wagon train was stopping he would keep the store open for a short time then close and open his bar. The men on the wagon train who saw his sign and were more curious than anything else. The men spent a short time and when the saloonkeeper ran out of beer they went home to their wagons.

The next morning all of the men who had drank the homemade beer had the runs so bad that they had to let their wagon partners drive. Frequent side stops were common. The beer had not matured long enough and it was taking a tall toll on the folks who had indulged. One man had visited the brothel and said he did not indulge. The women were all ugly and needed a good bath.

The third, fourth and fifth days were all similar. As the train headed west it was making between 20 and 25 miles a day. At the close of the fifth day they had traveled about 115 miles and were on the edge of a small town called Brinkley.

Brinkley had been a well to do town for a long time. There were several shops and the local people had developed an economy that was growing. This was a first time experience for the travelers to witness. The settlement was actually inviting.

Several of the local business people were quick to come out to the wagon train and invite the people to come into town and shop. This was a real challenge for the women to overcome. Most had started out with little money and to spend any here was not considered a smart decision. However, there were a few that went to look. Little was actually bought. Before they left Carl told them that these trail towns had a common practice that was to watch for. On many goods the price for the local people was one thing. The price for the travelers was normally much higher. Prices in larger towns were normally better and the selection was always bigger.

The local bar played loud music to advertise the fun to be had in town. These words of trail wisdom were understood and remembered.

The next day when the train pulled out the Army Lieutenant came to Carl and told him that he would send scouts ahead to make sure that there were no problems ahead with bandits. Before leaving Memphis a mail rider had reported that a band of about 10 men were causing problems in the area ahead and they were not sure what they were capable of doing to a wagon train. Carl appreciated the help and led the train forward.

In about three hours the scouts returned and reported that the bandits had been captured by a local group of citizen vigilantes and were not going to be a problem. They had attacked a settlement and were caught shortly afterwards. Apparently they were some old Confederate soldiers who were being led by a man who was wanted for murder and he was using them to advance his purposes.

The train moved on to the west. By noon of the next day they were on the banks of the Arkansas River. The town of Little Rock was on the other side of the river and there was a new bridge.

The bridge could be used to cross over. It was Saturday afternoon and Carl told everyone to bed down for the night. They were located in a small field about a mile south from the river bridge and the area had a few small settlements. Wagon trains were always welcome there and the local people were building a business from providing goods and simple services to the travelers.

The most popular place was a bathhouse and barbershop. The women wanted a hot water bath and the men were always glad to get a shave and some got a haircut.

One of the most valued items in the wagon's cargo was soap. Soap was always a special treat for everyone but using soap in a bathhouse was even more special.

That evening, several of the men and their wives cleaned up and had a party around the campfire. Several of the single men put saddles on their horses and went to Little Rock. They wanted to see the town. The wagon train was guarded by a few of the older, more conservative men who were not interested in nightlife or in spending money. They wanted to save every penny they had and not waste it on frills.

There were several fancy bars in the town and whiskey was easy to find. Four of the younger single men proceeded to get drunk. They were not troublemakers but the others with them saw that they needed to get out of town before the crooks drew them into a fight. Everyone got home safely. The evening was a welcome change for everyone.

Chalk was enjoying the trip so far and had been a quiet listener to the words and leadership that Carl was exhibiting. Carl gave him a lot of exposures to the problems that were happening was giving Chalk time to learn. One of these was trail care of the animals and for the wagons. Horses and mules will work hard if they are kept healthy. They need to be watched and any small problem needed to be brought to the wagon owner's attention at once. These concerns needed to be fixed quickly.

The most common problem was bruises and sores caused by ill fitting harness. A second concern was keeping good horseshoes on all of the animal's feet. The cattle needed to be watched equally as hard. Pink eye and loose bowels could put a cow down quickly and could infect other animals.

Chalk was at every wagon several time a day watching and teaching the drivers to watch for these problems. If you lost a horse, you lost a non-renewable animal. This was a major concern. If you lost a cow, the milk for the children was gone.

The other major concern was keeping the wagons in good working order. Covered wagons were made by large companies that used designs and materials that were intended to withstand a lot of trail punishment. The wagon axles were made from oak timbers that were selected for their strength. The tongue, doubletree and singletree components were also made from selected straight grain oak. Steel bands and straps helped to make them even stronger. Axles were made to have steel collars on each end that would allow a wheel to carry heavy weight and roll for almost endless miles.

The wheels were made individually with strong oak hubs, oak spokes and a segmented outer wheel. All of these parts were precision milled to make the into a strong and durable unit. Forged steel "tires" was installed on the perimeter of each wheel. The rear of the wagon had much larger wheels.

They were big for two reasons. A big, strong wheel can carry more weight in soft ground. They also are capable of crossing rough surfaces with greater ease. The front wheels were smaller. This was to allow for easier steering ease and to allow adequate and better side clearance when the wagon is turning. All of the wheels had metal bearing that fit onto matching metal fittings on the wagon axles. A large washer and nut held the wheel in place. Every wheel needed to be greased every few days to keep the axle bearing from galling.

If this happened the wheel and sometimes the axle would need to be replaced. There was a large pin in the end of the axle that had to be maintained to keep the nut tight.

Chalk learned quickly and his many trips up and down the sides of the wagons assured the drivers that their wagons were holding up. When any problem was discovered, the best way to fix it was quickly determined. If possible, the repair would be done at the nightly campsite. If it had to be done immediately, a place in the road was chosen and the problem wagon pulled from the train long enough to do the work. The repaired wagon would rejoin the train as soon as it was possible.

Chalk's primary job was to keep the train moving and to keep the animals healthy. Spare parts, axle grease and leather were all in the supply trailer and were dispensed as needed with each discovered requirement.

A positive relationship between Chalk and the wagon train members grew quickly. His easy availability to everyone gave everyone a real chance to see him do a good job and win their respect. Chalk had answers when the travelers had questions.

Sometimes the questions were about the trail. Often the questions were more about the west and what was to be expected when they arrived. His answers were often his opinions. He had talked a lot with Carl and had a lot of buzzwords that seemed to satisfy the travelers. He always painted a positive image and this positive attitude was always well received.

Another advantage was the chance to meet the young ladies. The train had several families that had both young men and women in their group. The fathers and especially the mothers were very protective of their children and were cautious as to whom they would build relationships. During the days, the younger people would often ride up front with their dad. A lot of the boys would ride horses along side the wagons.

The social scene would get a lot closer at night when the wagons were in a circle. Everyone had special chores on every wagon. The young people were a vital part of this family effort. Free time was not easy to come by but somehow it always happened in the evenings.

Chalk was a popular young man in most circles. In others, he was treated like a trail boss and that was as far as the relationship was allowed to go. Chalk had obviously dark skin and high cheekbones. It was no secret that he was part Indian. He was held in esteem by some for his knowledge of the trail but having any relationship with a young lady that was fair skinned was not to be considered. His education was by experience, not from a book and some saw this as a real demeaning situation.

The entire situation remained positive in general and Chalk knew that he had to keep a clear distance between himself and all of the young ladies on the train. After all, he was there to work and be a train leader, not to have a social life.

The young men had a completely different situation with Chalk. Chalk had skills and knowledge that every young man envied. He could shoot game with super accuracy, his animal handling skills and knowledge of basic survival were things they wanted to learn. His skill at driving a wagon was also well respected. Several times when the wagons were crossing streams the drivers would ask Chalk to take their wagon across.

He obviously had a lot of skill and backed it up with courage. The young men followed him when they could and helped with the tasks just to learn. Several of the older men saw this kinship developing and encouraged this relationship.

During the day Chalk would often ride off into a wooded area and hunt game. He always had several young men who always wanted to go with him so they could learn to hunt and shoot. Bullets were never wasted on just targets.

The only acceptable target to shoot was to hunt. In the event of an attack, bullets would be precious and everyone knew it. Chalk would track game and when it was in shooting range he would allow the fellow with him to take the first shot. If he missed, Chalk would do the kill. Most of the young men quickly became excellent shots and this was a point of pride for Chalk.

These relationships had side benefits. Several of the mothers always made extra food just so Chalk could have a little. They also did his washing and clothing mending. A couple of the more open-minded women actually tried to set Chalk up to meet their daughters. This was a problem. Chalk wanted to keep everyone at arms distance so long as they were on the trail. He handled it by making sure that there were many other people in the area when he would have conversations with any young ladies. The ladies parents and Carl understood the situation and never pushed anyone into a more serious relationship.

Chapter 6

Western Arkansas, the Woodland Trail

The Little Rock stop lasted until about noon on Sunday. Saturday night, a local church Minister who wanted to provide a Sunday morning Church service approached Carl. With some reservation, he agreed. There were many so called, self-appointed Ministers in the west that were nothing more than big mouth crooks. At about two hours after dawn the Minister came to the wagon campground and held a simple church service. He preached about knowing Jesus and how bad life in Hell could be. He also held a "save yourself" opportunity where sinners could come to his side and receive the blessing of Jesus. Some of the people were appreciative. Almost everyone attended. The people took up a small offering and offered it to the Minister. He refused the money and gave it to Carl to be used for the needy on the trail. He was obviously not looking for a handout.

At the end of the services the Minister asked if anyone in the train wanted to stay in the Little Rock area? He told them that after crossing the Arkansas River Bridge there was a small park on the other side of town where they could stop and look at maps as to where homestead locations were available. He also said that there were five wagons there waiting to hook up with their train and go further west. These wagons had arrived earlier from a northern trail and they wanted to go to Texas. In effect, he was a local messenger that kept up with the wagon train traffic. He also had a second motive, which was to get new residents for the town.

This was a common experience when a wagon train passed through a reasonably large town. The interest among the wagons was always high. Carl was open to such stops as long as they were quick and the wagons were not going to linger to shop. As expected, the wagons stopped for a few minutes, then all of them moved on.

The Army men were all present at the church services. When the wagons were ready to cross the river the troops rode ahead of the wagons. Just ahead was an Army post where the Army would have information concerning troops and wagon train travel conditions.

The Army actually maintained this site and a small garrison of men was kept there to assist everyone. They used this post as a place to report incidents on the trails. They also kept the local Sheriff under control. He was known to be a short-tempered man with a quick gun to teach his prisoners a lesson or two.

Upon arrival, the Lieutenant was called into the post Commander's office and was replaced as the Platoon Commander by an older soldier. This new Officer who had traveled this route before and was more experienced with command. He was a Captain and was also being assigned to the Army post at Fort Clark in Texas, the final platoon destination. Lieutenant Ramsey was reassigned to the Little Rock Post and his travel with the wagon train was over. Carl welcomed the change.

There were also 20 additional troops being assigned to the accompanying detail. They had two additional horse drawn cannons and an additional caisson full of ammunition to support the equipment. Army posts always had a supply of fresh horses and any animals that were sick or showing fatigue were replaced before the platoon would leave. This was common for the horses pulling the heavy wagons. The Army unit waited for the arrival of the wagon train.

When the wagon train arrived, in mid afternoon, there were several people who had looked at the maps available at the river crossing and were reviewed homesteading opportunities that were in the area. Everyone wanted to continue to the west. The wagon drivers from five other new wagons that were waiting saw the train pull in. They quickly made contact with Carl. Arrangements were finalized for their addition. They had come from down from northern Missouri and were going to an area near Dallas. Carl charged them a small fee and as he had told everyone else, no fees are ever refunded, for any reason. This was the rule of the roads and was commonly accepted by everyone.

That afternoon the train traveled about ten miles further west and circled for the night. The Army platoon stayed the night at the Army post and was to join the wagon train early the next morning.

The next morning it was beginning to rain. The wagons were covered with a light coat of tan mud from the dust that had built up on them during the trip in dry weather. It was still hot and the humid air felt like a big wet glove all around you. Comfort was not the order for the day. The trail had become slick but the rain never made it so wet that mud holes became a problem. It was Monday and Carl wanted to get moving to the west quickly. He saw storm clouds in the area and knew that there were several small streams to cross in the next 50 miles.

The Army detachment arrived on schedule and the full train proceeded west. The area west of Little Rock was hilly. Hills were not all bad, as they were high places to travel and let any rain run off in the many streams that were in between them. The trail was crooked and followed the upper sides of ridges and only crossed a stream at a conveniently shallow place.

The ground elevation was a little higher than the flat plane just west of Little Rock and was starting to show a thick covering of large, tall, majestic pine trees. Trees were good news as they were shelters from the wind and they were always full of game.

Trees also were good places to find nuts and other things that could be eaten. Dead fall trees would provide firewood and the trails that were cut through the forest were always easy to follow.

The sun was shaded sooner in trees and travel days were by necessity shorter. As fall was approaching the days were growing shorter and the amount of time spent in campsite was longer. The real bonding of people began in the nights spent in the pine tree woods.

The wagons that had joined the train in Little Rock were people who had been living in row crop farming communities. They had brought seed and hand tools to start a small farm in the rich black dirt of the area found along the Trinity River in north Texas. They knew of the area from letters from people who had gone before them.

They were already bonded into a close small group and were focused on getting to Texas in time to build a small house before the winter cold got too bad. If everything went well they should arrive by late November. They had this target firmly fixed in their minds.

Carl warned them that this could be a bit ambitious. The route was not always a fast traveling trail. In fact, he had seen fall rains stop a train for days and even a week one time.

The small streams in the area could turn into impassable rivers with a heavy rain. The resulting mud would let the wagons sink on the trails and the train would simply need to stop and let the ground dry out to a passable condition.

As luck would happen, the heavy rains did not come. The few days of wet weather that did happen were not intense and the wagon train was making good time. The several streams that required crossing were low in their banks and crossing was tricky but never a complete train-stopping situation.

Chalk had learned how to "read a river". Deep water always flows slow and shallow, fast running water indicates a less deep stream. Many of the rivers in western Arkansas were deep in many places but over time small island were built up in the middle of a flow that were dry and even had trees and grass growing on them. The headwater side of such an island had a split in the stream where one side was always deeper and the other side was shallow. Another good condition was the presence of a lot of river rock in the shallow stream.

When an island like this was found Chalk would scout the entire island and see if wagons could cross safely. River locations like this were always wider and the water speed was normally faster. Crossing point also had to have riverbanks on both sides where a wagon could enter and exit the water.

Several nights were spent in wooded country. The hills were not steep and the wagon drivers had become masters of keeping the wagon under control during the downhill slopes. On several occasions the wagon wheels fell into cracks in the rocky trails.

Often the wheel was simply stuck. On two occasions the wooden spokes had broken and the wheel had to be replaced. This was hard manual work and everyone that was able pitched in and helped. The people in every wagon had become unified as a solid group and hardships for one was shared by all. Changing a wheel was dangerous work. The axle had to be jacked up, the old wheel removed and a new wheel placed on the axle. Wheels are heavy and jacking was always dome with a long pole being used as a lever on a pile of rocks or what ever was available. A wheel could slip and damage the hub if it was not installed properly and all of this work had to be done slowly to get it right.

The nighttime campfires were becoming fun for many. The Kentucky mountain people were often skilled in playing music and in folk music style music singing. The songs were often gospel in nature and it seemed everyone was always having a good time listening to the music. Fiddles, banjos and guitars were all commonly played instruments. Several of the soldiers, especially the black men, had great deep voices and knew a lot of spiritual music. They were always in demand.

After the music started the women would have snacks and fresh drinks for everyone. The men often opened a bottle of whiskey and let their hair down for these occasions. When a familiar song was being played everyone would sing along. Solo singing was also common. Drunken men always wanted to sing and they soon would become a big part of the fun.

On one such evening Carl was asked to sing a verse of a well-known song. He resisted at first but after prodding from the people, and a few good shots of whiskey, he sang a verse to the Kentucky waltz. After it was over Chalk told him to go sing to the horses, they needed it more than this crowd. He was never asked to sing again.

The soldiers from the Army platoon were always invited. They were given much more liberty to mix with the wagon folks by the Captain. They liked this and soon they were on a first name basis with many of the people.

The Captain was also asked to sing and his voice was clear and had a romantic ring. The young women were all impressed. A man in an Army uniform that had a post of responsibility and could sing, wow, He soon became a train celebrity. He was single and this was soon well known by all. He also was a good dancer.

When the fire burned down the whole community would retire and the camp guards would take over. For security, the campfire was maintained at a low level all through the night. The same fire was available in the morning to brew trail coffee. Coffee was a staple for all of the men. The morning cup of mud and a biscuit were often breakfast. This morning diet was commonly accepted as good trail food service. The guards would sit by the fire to warm up, keep a coffeepot active and take turns walking the perimeter around the wagons. The nights were cool and the moon and stars were awesome.

On one such night the guards were doing their job when a lot of noise was heard out behind one of the wagons.

Both guards responded quickly. They saw a shape that was moving but could not see what it was. One of them went to the fire and got a small torch to light up the area. They drew their pistols and approached the end of the wagon. What ever was there was not moving and was not making any more noise. They went into the area where the noise was coming from and there was nothing. All of a sudden a large crash was heard and a big black bear came charging toward them.

They fired a shot into the area and the bear stopped. He was not afraid of the men but the gunshot provided a lot more than he wanted to deal with. They held their torch a little higher and the bear turned and ran back into the woods. When daylight came it was discovered that the bear had been trying to get into a wagon where some fresh biscuits still smelled good. Everyone understood the danger of leaving any food where a bear could smell it or find it. This had been a close call. From that night on, the last nighttime check was to make sure all of the food was properly put away.

Bears were not the only night robbers. Coyotes and raccoons were similar in many respects but they were never a threat to people like a big bear.

On October 18th, the train reached an outpost named Hope. Hope had a small number of buildings but appeared to be growing. There was a Church, a general store and a rip-roaring bar that was open all day and all night. The train set up camp outside the town and Carl told the people to beware if they went into town. Several people had been gunned down there in the past and the Law officers were not to be trusted.

Carl wanted to give the train a rest as within the next day or two the Red River was going to be crossed. The Red River was always changing its flow and this made it a hard river to find a safe and reachable place to cross over. The Texas border was about 20 mile past the river and this knowledge gave everyone a real boost.

A small group of the men went into town. They needed to see for themselves as to what was there. When they went into the general store there were several things they wanted but the prices were so high that they passed up the place. On the way out of town a man stopped them and wanted to know what was wrong. They said little, left the town and avoided any conflicts. Carl saw them coming back and told them that the town might send people to the campsite to cause trouble. The Army troops set up a full perimeter guard for the night and nothing happened. Carl said that Army uniforms were probably why nobody bothered them. This was a bad place. The next morning everyone was ready to roll as soon as the sun was high enough to see the trail.

In about 3 hours they were all assembled on the banks of the Red River. Chalk had scouted the riverbanks, both up and down stream and had found a place about a mile to the south where crossing was going to be possible. The train proceeded to the point and the Army troops, wagons and all crossed first. This was the widest water crossing they had made so far and the distance running in axle deep water, more than anything else, was what concerned the wagon drivers. The bottom was a combination of sand and rocks. The flow slow and the water was crystal clear. The bottom was visible for most of the way across. The wagons started and in about two hours all had crossed.

There was one incident where a horse spooked when a floating tree branch came up right in front of him but the driver and the men on the next wagon behind the horse calmed him down. The horse soon was fine and the crossing went forward.

When they reached the opposite shore the train had to travel up river for about a mile to get back on the main trail. Everyone was relieved and they pressed forward. The town of Texarkana was straight ahead. This was a milestone and turning off location for the group that had joined the train at Little Rock. Texarkana was a settlement where the main street ran north and south down the town center. Arkansas was on one side and Texas on the other.

It was near nightfall when the train reached the outskirts of town and everyone was excited to finally be getting out of Arkansas. Texas was the advertised place where dreams were to come true and just being there was going to a thrill unto itself. Arkansas was seen as a place where fast talkers and slick merchants were far too common.

That night the wagon train camped in Arkansas and the people were all eager to get to Texas. Carl made a trail- side rule that nobody was to ride ahead and that night and the next morning the entire train would ride into Texas with the Army troop in front. They had an American Flag and a Texas Flag that they would carry in the front formation.

Several of the wagons had flags from their home states and proudly put them on poles cut from the local woods. They were proud of where then were coming from and wanted to show off a little. This was as the opportunity to have some fun. The whole train looked like a small circus and the people dressed up in clean clothes and tried to look their best.

When a wagon train arrived in town, Carl knew from past trips, the local people would come out to the street to wave and welcome everyone. New wagon trains were always greeted and welcomed with a lot of friendly smiles and hardy handshakes. Carl had several old friends in town and he knew that the people on the train would be treated well and fairly. He always called this destination the trail highlight of the trip as everyone was at his or her highest level of excitement.

The memories of this day were to last a lifetime. Carl told everyone where to shop and said they would be allowed about an hour to buy supplies and to see the town. There was a large parade ground type of clearing near the center of town where wagon trains could safely park.

The Army troop would stop briefly in the downtown area and then precede to an Army post about 5 miles further down the trail to the west,

The wagon train stopped, the settlers shopped for about an hour. Several local merchants were showing off their merchandise and inviting the people to come in and look. The ladies bought a few things and the men bought supplies to assure they were going to have enough to make the next leg of the trip. Then they all traveled on to the Army post. This post was also another place where people going to different destinations would drop out of one wagon train and join up with the next train going their way. The resident Army Officers had a group of nice homes located on the north side of the post. There were barracks buildings for the soldiers and extra barracks for the soldiers who were just passing through. A tradition was that the wagon masters were treated to a good meal and an evening of friendship with the Officers. The soldiers who were post regulars would cook bar-b-que on an open pit and all of the settlers would all be invited.

A large open shower area was available for the men. The women were treated to smaller private shower rooms where they could wash and take a few hours of rest from the trail.

Wagons were not fun to ride in. They had no springs and were never still. The road bumps were all transferred directly to the load, including the passenger's butts. The driver's seat had a simple spring on each side. They did little to improve the ride.

The Army post always had the latest news concerning the trails. They also had the reports from mail riders who were using the post to secure fresh horses. The stagecoach lines that operated out west also stopped here and they often brought mail and had the latest news. This was the last good place to find out what a wagon master needed to know before venturing out to the western areas that were beyond.

The information may be a few days old but it was better than no information. Often, trailside information was inaccurate and flavored by the opinions and local issues of the people who were living in the different areas. Maps were also available, at a small cost, and the wagon masters were always eager to reach this post.

That evening the few people that were leaving the train were instructed to pull there wagons aside and park them in a holding area where they could wait for a train going their direction. It was considered dangerous to travel further west alone as bandits watched for single wagons and plundered them at will. However, a few wagons did often go alone. It was always safer to join up with a train. The original train added the new joining wagons and put them in an order for rolling out the next morning. Carl held a group meeting to make sure that everyone was aware of trail rules.

Often there were two wagon trains in the parking area at the same time. Seldom were they both going to the same destination. In situations where a settler wanted to join a specific train they would pull into a special area and wait. When a train they wanted to join arrived they would join. People who had become friends and were parting would say good by and sometimes there were tears.

Others were forced to wait and hope a train that was going their way was coming down the trail. In some instances where there were no new trains. The wagon family would commonly go into Texarkana and find work. Many of these people never left the area and found a place in the local economy.

There were now 19 settler's wagons plus the supply wagon in Carl's final train make-up. Five were going to an area south and east of San Antonio. They were planning to settle in this area and homestead land along the rivers that had heard was common in this area. These settlers were largely of German decent and had trades and skills to start life in a new home. Two were Jewish Doctors and they had all of their tools and patent medicines in their wagon. The rest of the wagon train was going on to southwestern Texas and were following the dream that Carl had carefully built in their heads.

The final evening before the train was to leave the two men from Mississippi who were Carl and Chalk's supply wagon drivers came to Chalk and said they did not want to go into central Texas. When questioned as to why, they said they were "wanted posters" there that might have their pictures on them. It was obvious that they had a past they did not want it to catch up with them. They were paid for their work, collected their personal belongings quickly disappeared into the crowd.

Carl went into Texarkana and found two Spanish-speaking men who were hired to drive the supply wagon. Both were originally from Mexico and were in Texas as a result of being involved in cattle drives. They were strong, big and ready to go back to south Texas. Carl spoke broken Spanish and he had no trouble in finding a common, broken English communication with the two men.

Another wagon driver came to Carl and said he had a major problem. His wife, as she had been identified, had deserted him and gone to live in Texarkana. He said she was not really his legal wife but had come with him to escape a dance hall owner and a past "loose life" in Memphis. She was not cut out to become a rancher's wife and had just told him was not going any further. He had wished her well, given her a small amount of money and taken her personal things off the wagon. She had paid a local rancher to haul her and her belongings to town.

The wagon owner said he wanted to hire a helper as soon as he could. Carl told him that he would share his two supply wagon drivers with him for a few days and he could pick up a helper down the trail. This arrangement was fine with everyone and he did find a helper within a few days. He obviously had grown tired of the woman and was glad to finally be rid of her.

Two wagon drivers became sick but chose to travel on. They were not willing to stop now, as the impact from arriving in Texas was greater than the thought of stopping just to get well. Over a few days they recovered.

The Army troop stayed intact and at dawn the next morning they sounded revelry. Everyone was ready to pull out. Everyone in the train was now excited at the fact that they were finally becoming real Texans.

Chapter 7
Texas Trails and Trials

The wagon train headed straight toward the west. It was clear the trail had been traveled many times. Wagon tracks were deep and the side of the trail was clearly marked with hand made sign as to when others had gone before. Chalk took a small piece of wood from his supply trail and inscribed the date and the number of wagons that were heading to south Texas. He also added, "Harmony and Goodwin" to the sign in bold black letters. He proudly nailed it on a big oak tree that was hard to miss for anyone heading west.

Chalk was riding near Carl when the train got to a milepost marked "12 miles", west of the Army post. Carl explained that the trail split here and all of his train needed to be directed to make the change at the milepost. In the past there had been a couple of wagons that had fallen back from the main train that went the wrong way. Carl said that this caused major problems and must not happen again. The split in the trail was marked but weeds and grass often covered the small sign. Chalk took the wagon list and stopped at the trail junction, He checked out every wagon as it passed and made sure the entire train was on the right trail. The Army followed behind and brought up the rear.

Carl was a little nervous the next day and Chalk picked up on the way he was acting. The Commander at the Army Post had heard that there were bandits in the area just ahead. Carl knew that they were known to have robbed two stagecoaches. He also knew that a straggling wagon was a popular target. Wagon trains were not as easy to take over and the tactics were never the same. The bandits would block the trail by cutting a tree and placing it across the trail. When the wagons arrived and they were stopped to clear the trail the bandits would attack. They then would disappear into the woods and the train was left with problems.

Carl asked the Captain to put several of his troops up front
and to mix others in with the wagons. The Captain agreed
and soon the wagon train was a mix of wagons and soldiers.
Carl thought that the presence of the Army would stop any
attacks. The people in the wagons were all informed and
they were nervous. Everyone who had a gun kept it loaded
and within easy reach, just in case.

The weather was getting cooler and the days were continuing
to grow shorter. For this reason every day was becoming
more pressured to get to the south part of Texas as soon
as they could. Travel was scheduled for every day, all day
Sunday included. The people were told that early winter
storms in the area could come at any time and when they
were in the area, snow and ice were major concerns.

The trail went south toward a small town named Marshall.
The trail was following flatland and planned to cross a
river bridge located about 10 miles south of town. The
Sabine River was never predictable and could go into a
flood stage with a small amount of rain. The bridge was not
always passable. If the river was in a normal fall shallow
pool, you could cross. Luck held, and they crossed with no
problems.

Marshall was a typical small Texas town. The merchants
were all eager to sell supplies and local whiskey to a wagon
train. Most of the merchants were honest and were sincerely
trying to help the settlers. There were several small metal
working shops in the town and they were making spare
parts for wagons. They also were producing simple farming
tools, rakes, hoes and shovels. Sodbuster plows were in
demand by the local farmers and were being turned out in
large numbers. It was common for the local merchants to
come out onto the streets as a wagon train passed and set
up displays of things for sale.

The wagon train reached Marshall. It never stopped but
went straight past Marshall and to the bridge on the river.
The local Sheriff was in the street.

Carl told him they were in a hurry and did not have time to stop. Stopping would not allow them the time they needed to get to the river, cross over the bridge by nightfall and be safely on the other side.

The lead wagon finally reached the river. Carl rode across the low water bridge on his horse. He felt the bridge was safe and waved for the first wagon to come across. The water was near the top of the road surface but with a good driver, it was easily passable.

Carl's biggest fear was that bandits might try to fire shots and spook the horses while they were crossing. This could cause a major problem. All of the wagons finally crossed the bridge and the Army followed towing their wagons and cannons. The whole train found a small but ample clearing about two miles past the river and camped for the night. The ground was muddy and there were a lot of snakes.

Chalk noticed that there were a lot of buzzards circling in the area south of the campsite. Buzzards were commonly seen flying near the trail but these birds were landing in an area about a half a mile ahead. When the wind would blow from the south there was a bad smell blowing north.

Carl and Chalk were concerned and rode ahead to check out the cause. What they found made them sick to their stomach. There were two wagons on the side of the road. They were turned over on their sides. About 20 yards back in the woods there were 4 dead human bodies, two men and two women. You could tell by the clothing they were wearing. The buzzards were feeding on the remains. Chalk shot several of the buzzards and lost his stomach from the smell. After they recovered a little, they rode back to the wagon train and got the Army Captain in a corner. They told him it looked like the wagons had been ambushed, robbed and then the people were walked into the woods and shot. It was a deed that looked like bandits were to blame.

The Captain took a detail of men, plenty of ammunition, shovels and returned to the crime scene. The remains were buried and the Captain recorded the grizzly details of the scene. Before leaving, he delivered a short Christian prayer and asked the men to sing "Amazing Grace" with him. The names of the dead were never known and there was nothing found to provide any identification. The bandits had stripped everything of value from the wagons and the people.

The detail returned to the wagon train and an increased detail of security guards was placed all around the wagons. The cannons and Army wagons were put in the center of the wagon circle and everyone was told to stay within the camp circle. There were to be no exceptions. The night came and the train settled down to an uneasy night of sleep.

The next morning came under a gray and low cloud sky. The wagons hitched up and pulled out without having any breakfast. The Army troop was leading the way as well as being spread throughout the wagon train. The train passed the death site and never stopped. The men kept the women and children in the wagons with the curtains closed. The odor of death was still present and they passed as fast as possible. All of the wagons were about 5 miles past the site and they pulled up long enough to allow the women to feed the children and the men to take care of the cattle. Milk cows must be milked on a regular schedule to keep them giving milk. Not milking them also can lead to serious and quick health problems.

The train then resumed travel and headed for the town of Henderson, Texas. They arrived about an hour after noon. The Captain went to the local Sheriff and informed him of the situation on the trail. The Sheriff told the Captain that there were several men living near the river that were raiding small groups of wagons. Murder was a new part of their bad behavior the Sheriff was upset. He told the Army Captain that he knew of most of the local bandits by name and they were very dangerous.

He also told the Captain that the trail south to Waco had reports of a band of Comanche renegades doing similar raiding. They had been known to steal young girls and to kill everyone else. All of this was reported to Carl and Chalk.

They were deeply concerned but did not want to add additional fear to the people in the train, especially the women. Instead, they called a camp meeting and stressed the danger as was seen on the trail just traveled. Everyone was restricted to the immediate campsite and only a few men, accompanied by soldiers, were allowed to go into town for supplies. All of the men were told to wear guns and to keep them loaded.

The wagon train was told to plan for as much travel per everyday as was possible during daylight hours. This camp rule was to apply until the train arrived in Waco.

The trip to Waco took five additional travel days. Every day was stressful and the wagons were pushed as hard as they would go. The biggest holdups were the slow moving cattle. The mood in the wagons was laced with fear and stress. The nights were equally tenuous. Having the soldiers with the train gave everyone a better sense of safety but fear was still everywhere.

The last day before arriving on the outskirts of Waco the soldiers who were patrolling the trail in front of the train saw several Indians on ponies riding near the trail. When they spotted the soldiers and they quickly disappeared into the woods. No shots were fired and no confrontation happened.

The Brazos River flowed north of the area of downtown Waco. Waco had constructed a single lane bridge over the river about a half-mile east of town. Every wagon had to cross by itself, as the wood and stone bridge was not capable of holding an excessive amount of weight.

Chalk took his supply wagon over first to test the span. He made it with no problem. The cattle were then led across one at a time as the bridge had very short side rails and not spooking the cows was vital. It took about four hours to get all of the wagons and the Army troops over the bridge. The last wagon crossing was a point of celebration for everyone.

There was a large campground on the backside of a local College, Baylor, where the wagons were pulled into a circle. The School was gracious to the settlers and gave them a big meal, access to hot water showers and fresh hay for the animals. The wagon train stayed there for the rest of the day and the night. The next morning they then set out on a trail going to an Army post about 40 miles to the southwest. The morning was blacker than most. Dark storm clouds were overhead. By about 9 o'clock it began to rain so hard that the trail turned into a muddy fluid. The rain was cold and the wind made it feel even colder. By nightfall they had only gone 18 miles. The train found a field and circled the wagons. There were several cattle ranchers in the area. One of them came out to welcome the train. He brought apples, pecan nuts and fresh cut cabbage in the back of his wagon.

By morning the rain had stopped but the trail was still slow. The horses were slipping and loosing their footing as they pulled the heavy wagons up even the slightest grade. Carl saw the bad conditions and recognized that they were not going to improve. He circled the wagons and told everyone to plan for a rest stop until the trail was passable. Two days passed.

The center of the camp circle was always lit with a campfire and the musicians again were making music. A local rancher who liked to sing heard the music and came in. He sang a lot of cowboy songs and he played a mean harmonica. The whiskey on everyone's wagons began to appear and the fear that had been so common were become just a bad a memory.

On the third day the trail was drying and the footing for the horses was better. The wagon train pushed on to the Army post. This stop was a final dropping off point for several wagons.

The wagons that were going to the San Antonio area needed to go almost straight south. Carl and Chalk were going further west to pick up a trail that went to a small German town named Fredericksburg.

A few more wagons were waiting at the Army post to join Carl's train. They were glad to see this train arrive. A total of 28 settler wagons and the Army troop were going to follow this western trail.

Carl called all of the wagon drivers together and held a group meeting. He realized that this group did not have a wagon master. Carl asked the group going to the eastern trail to pick a train leader. Carl knew that every train must have a designated and recognized leader or it would have problems. He told them that there was a well-marked cattle trail that went almost to Austin, the Chisem Trail, and this was easy to follow. From there on south there were several trails that went to small towns that were all just being settled. He was personally recommended a German town called New Braunfels. He drew them a simple map and helped them plan the remaining trip.

On south, there was San Antonio; Alice and a small place that was still just a wide spot on the trail called Dilly.

There were many small settlements springing up along the several small rivers in the area and most were in areas where the land was good for either growing crops or running cattle.

To the west of Austin was an area that the natives called the hill country. This area had a lot of good cattle land but the soil was too thin and rocky for raising row crops. Further west, in Johnson City there was deep soil and the ground was rich. But, the further west one went, the less the supply of water.

He then told his wagon drivers that they were going to leave early the next morning. The Army Captain was anxious to move out and this helped make the decision. Several of the soldiers had been drinking and the Captain knew that additional free time could only make the problem worse.

The weather was turning colder and the train left on time early the next morning. They wanted to get to a small town called Llano within the next week. Weather and trail conditions were good and every wagon was able to make a good distance for the first day.

The weather turned windy, but it was finally dry. The travel as planned was running on schedule. The trail was now more open and large Spanish oak trees were on the hills and in the fields. Prickly pear cactus was also everywhere. Large groups of wild turkeys were seen often. White tail deer were everywhere and many of the low water crossings were dry. Travel was relatively easy but still a lot of hard work.

Routine trail life seemed to be an easier routine for Chalk. He had come a long way under Carl's leadership and he was actually feeling good about himself in learning trail management. This feeling was a strong and empowering experience. The closer to the end of the trail the train got, the greater the energy within him became.

The people in the train had all become his personal friends. The young men all were looking up to him as a hero. The success of getting to south Texas, safe and on a respectable schedule was a powerful feeling for everyone. Chalk was especially happy and was becoming a complete and self-confident young man.

Travel was now becoming a daily routine. Standing as a security guard was less eventful. The Texas Rangers and Army had already cleaned out the worst trail bandits. The Indian raiders were being forced further west and the trail threat concerns was going away. Nighttime camp conditions were now less stressful and actually were becoming fun. This situation gave Chalk a lot of time to think and reflect about his past. The availability of some free time in itself was a luxury.

On the other side of the fun was reality. When the wagon train left Memphis everyone was clean cut, shaven, wearing clean cloths and generally healthy. The horses were strong looking, in great shape and had a little fat on their bones. Now, most of the men were wearing long hair, had shaggy beards and their clothes were worn so badly that the patches and mending were the only good looking parts left.

Most of the women were likewise showing the signs of trail wear. There was no lipstick, no well-managed hairstyles and their dresses they were wearing were worn and patched the same as the men's clothing. Everyone had developed severe body odor. After a while it became accepted as a part of being on the trail.

The horses were still able to pull the wagons but had become lean. They were marked from harness sores and from cuts and bruises suffered on the trails. The cattle were thin. They were walking with much less purpose and less speed. Often they were being pulled up to speed by the halters that held then to the backs of the wagons.

The best looking group was the children. They were still wearing big smiles and were often more active than their parents. Youth was a blessing on the trail.

The experiences from the trails had hardened everyone. Trail experiences and training were an education in how to survive. They were going to need this in the new roles they were entering as settlers.

On the trail one of the young men driving a wagon that had come all the way from Memphis got really sick. He passed out while driving and suddenly died. His wife was overcome with grief and had several sessions of crying and fainting. The other women in the train came to her side and offered their help in making her stable. The men found enough lumber to build a simple coffin and line it with a quilt that one of the women had made. His name was Walter Anderson.

A simple funeral was held and the grave was covered with native stones and a simple cross. The Army bugler played taps. The man's name "Walter Anderson' was painted on a simple wood cross. When the service was over the train moved on to the south. Carl took one of his Mexican drivers from the supply wagon to drive the widow's wagon.

The widow was not sure of what to expect or do in the future. Several of the women on the train took turns of having her ride with them and allowed her the time it took to regain her composure and to think for herself about her future. Carl offered to have his driver take her wagon as far as train was going and would help her get a job in a city somewhere near the area where he lived in. She was barely 30 and had a college education. Carl suggested that she consider her future for a few days and them make a decision. Her name was Wanda Anderson.

Chalk watched the grave digging, the funeral and the final closing of the grave. This event brought back memories of his Mother's funeral and the work that Digger Maggard had done to place her remains into the earth. The realization that life is precious and how much he appreciated the friends and people who had been important to him during his life

Chapter 8
Arriving In South Texas

Finally, the wagon train pulled into Llano. The Llano River was on the north side of the town and Carl decided to cross as soon as the train arrived. It was mid morning and the water was seasonably low. The crossing was easy. The riverbanks were sloped which made it easy for the wagons to enter and exit the crossing. The river bottom was rock and the water was barely flowing. The Army troop crossed after all of the wagons had safely crossed to the other side. The town was similar to Waco but much smaller.

Local merchants were out in force. The local political staff was equally obvious. Camp was set up south of town. There were several cattle corrals in the area. Longhorn cattle were common sights in the fields and were a popular breed in this area. The horns on these animals were gigantic when compared to the cows in the train.

About an hour before night fall the local Mayor and Sheriff rode their horses into the campsite and found Carl. They were very friendly and wanted to make him and everyone in the train to feel welcome. Carl called everyone together. The Mayor was outlining the best shops and facilities in the town and the Sheriff was assuring everyone that they were safe and had nothing to fear. They invited Carl and Chalk to have a drink at a local saloon and told the wagon people that the town would stay open late into the evening for anyone who wanted to shop. Wagon trains seldom stopped here for more than overnight and moved on the next morning. This was a common stop over practice.

The train spent the night and left camp early the next morning heading toward Fredericksburg. All of the wagons continued south. The trail followed gently rolling fields and went through countryside that was covered with yucca plants, mesquite trees and an ever-increasing number of cacti. The trail was well traveled and easy to follow. Wildlife was plentiful as were all type of fall wildflowers.

The number of local ranches was increasing and barbwire fences were becoming a more common sight. This area was obviously prosperous and the stories that Carl had been telling started to look real.

The trip from Llano to Fredericksburg took two full days. The campsite for the first night of this trail was in a flat spot near a big natural pond. A local rancher came over and made them welcome. He had several Mexican men with him who were cowboys. Everybody was friendly and the settlers were discovering that the Spanish language was common in the area. The pond had attracted a lot of ducks and geese. Chalk was a good shot and there were four fresh geese and 4 wild ducks for supper.

Wanda Anderson was beginning to gather her thoughts and was thinking about the future. She went to see Carl. Chalk and Carl were busy working on a trail problem when she arrived. Carl asked her how she was doing and wondered what she wanted to do. She said she wanted to go to Bandera, Texas and find a job and a place to live.

She knew that the other settlers in the train were planning to find homes in that area and she would at least be among friends. She also knew that Carl was well known in the area and he would be available if she needed a man's advice in the future. Chalk noticed that she was still not herself and spoke up offering any help that he could provide. She thanked both of them and went back to her wagon.

The next day the train pulled into Fredericksburg. The campground was near the center of town. The wagon train formed a circle around a tall permanent flagpole. The Army troop set up camp just to the west of the wagons. There was a small Army post on the east side of town and the Officers came out to welcome the new soldiers to the area. Buildings in the town were impressive, there were several large limestone churches, many stone homes and the whole town was immaculately clean. Most churches had tall steeples and had a cross on top. This construction indicated that the Catholic religion was strong in the city.

White limestone was the primary building material for the better business structures and home sites. Large oak trees and an occasional palm tree were on the sides of the streets.

Most of the new settlers went to the shopping area and spent time looking at items in the stores that lined the main street. The most populated street was a wagon trail heading toward west Texas. There was a three block long area full of stores selling hardware and trail supplies. Boots were the popular footwear choice for men.

Several boot shops were in the main shopping area. Some shops had boots that were made ahead to standard sizes. Every shop would make you a pair of custom boots but they cost more and the buyer had to wait for delivery. Women's boots were more dressy but did not offer as many styles and sizes.

Carl often shopped in several of the local stores and he was on a first name relationship with many of the locals. A large German majority had settled the town. Beer was brewed locally and German food was available in several local restaurants. The men were soon drinking big schooners of cold beer and eating sausage and cooked red cabbage. The women were less inclined to drink the beer but enjoyed the many German dished that were available.

Another welcome advantage that was found in this town was a small hospital. The also had a large hotel. The saloon area was a great place to meet local people. There were several doctors available and the local people were generally healthy and were living to be old people.

The Pedernales River flowed on the west side of the town. This river was never a dependable source for water, especially in the late summer. Spring rains often put the river in flood stage

Area ranchers had dammed up places where water could be retained and built fences to assure that only their cattle were able to gain access. They called these impoundment's "tanks". Hunting around tanks was easy in the dry months. Wildlife would go to the water when other water supplies were gone. Snakes were also common in these areas.

The area around Fredericksburg was hilly and had many cattle, sheep and goat ranches. The cattle were being raised for beef. Sheep and goats were used for wool and food. Cabrito is goat meat and is a standard part of many Mexican diets. Area ranchers were both Spanish speaking and English speaking folks. German was also a common language in many places.

Fredericksburg was the area's economic center. This town was the trading center for area ranches and was also the most economically advanced town in the "hill country" part of Texas.

In Memphis, there was one wagon that was loaded with a cargo so heavy that the team pulling it had to have 4 horses. Few knew what was being transported in this wagon. This wagon was always an issue in crossings and in muddy roads. Weight was a problem on any trail that was less than perfect.

The settler driving this wagon went to several key people in Fredericksburg and inquired as to what new towns in the area still needed a local newspaper. He discovered that the town of Kerrville was still without any major printing companies. Kerrville was about 25 miles south of the current campsite and was on the trail to Bandera. He then went to Carl and asked him what he knew about the town.

Everything Carl said was positive and this was helped the settler to decide to settle in the Kerrville area. Carl warned him that the Guadalupe River flowed on the south side of the main town area and was known to flood often from spring rains. For this reason the main section of town was built on a high section of ground. If he were to set up a shop Carl suggested it be in the area on this high ground. Another important positive in Kerrville was the availability of a good medical clinic. There was also a trail from San Antonio heading west that went through the town. The trail traffic was helping the town grow. The decision was finalized; he would leave the train in Kerrville.

The next morning the train left Fredericksburg and arrived in Kerrville about an hour before nightfall. The wagons circled and made camp for the night. The heavy wagon stayed with the train for the night and word quickly spread that this settler, his wife and two teenage sons were going to leave the train there.

Many of the settlers were quick to come by their wagon and wish them well. The mutual support of each settler for the others was strong. They had endured much together and were each concerned for the future of the others. This bonding and the relationships that had been formed on the trail lasted the rest of these people's lives. Common concern and common objectives had built friendships and sincere caring. The west was built with many such relationships.

The next day the train was scheduled to arrive in Bandera. Carl was growing excited, as was everyone else. Carl had brought 3 other trains to the area over the past 7 years and was a hero in his hometown. His wife was running a general supply store on the main street of Bandera. His two sons and a crew of hired cowboys were running his 4000-acre cattle ranch. Many of the local shopkeepers in several local towns had traveled to the area in response to Carl's leadership. They were all his friends and everybody respected him.

Carl knew this would be his last wagon train and in many ways was happy to be going home. However, he was also sad that this was going to be his last train. He had really enjoyed these trips and the many people he would meet and the experiences that went with the job.

Carl hired a friend from Kerrville to ride ahead and tell his wife that the wagon train, and the Army troop, would be arriving late the next day. He wanted the new settlers to feel welcome and he knew that everyone in town, and from the nearby ranches would come to town to welcome the wagons. Having an Army troop with them was an added bonus.

The lone rider left about 5 PM and was in Bandera by 8 o'clock. He found Carl's wife, Charlie. She was excited to learn that her husband was coming home. The sky was almost lit by the light from a full fall moon and the atmosphere of high expectations in everyone's last night on the trail was intoxicating.

The rider returned to the campsite early the next morning and informed Carl that everything had been communicated. His wife was going to inform the local residents of the arrival. She told the rider to tell him that his ranch hands would have a bar-b-que dinner ready for all of the travelers and the food would be ready when they arrived.

Chalk took all of this in and was enjoying the moment. Carl was not only his business partner but Chalk had come to think of him almost as his father. He was happy and felt privileged that Carl allowed him to be his partner.

The next morning came and the familiar Army bugle sounded the wake up call. The local people in Kerrville watched as the wagons pulled out. Many stood by the side of the trail and waved. They people on the train had made close friends with many of the soldiers. Everyone knew that to time was near when they would be riding on. Finally, the camping area was empty with the exception of the remaining single wagon, his horses, cow and the pioneer family that was staying in Kerrville.

Within a few minutes the local Kerrville people were coming to the wagon and offering food, advice and friendship. All of the local residents wanted to make them feel welcome.

The final 25 miles seemed to fly by and the spirits grew higher with every step of the horses. There were two small streams to cross. Both were near dry and the crossings were easy. The settlers were looking at the wide-open fields in some areas and the virgin timber stands in other places. Wild turkeys crossed the trail in two places and the colorful population of birds was singing in the trees.

About 5 miles from town Clay stopped all of the wagons and the Army troop. He asked them to all come together in a small open area and to make themselves comfortable. He wanted everyone, Husbands, wives, children and all of the soldiers to be present.

Carl thanked everyone for the many deeds and expressions of hope they had provided for him on the trail. He also told them that they were going to be welcomed by the townspeople as they arrived. Carl wanted the Army troop to lead the procession into town. He asked that the troops line up in the main street, let the wagons enter the camping are and then follow them to this location.

Carl told them when they arrived in town that they all pull their wagons into a final circle in a large open area just a short distance from the center of town. He was going to lead the way. There was a big field there and wagon trains were always special guests. They could park there until they had decided on their further plans. His last words were a short prayer for everyone's safety, for the fallen settler, Walter Anderson, who had died on the trail and for everyone's success in the future.

Just as he was closing a pair of horsemen arrived from the south. They were Carl's two sons and they had come to greet their father. When they dismounted they hugged their Dad and made him feel very welcome. Carl introduced them to Chalk and to the assembled crowd. Carl told his sons that

Chalk was his business partner for this trip. Everyone was happy and the wagon train people applauded Carl, Chalk and two his sons.

Carl asked the Army Captain to move his troop, cannons and wagons to the front and led the train into town. They had American and Texas flags and were a real positive symbol of the spirit of the new west.

Carl and Chalk, along with his two sons would ride next in line. The wagons would come next followed by the final wagon carrying the sign "Harmony and Goodwin".

Everyone put on their best smile, cleanest clothes, if they had any and fell into line. The wagon train pulled out for the last time and the men were shouting and whooping it up as they rode.

About a mile north of town there were a few families setting along the side of the trail in open wagons. They waved and threw flowers into several of the lead wagons. Carl recognized them, nodded his head and smiled with appreciation. The closer they got, the more people were on the trail waving and making noise. The train entered the north side of the town, rounded a curve in the trail and the final stopping site slowly came into view. The trip was just about over.

Carl, Chalk and his sons rode ahead and caught up with the Army Captain. Together they rode into the campground first and made sure the others knew where to enter. The Army troops stopped on the side of the street and watched as the wagon train moved to the rear area of the camping area. The troops moved into the campground formed a long line in front of their wagons and cannons. The whole procession was on the campground and stopped for the last time in about 15 minutes.

All of the wagons were parked and the drivers began to unhitch the horses. A local rancher had supplied a supply of oats and hay for them to eat. When the last wagon was parked and settled in a group of men came from across the street and greeted Carl and his lead group. A Minister was in the group and he asked Carl to have everyone gather, as soon as the horses, cattle and other shut down chores were completed.

Carl passed the word and everything went well. The settlers and the soldiers all gathered at the front of the area and the Minister gave a prayer of thanks for their safe arrival. He also told them of several different denominations of churches that were in the town and assured them that they were welcome to attend at their convenience.

The Sheriff and Mayor showed up just as the Minister was closing. Both said a few words. Carl got up and stated that everyone was invited to a big bar-b-que dinner that had been prepared just for them. There was plenty to eat and the beer supply, he promised, would be almost endless. The cowboys had brought the food to the camping area in the ranch chuckwagon. A spare wagon was also loaded with food and drink.

Carl said a few last words to the assembled group. As he was closing Charlie joined him and he proudly introduced her to the crowd. Charlie addressed the women in particular and told them that she would be available to answer questions and give advice after the meeting was over. Chalk also expressed his thanks and wished everyone well. Everybody had their fill and bedded down for the night. For most, they were near the place they would soon call home. It was a welcome feeling for everyone.

The Army Captain came to Carl's side and thanked him for the safe passage he had taken them through and he handed him a brand new Army Rifle. He also handed another one to Chalk. He said his men had suggested that they both have these rifles as they had earned them with their leadership. Chalk now had two rifles. He had always carried his first rifle from Kentucky with him and now he had an Army issued rifle.

The Captain discussed the trail from Bandera to Fort Clark with Carl. He was comfortable that his men and he would have no problem in getting there. They planned to pull out the next morning and arrive at the Fort late the same day. That was an aggressive plan.

Carl asked Chalk if he would like to spend the night at his ranch. He told him there was a nice warm bed available and the food was always good. Chalk was not book schooled but he knew that Carl needed to be at home with his wife, alone, for a few days. Time has a way of making reunions very special.

Carl was also aware of the stress and pressures on widow Anderson. She was alone and still afraid of what she was going to do. She needed to be with another woman who could help her find herself and go forward. Carl found her wagon and she was inside in a corner looking at a picture of her deceased husband. She was crying. Carl saw her before she saw him and in a soft voice said, " You are welcome to come to my home for a few days and get some rest".

She dried her eyes and looked him in the eye and said Thanks but your wife must need you tonight more than she needs company. Thanks and let's talk tomorrow. Chalk was near Carl and overheard the conversation.

He went to the Mayor and told him about Widow Anderson and asked if there was anyone who could put her up for the next night or two. The Sheriff and his wife immediately went to the widow's wagon and gave her a warm smile. She responded and climbed down to greet them. They told her to get a few things; she was going home with them.

Chalk was nearby and told her that he would take her wagon to Carl's ranch and make sure everything inside and the horses were all safe for the night.

Chalk drove the widow's wagon and one of the Mexican drivers drove the supply wagon and they followed one of Carl's sons to the Harmony ranch. When they arrived all of the wagons were parked next to the ranch house. The strong boxes, one being Carl's, one being Chalks and the third one from Widow Anderson's wagon were carried into the house and put in a safe place. Chalk rode his horse back to town.

When he arrived in town he went back to the bar-b-que dinner, had a few cold beers. While Chalk was mixing with the crowd Carl found him. Carl told him that as soon as he had a little time he would figure out what this trip had done in profits. He then would split the profits right down the middle and pay Chalk.

He assured Chalk that his strongbox would be safe at his house until Chalk wanted to get it. On the trail Chalk never discussed money with Carl. But now they were in a safe place and the trip was over. Chalk told Carl that he had several thousand dollars in gold and the deed to a farm in Louisiana in his box.

He had won the deed in a riverboat poker game. He had also won over $20,000 in gold coins over time. He had never spent anything and he was not certain as to how much money he actually had. The bottom line was that he considered himself "well off" for an uneducated Kentucky half-breed.

The evening settled in. Carl was home and went to his ranch to spend the night with his wife. It was only about a mile from town and an easy ride. Chalk got a room in a small hotel and took a long warm bath and went to bed.

The next morning the bugle called the soldiers to order and they prepared to leave. Carl and Chalk were both there before the troops pulled out.

Carl and Chalk gave the Captain a custom made knife that had been crafted by a local citizen. He accepted the knife, gave Carl and Chalk a last hardy handshake, mounted his horse, called his men to order, gave a crisp salute to Carl and Chalk and made ready to pull out. As they left the campground each soldier saluted Carl and Chalk as they passed in front of them. This was the highest compliment they could pay them.

The widow Anderson came to the good-by event. She waved at every soldier as they passed. When the Army troop was gone Chalk asked her to join him for a cup of coffee and some breakfast in a nearby café. She gladly accepted.

As they eat she began to talk about her former husband; He was a lawyer who was originally from Nashville, Tennessee. He got his college education at the University of Cincinnati. He was two years older than Wanda. She had met him in Cincinnati, Ohio, which was her hometown. She was a teacher and they met at a school social.

They had fallen in love quickly and in a short time they were married. Her parents were not in favor of the marriage and after about three years Walter and Wanda had decided to leave town so that they could be away from her parents. Going to the west was an exciting place for both of them to find a new and interesting life.

Her husband had already made a lot of money in the legal field and she told Chalk that there was over $30,000 in her strongbox. She wanted Carl and Chalk to help her safeguard this money and to be sure that it was not put into a crooked bank.

Chalk liked her and was drawn to her by her honesty. She obviously trusted and liked him. After all, she was lonely and all of the ladies on the wagon train had husbands. They were friends but they wanted to spend this time with their husbands and children.

Chalk was also alone. He was never concerned about being lonely while he was working but now he was at a point where he had nothing to do. It was a time to just relax and find a new life. As they parted they agreed to have coffee again, soon, and to be good friends for the future. It was a time to set back and smell the roses for a while.

The wagons slowly came to life and soon everyone was soon walking the streets and looking the town over for what it had to offer. The many events of the next two weeks gave everyone a place to go and the wagons were slowly pulled away. Each individual settler found a place to start and they were not disappointed with their new situation in Texas.

The choices that each settler made for their future were all different. Everyone was excited and anxious to get started. Chalk was now in Texas and ready for what ever would happen next. That part of his life *is another fantastic story.*

In A Time Before Ours

Chalk Goodwin and His Early
Experiences in Texas

Book Two of Four

Kenneth Orr

Chapter 1

Getting Roots and Reason

Bandera, Texas was a friendly small frontier Texas town. The local people were basically God fearing church people. Many were Hispanic or from Hispanic roots. They were all involved with the daily affairs of life, family, church, making a living and being good citizens. Their local social circles were small, but everyone was united. They trusted each other and cared about the well being of their neighbors. Out in the surrounding prairie lands, especially to the west, there were cattle ranches with large herds of beef cattle. There were also ranchers who were also raising sheep. Both types of ranches always had large herds of goats. Chalk had never lived in a place where the entire economy was based on livestock. It was different and it was a welcome experience for him.

The central part of town was not large. The dirt streets were well packed and dusty from the weight of wagon wheels and the pounding of both horse and cattle hoofs. Cattle were often brought to town to be sold in the livestock auction that happened regularly every two weeks. Cattle were sold by auction. The sale barn was a place of constant dealing and constant discussion between the ranchers and buyers. Young calves were brought to the sale on a regular basis. Local ranchers would buy them to raise and fatten up for the markets. Older cattle were sold to packinghouses in San Antonio for slaughter. The packinghouses would send a buyer and a small group of cowboys to bring them home.

"Sale Day" was a big experience for everyone. The local cafes, of which three were located near the sale barn, all did a lot of business. They would always have plenty of food and cheap beer to sell. The ranch supply stores would set up sidewalk displays featuring "sale" merchandise for the ranchers to buy. The ranchers would sometimes bring their wives who would shop while the men dealt with the cattle.

They would buy cloth, buttons, clothing patterns, yarn and kitchen items. They also would buy toys and hard candy for the children. Money from the cattle sale often never got home but was exchanged for flour, sugar liquor and coffee beans. This local economic cycle was well established and was all centered on the "sale".

Chalk was intently interested. His first few sale day experiences helped him learn that the best deals were often made in the streets around the sale barn. Ranchers could save paying a sale commission if they sold their products directly and skipped the middleman. Some local merchants would set up a table and place all kinds of goods in full view to attract customers. The old-timers were always seen cutting deals and talking to lifelong friends. The day was always a real big Bandera happening.

Chalk had gone out to Carl's ranch to spend a few days and got the hang of the ranch style of life. The one common effort from everyone was hard work. Carl's wife, Charlie, her full name was Charlene but she preferred to be called Charlie, would get up early, fix a morning meal, get dressed and ride to town to open her "General Store". Charlie had a staff of housekeepers who cooked all of the meals except breakfast. She kept that meal for herself.

Carl would get up at about the same time and get dressed for the work he was going to be doing. Their two boys, Jim and John, were 22 and 26 years old. They still lived at home and worked on the ranch. Some days Carl would go to the bunkhouse and ride with the cowboys. He loved to see the ranch and to be out with the cattle. On other days he would ride into town where he was always involved with buying and selling.

Carl was a cattle broker of sort. He would sometimes lend money to local ranchers for operating expenses. In exchange he would get guaranteed lower than market prices on the borrower's cattle when they were for sale. He was like a cattle banker and had a reputation for being fair and honest with everyone. He had many friends in town and he often would go to lunch with one of them. That's where a lot of the deals were made.

The two sons would always go to the bunkhouse, plan the workday for the cowboys and work along side them. On some days, work would be planned for two, three or four days working out on the range. This was always the case when they were rounding up calves, branding, mending fence lines and rounding up cattle to be sold.

Branding was a selective effort. It a cow was going to be raised on the Harmony Ranch, it got branded. If it was going to be sold at the sale or put into a cattle drive, branding was not inflicted. Sometimes they would ear tag these cows and turn them loose again.

There was a middle aged Mexican man who rode with the cowboys. He drove a special wagon, called a "chuckwagon" that was set up to provide food in the fields, fresh water and basic medicine when a cowboy took sick.

There was usually a second wagon for work supplies and tools. There were always a supply wagon with barbwire, cedar posts and tools.

The camp cook's place was always special. Hungry cowboys were always hardy eaters and he fed them well. He always kept a few snacks available to put in the saddlebags to make the day a little more enjoyable. The favorite was hot and spicy beef jerky. Coffee was always available and it was always HOT.

Chalk went out into the fields with the cowboys several times. He enjoyed the work. Carl had told Chalk that he would help him set up a small place of his own when they entered into the wagon train deal he had cut with him. But before anyone made any decisions he wanted him to have some experience in the field and see how well he fit into this lifestyle.

Chalk had become a skilled poker player. As a part of his work he lived in the cowboy bunkhouse. It was common to see the cowboys gather around one of the dinner tables and shuffle the cards. Chalk was always interested in a good game.

His skill, most of the time, allowed him to win more than he lost. In some games it was obvious that who ever were betting into him was an amateur and was not going to win. If he was ahead in winnings he often took the opportunity to fold his cards and not show the hand he had. He did not want to take large amounts of money from his friends. Money was not plentiful and friendship was more important.

Carl was also true to his word on money matters. After doing the accounting for the wagon train trip he saw there was a profit of $ 5,990. The Army troop had paid him $1,500 for escorting the detachment into Texas. The Officer in charge had never been out west and needed a seasoned leader to keep them on the right trails. The other wagons had paid several hundred dollars each and the entire fee charges were paid in coin. He split the total amount down the middle and gave Chalk $3,000 in gold coins. The money went into the strongbox that was still stored at Carl's ranch.

It was December and Carl and Charlie were figuring out his property tax bill for the ranch, the General Store and for other property he had bought in town. Chalk thought about what was happening and remembered he had won a place in Missouri earlier that spring while gambling on the riverboat. He went to his strongbox and found the deed he had been given.

When he dug the deed out and it was still carrying the name of a Mr. Earl Webb. The County and all of the property description were clearly outlined on the deed. Chalk took the document to a local lawyer and told him how he had come to own the land. The lawyer agreed to contact the tax agent in the land's location and get everything in good order for him.

Chalk gave the Lawyer a retainer fee, left the document with him and put the lawyer to work. In about a month the lawyer contacted Chalk and asked him to come into his office. Chalk went to the office and the lawyer told him that the land he had won was a real can of worms. He had contacted the tax people and found that the taxes were already paid. He had also learned that Mr. Webb was renting the land to some sharecroppers.

The lawyer, having learned the facts, contacted local Sheriff in the county where the farm was located. The Sheriff assigned one of his men to investigate the situation. They knew Mr. Webb from some previously experienced several slick deals and wanted to get to the real truth on this one. What he found was a real surprise.

A big bank in St. Louis had previously repossessed the farm from a family that could not keep up with the payments. Mr. Webb was the agent for the bank and he handled the whole deal. When he had the Sheriff take ownership from the previous owners he had substituted his name on the new deed as the new owner, not the Bank in St. Louis. Mr. Webb then found renters who were told he owned the farm and all of the surrounding farm land. They were currently paying rent to Mr. Webb.

Chalk asked the lawyer what to do, he had never been involved with a crooked deal like this and he wanted to resolve it quickly and with honesty. Chalk had a deed that bore Mr. Webb's name and a hand written assignment, with a credible witness's signature giving the place to Chalk. The lawyer contacted the Sheriff that had the whole story on Mr. Webb. He sent him authorization to contact the St. Louis bank and to do what was necessary to fix this problem. About a month passed.

Again, the lawyer contacted Chalk and asked him to come by. Chalk responded quickly. The lawyer had a nice long letter from the Bank President of the St. Louis bank where he outlined a trail of fraud that had been going on for several years. It appeared that Mr. Webb was considered to be a star bank employee who had a good record for recovering property when the bank had to inforce foreclosures. Over the past three years he had handled over 200 such situations. Most of these were in the area near St. Louis and were handled with no problem. However, several were in places that were farther out of the way and they were often in places where the bank had little or no other interests. These remote locations were in communities where local officials were slow to change records and often were never followed up to assure everything had been properly transacted.

Mr. Webb had taken the opportunity to insert his name on several such places and upon a closed-door audit 33 such transactions were unaccounted for.

The bank also discovered that all of the supporting paperwork for the 33 transactions was missing from any file. He was making a fortune from rent and from the sale of a couple of these properties. All of these transactions were fraud.

Some how Mr. Webb had discovered that this investigation was going on. He obviously had a partner somewhere in the bank and he was alerted when the questions got too complicated to answer. On the day when the bank President planned to confront, him he never came to work.

The Bank President called the local Sheriff from St Louis and told him what was happening. A warrant was issued and together The Sheriff and Bank President went to Mr. Webb's home.

Upon arrival they discovered that Mr. Webb, his wife and most of his personal belongings were gone. He had a wagon that was easy to identify. It was painted white with a red canvas cover. It was not easy to hide. The Sheriff contacted other local law officers requesting help in locating the wagon and this man. The next day he was found in a hotel about 30 miles west of St. Louis and the local Sheriff made the arrest.

The Bank President was glad to find out about this crook and in appreciation to Chalk and to the professional way that he had handled the situation; he ordered the bank to issue a new, clear title to Chalk Goodwin. He also ordered the bank to pay all legal fees for Chalk's lawyer and to inform the renters of what had happened immediately.

Chalk relayed all of this information to Carl. Carl was shocked. The whole experience put a fear of big city bankers into both of them and they went out of their way not to go to any bank in a big city for any business.

The realities of life were becoming clear to Chalk. He was learning and he was quickly growing into a 'street-smart' young man. He also was enjoying being in Texas and being among people he trusted and could, with honesty, call friends.

Chapter 2

Meeting Local People

Chalk stayed with Carl, living in the bunkhouse and working with the cowboys, for a couple of months. This was hard work but it was still easier than the hard work involved with supporting a wagon train. The food was always great, especially the Mexican dishes that the bunkhouse cook served. Refried beans, rice, hot peppers and flour tortieas were served at every meal. Beef, chicken and cabrito were the standard meats and on special occasions a roast pig or turkey was served.

Carl told him to stay as long as he wanted. Chalk was never one to overstay a welcome. He was strongly independent and one day while in town he found a small house that he could rent. The outside was weathered white stone and the inside had all of the room and conveniences that he wanted. It was furnished with good locally built furniture and the only thing he needed to bring was bed sheets, towels and his clothes.

Carl told him the house belonged to a friend and he was an honest and fair man. The rent was cheap and the location was only a few hundred feet from the main section of town. Chalk rented the house, moved in and made himself comfortable. He liked doing cowboy work but he felt that he could do more being in town doing something to allow him to meet more people. A "cowboy" life is a great way to get to know cattle. But, cows are not much fun to talk to, and they never talk back.

The main section of town had Charlie's dry goods and supply store on the main corner. There was a big saloon and restaurant next door and on up the street there was a livery stable and a blacksmith shop.

Charlie had taken a real liking to Wanda Anderson. Wanda was young enough that she could have been her daughter. Charlie and Carl had two boys, no girls. That was great for Charlie, she had always wanted a daughter, but not so great for Carl.

Wanda was offered a job to work in the dry goods store and she gladly took the opportunity. This job was a way to get established and to start putting her life back together. Wanda had found a room to rent and had parked her wagon out on Carl's ranch.

Chalk was a frequent patron to the local saloon, not so much to drink but to eat. The food was mostly Mexican style and he loved it. He could cook, but he had rather buy lunch and dinner than to cook. Chalk got to know the blacksmith and they were both friends from day one. He offered Chalk a part-time job to help out with the horseshoe business and to mend broken wagon parts.

Chalk took the job offer and soon was busy fixing things, meeting people and doing something that was worthwhile. He had got to know the Sheriff who always seemed to have a blacksmith job to be done. The relationship led to Chalk being offered a deputy's Sheriff's job on a part time basis. Between serving blacksmith customers and working part-time at the jail, Chalk quickly met a large cross-section of the local folks. He also had the opportunity to wear his badge when in the saloon. After all, he was on call if needed 24 hours a day. This proved to be a positive situation and when he came by to eat, the owner would never accept money from lawmen.

Another chore that went with being a Deputy Sheriff was keeping peace at the saloon. A lot of cowboys would come to town, especially on weekends, and they all wanted to party. The saloon was always their primary target. There were always a lot of young ladies there who were also in a partying mood. The potential for being rowdy with this mix was automatic.

Usually there was a fight or two every night and the cause was normally over some gal that more than one cowboy had his eye on. The saloon owner had a bell he would ring when he was concerned and the sound was easily heard at the Jail. Chalk would stroll in and walk among the people just to let them know they needed to get their act together. If that was not strong enough, he would go to the troublemakers and tell them to get out of town, right now. If this advice did not stop the ruckus, he would drag one of them out into the street, handcuff him to a horse trough and then go back in and get the other one. Chalk soon had a reputation as a man not to cross. Those that did were always sorry.

Sometimes some drunken cowboys would want to shoot up the place or shoot each other. If this got out of hand before he arrived he would shoot a couple of rounds into the air and try to stop the situation before it got deadly. Anybody that shot a gun and was acting in an unsafe way always spent time in jail. The local people knew he was in command and if a posse was ever needed, the local men were quick to follow his lead.

The High Sheriff was always available but let Chalk build his reputation. That made his job easier. The local saloon was a favorite spot to contact young women. It was also a place where the local Church people described as a den of sin. Chalk did not want to get the local people, both church going and others, down on the saloon, as it was also a good place to get a good family meal. When the cowboys would get all liquored up and fight over some gal Chalk would put them in jail and when they were sober they were fined for fighting. The fine money was often used to support several local Church activities. This approach kept everyone happy.

A lot of young women worked as bar maids. They were common targets for some lonely cowboy. The women simply disappeared when a fight broke out. It was rumored that several of them worked at a local "boarding house" which was known as a place where cowboys could find "easy" female pleasures.

The General Store would normally close at about 6 PM. When business was slow, sometimes the doors would be locked earlier. Wanda Anderson was living in an apartment house that was about two blocks north of the store. She had to walk past both the saloon and the blacksmith shop to get home. When passing she would always look in both and hope to see Chalk. Chalk was aware and would make sure to be "available" when she walked by. At first, it was just big smiles and an occasional "Howdy". That grew into more and soon the two were eating their dinner meals together two or three times a week.

At work, Wanda would ask Charlie a lot of questions about Chalk. She was interested in his past and if he had ever mentioned her to Carl. Charlie saw that this relationship was growing stronger and she made sure that Wanda knew Chalk was part Cherokee Indian. As it turned out, Chalk had already told her a lot about his childhood and his parents. Carl was also aware of the relationship and had no issue with either of the people's best interests.

He knew they were both adults and would not expect anything less than an honorable relationship to develop. Carl also knew that Chalk was still an adventurous young man and might not be ready to settle down with a wife.

Chapter 3

Finding Each Other

Over the winter the relationship between Wanda and Chalk grew stronger and by spring it was obviously more than a passing friendship. Both were in their late 20's and each really were feeling a strong pull to take the next obvious step. However, both wanted to be sure that they were doing the right thing. They carried this level of friendship forward and continued to discuss possible plans for living together as a married couple. Both of them were still testing their own feelings.

There were several other young men and women in Bandera who had hopes of becoming romantically linked to both Wanda and Chalk. Why not, they were both good looking and upstanding young people. They both knew this and discussed it openly between themselves. They started to go to a local Lutheran church together and met a lot of single people their ages. This only worked to build a stronger relationship between the two and gave them reasons to become more sincere to each other. They both continued to work in their jobs and saved their money with a passion.

Chalk had made friends with several local men of his age. They had a lot of local knowledge and often did things as a group. The big thing to do was go to Mexico, buy tequila and have a party. Chalk was invited to go on one of these trips. The horseback ride was a full day each way and the time they spent in traveling was always full of small talk and generally men's topics. The arrival at the border was always an event as the crossing was always an experience like none other.

The Mexican saloons were always glad to see "Gringos" ride up. The price of liquor always went up and the local street merchants would go into action. After a drink or two the group would often go to "Boys Town" which was an area where young women were available and willing. For a small fee a cowboy had a room, a girl and a bottle for the night. Some would pay up and disappear for the evening. Others would look and go back across the border to Eagle Pass and get a room. There was no fear of foul play in either town as long as the cowboys did not start a fight.

The next day was normally a time to sober up and about noon they would start back to home. The trip was always a lot of bragging and story telling. The trip would last into the late evening hours but after a night's sleep it was back to work on Monday morning.

Wanda had sent her parents a letter telling them of her husband's death. She also told them that she was in Bandera, Texas and was building a new life there. The first letter was sent soon after the wagon train arrived in town. At that point there was not another man in her life. A return letter came back in about three months telling her that her Father had become very ill and died. Her mother wanted her to come back to Ohio and spend time with her. Wanda was torn as to what to do but when Chalk started to show an interest she sent her mother a letter telling her that she was staying in Texas and was going to find another husband someday. She never heard from her Mother again.

Wanda told Chalk about the last letter and told him that he was probably the man she wanted to call her husband. Wanda discussed her marriage to her first husband and it was obvious that she had loved him deeply. She had overcome much of her loss and was now ready to start over. Chalk understood and told her that he was sure she was the Lady of his dreams but was wanted to be sure that people in the community would accept them as a couple. Her husband had been dead for a relatively short time and the time for grieving was expected to be extensive by most people. He also knew his dark skin and her white skin could be an issue with some people. Some of the local people thought Chalk was of Mexican decent from his skin color and black hair. He never denied being an Indian but never made any big deal about it either.

Both of them were sure of themselves but wanted to fit into the community and not become outcast by anyone. As time passed they were seen together often and it was clear, they were in love. Together they decided to go visit with Carl and Charlie.

They needed to talk to an older couple that understood how they were feeling. They knew their advice would help them decide the right thing to do. Wanda asked Charlie if they would help them with this situation and asked if they could come out to the ranch for advice. A time was set and life went on.

Carl's ranch was located on land that was next to the Medina River. The river was always running but would slow to almost no flow in the hot and dry months of summer. There were many large cypress trees on both banks and the cool shade and easy blowing breezes made his ranch house a place of comfort. Carl had the Mexican housekeeping staff fix the best possible dinner he could create and the ranch house was set for a very easy and fun evening.

Carl and Charlie met the couple at the ranch gate and had a special wagon with bales of hay and small refreshments. The wagon that Chalk had driven to the ranch was turned over to a driver and followed the party wagon. It was the same wagon that had "Harmony and Goodwin" painted on the side panels. Chalk had removed the canvas cover and this made it an open-air treat in which to ride.

Carl, Charlie, Chalk and Wanda were seated in the rear and a gaily-dressed Mexican cowboy drove the wagon on to the ranch house. The trail from the gate to the ranch house was about a mile. The road ran on the north bank of the Medina River. The evening sounds of bugs, birds and blowing trees were everywhere. When the wagon arrived the were mariachis singing at the front door and cold drinks were quickly served by Spanish ladies in colorful dresses. Wanda and Chalk were really surprised.

Everyone went into the house and walked down the candlelight lit hallway. The couple was taken down the hall to the big dining room. The table was set with beautiful glassware and traditional Mexican dishes. The music was soft, low and beautiful. It was no secret that the two were in love but needed a push to make the final decision. This surprise reception was overwhelming to both of them.

Dinner was served and everyone enjoyed the food and drink. After the meal Carl suggested they go sit on the front porch veranda and relax. They were all seated and again the dinner staff served drinks. Chalk then began the conversation. He asked both Carl and Charlie to tell them what they thought about him and Wanda getting married.

Carl stood up walked over to Chalk and sat down next to him. He said that he loved him just as he loved his own sons and his future was as important to him as it was for his own sons. Charlie went over to Wanda and sat next to her. She told them both that Wanda was the daughter they had never had. Wanda expressed a similar feeling for Charlie and Carl. Carl then said that nothing would make them happier than having them marry and live their lives as one family.

Chalk turned to Wanda and said to her in a shaky and tender voice that he wanted her to be his wife. Wanda cried. The tears were not reflecting sadness but joy. She said nothing would make her happier and she was ready to become his wife.

Chalk got up walked over to Wanda and helped her up. He gave her the biggest hug he had ever given anyone. Carl and Charlie both were crying and they hugged both of them and told them they were happy for both of them.

Carl was a fox. It was obvious to both he and Charlie that the evening would turn out this way. They had a well-kept secret. Carl went to Chalk and said follow me. So far the whole evening had been spent on the East Side of the ranch house.

They slowly walked around the porch to the rear of the ranch house and there were a lot of horses and lights in the cowboy bunkhouse. The bunkhouse was about 150 yards from the ranch house. Everything was almost midnight quiet.

The bunkhouse was shaped like a big letter "T". The front section, the leg shaped section of the T, was actually a large dining area. All of the cowboy bunks were in the back section. Carl treated the back section of the bunkhouse as a home for the cowboys and never infringed on their privacy. Carl and Charlie and Chalk and Wanda slowly walked to the door where the cowboys normally entered to have meals.

Carl opened the door and the crowd that was inside was almost half of the towns leading citizens were inside. The silence quickly turned into friendly noises, as everyone was there to celebrate. They were all there to help the couple party and to wish the couple well.

There were long tables down the center of the room and chairs lined the sides. The same Mexican dinner staff showed up quickly and the beer, wine and whiskey flowed. The women that did not drink were given iced tea and punch. Cookies, cooked dishes and Mexican pastries were on several tables.

The party lasted until about midnight and the crowd left. Carl told Chalk and Wanda that there were two rooms ready for them to sleep in and they were not going back to town that night. That was a great plan as Chalk had found a few too many drinks.

The next morning was a workday. Chalk hitched the horses and drove the wagon to the front door. Wanda joined him for the trip back to Bandera. Carl and Charlie were wishing them well and waved goodbye as they pulled away. Their conversation was quiet and very private. Chalk drove a "slow wagon" as he had a really serious headache.

The next week was spent with seemingly endless excitement. Carl had told Chalk he would set him up in Texas when they arrived. So far, this was still an open issue. He came by the blacksmith shop and took Chalk to lunch. He told him that he owned a tract of ground, about 50 acres, five mile south of town and there was a nice home already built there. He told chalk he would give him and Wanda this home and would also give him a small herd of cattle to get him started in the cattle business. The cowboy work was not a problem as there were many cowboys in the area that were always looking for a job. He asked Chalk to discuss this with Wanda.

That evening Chalk took Wanda out to eat and they discussed Carl's offer. After dinner they rode out to see the house. They soon agreed to accept. They then began to discuss wedding plans. Both were not into big parties and outlandish preparations. They both wanted to involve Carl and Charlie in their wedding and thought it proper to ride out to ask them to join them for the formal ceremony.

They went out to Carl's ranch the next evening and discussed their plans. Carl spoke up and said lets hold the wedding here at the ranch and we will be glad to give you this as a wedding gift. All of this was overwhelming to Chalk. But, he and Wanda accepted the offer. He knew Wanda was equally pleased. The date was set, the minister was selected and a guest list was drawn.

April 15th was selected as the wedding date. The wedding would take place at 6 PM. The day was a Friday and it would allow people to come and still be able to have time for their other planned weekend events. The Texas spring weather was wet. Beautiful wild flowers were everywhere when the wedding day finally arrived. It was a perfect day.

The night before the wedding Carl had a party for Chalk. It was an all male event and of course there was a lot of male talk. Carl had invited several of Chalk's close friends and the group was a reflection of all of the people who Chalk had made friends with, on the wagon train, in the local community and even a Sheriff from a nearby local county. When it was over Carl sat down with Chalk and asked him if he was still sure. He said yes, of course. Carl told him that he had a shoulder to lean on in him if he ever needed one. Chalk thanked him, had a final drink together and went home to his rented house.

Wanda and her friends had a similar party but the talk was more about having kids and homemaking. She had a good group of friends and they were all happy for her.

The next morning Chalk went out to the new house and made sure that everything was in good order. He met a neighbor who told him that the next place up the road was a family that had been on Carl and Chalk's wagon train. They went over and sure enough, it was a family from just east of Memphis. Their family name was Tobin. They welcomed Chalk to the community and asked him to bring Wanda by. They already knew her and this was a first step for a strong relationship in that community. They had three kids and another one was on the way. Joe Tobin was a carpenter and was working in town for a lumberyard. They had homesteaded a 2000-acre tract and were just getting a new ranch house completed.

The wedding day had finally arrived. At about 4 PM Chalk went home, put on a suit and put all of his clothes in a small box. He put the box in his wagon, hitched the horses and drove to Carl's ranch. The wagon was the same one that they had bought in Memphis but was soon becoming a normal part of Chalks daily life.

Carl was already dressed and a reception for wedding guests was about to begin. Over 200 people came. This was a very large crowd for Bandera, Texas, for any event. Wanda arrived in a friend's coach and went into the back door. Charlie took her to a back bedroom. She got dressed and had a small fun time with the three girls that were also a part of her wedding. The Preacher arrived and he got the layout for the wedding all mapped out.

At 5 PM a group of Mexican musicians began to play soft and subtle love songs. They had guitars, a couple of horns and a sweet sounding violin. There was no singing, just instruments. At 5:55 the preacher called Chalk to stand by the small alter and he came forward with one of Carl's sons as his best man.

The guests were everywhere and they gathered into a large standing crowd with an open aisle down the middle of the room. Charlie was seated in the front row and an open seat was left for Carl. Neither Wanda nor Chalk had any family. Carl's family filled the void for both of them.

Promptly at 6 PM Carl stepped out from a bedroom with Wanda on his arm. She was wearing a new white Mexican style dress and carrying a single red rose. The musicians started to play the wedding march. Chalk turned and saw her coming. He was very happy, but he was nervous. Wanda had been in a prior wedding and knew that Chalk was nervous and when she reached him, Carl placed her next to Chalk. She took his hand, squeezed it to silently to say how happy she was and they faced the preacher together.

The service was short, simple and basic. This was what they both wanted. After vows were exchanged, Chalk took a ring from the best man, Carl's son Jim, and put it on her finger. She got a ring from one of the women who had joined her and placed it on Chalk's finger. The preacher proclaimed that they were now Man and Wife.

Then, the festive music began. Several wedding songs were played and the band had prepared a special love song for them. The wedding party then went to the bunkhouse eating area where a magnificent reception was planned.

The party lasted until at least midnight. At about 10:30 Wanda and Chalk sneaked out back and took a breather. They had one of the cowboys pull their wagon up to the back door and load the wedding gifts into the back. At 11 PM they told every one thank you, hugged Charlie and Carl, and went to their wagon. They were on their way home to the house that Chalk had just moved into.

Chapter 4

A New Family Begins

The next few weeks were full of excitement and surprises. The house was fine but the area around it was full of overgrown bushes and weeds. The weeds were perfect places for critters and snakes. Chalk hired a couple of helpers and clear-cut everything back from the house. There was a clear area about 20 feet wide on all sides when they got done. In the process they killed several snakes and an armadillo.

The house was comfortable but the summer heat made it uncomfortable in the heat of the day. It had a separate kitchen off to one side and the area in between was called a dogtrot. This area was always less hot when the breezes were blowing. Chalk had screened the area in and put a comfortable big bench in the area. The cooking food in the evening always made the place smell wonderful. Soon a table and chairs was added and summer meals were served there on hot days.

About a thousand yards to the north there was a drop in the land and at the bottom flowed down to the Medina River. There were giant cypress trees on the banks and in several ways this place was much like Carl's ranch. To get to town there was a low water stone bridge that had been built about 5 years earlier.

Wanda and Chalk kept their current daytime jobs. In the evening they both worked to fix up the house to their liking and to make sure the fences were strong enough to hold livestock. Chalk hired two cowboys to build some new fences and to fix up the barn. It was basically in good shape but had some roof leaks and needed all of the doors replaced. Within a couple of months the place was looking much better and was ready to receive cattle. Carl followed the progress and when Chalk said everything was ready, Carl would have his cowboys deliver the cattle.

Chalk went to work at the blacksmith shop on Tuesday and Carl was in the dry-goods store. He saw his horse tied up outside. Chalk went in and found Carl. He was in the back having coffee with a friend. Carl saw chalk and invited him over. He introduced the man as Federal Judge Goodman from San Antonio.

They all had a cup of coffee and Carl told Chalk that the Judge was there to see if he would consider running for a Judges job. Judge Goodman was a Federally appointed legal official and worked out of San Antonio. Bandera did not have any resident Judges but had a circuit Judge assigned to hear cases. Hondo City had become a county seat and local law cases in Bandera were commonly tried there. The circuit judge only got to Bandera about once every 5 or 6 weeks.

The Federal and State legal departments wanted to add a local Judge who would work with the circuit Judge to hear cases when they were actually placed on a docket. This job would require Carl to travel to Hondo City and San Antonio on a regular basis. Carl listened but wanted time to consider accepting this responsibility. In Texas, a Judge that made enemies in court was often found shot in a dark alley. It was also common for Judges to become aligned with other political figures who often had money interests as their objective. Carl had made friend in many places and his reputation as being a man that was not "for sale" was well known.

Carl had already told Judge Goodman about Chalk and how he was working as a deputy and a blacksmith. The Judge told Chalk to keep a firm hand on the legal problems of the county, as it had been a place where the law was never really very strong. There were over 50 open cases on the court docket and most of them were for shootings, stealing horses and robbery. Stealing cattle and horses was a common but not well enforced crime for the whole area.

After coffee, Chalk went to work at the blacksmith shop. In about a week Carl came by and told Chalk that 40 head of prime quality cattle, 39 cows and a good bull, were going to be taken out to his place that evening. Chalk thanked him and told him how much he had appreciated all that he and Charlie had done for him and Wanda.

The cattle arrived and were put into a pasture. They had plenty of grass and a big tank of water. The bull was not immediately "at home". He tried to get loose and broke down a couple of fences. In about a month he settled down and was not snorting or trying to get out of the small fenced area.

Much of the area west of Bandera was open range. Cattle commonly ran loose and the only fences were often several miles apart. Cattle were a big and growing business. Chalk saw this area as a prime opportunity if he wanted to expand his operation. However, he wanted to fence his land and not have other rancher's cattle mix with his.

Texas had declared independence from Mexico on March 2nd, 1836. They set up the area as a Republic, independent and self governed by local residents. In 1845 they joined the United States. They immediately became known as the "Lone Star State". Mexico had not agreed to any boundaries for the western territory. These would not be determined until the Mexican American war and the signing of the treaty of Guadeloupe Hidalgo.

Small towns like Bandera were still being settled and were a key part of the development of the western Texas identity. Bandera was actually settled in 1852 as a Mormon colony that was cutting cypress trees and making roof singles. There were still several local craftsmen who were doing this type of work but the cattle industry was taking over. There were also a lot of people from Poland settling in the area and they brought their skills of wood and metal fabrication with them. Most ranches were self sufficient for many of their needs. However, sugar, coffee, salt, cloth, tools and fence wire had to be bought in town.

Over half of the wagons that had come to the Bandera region had gone further out west. There was still a lot of land to homestead just a few miles further to the west. Plenty of year round water was available, especially along the Rio Grande and Pecos rivers. Water was always a major concern to everyone. Cattle had to have water. To settle on land that was not on a good river or creek was not going to work. Over time water shortages would become a major problem and the ranch would fail.

By 1876 an annual cattle round up would be held in the spring and then a cattle drive to the north would be undertaken. The trail ran from Bandera to Dodge City, Kansas. Carl had been active in organizing this drive and his cattle brokering had made him a lot of money. It was now 1894 and over the past several years he had made a lot of money.

Carl would spent his spring in setting up the cattle drive and getting it rolling. He then would travel to Cincinnati, Ohio, spend a few days gathering people who wanted to go west. He would then ride a riverboat to Memphis where he would finalize his wagon train, buy a wagon for his supplies and get all of the new pioneers set up to go west. His trail boss life was now ended. The railroads were finally coming to the southwest and wagon travel was not the best way to travel long distances.

The trail drive was still a popular and economic positive for the cattle business, but the railroads were coming west at a very fast pace. There were now tracks to the areas near San Antonio, Dallas and Fort Worth. They would soon also be coming to other western towns.

All of these cities were building large cattle processing yards and were encouraging the railroads to come as soon as possible. By 1895 the cattle drives were going both to San Antonio and to Fort Worth. The yards at Fort Worth became so big that the unofficial name of "Cow Town" was coined for the city. This period was the heyday for the Texas cattle industry and became the basic lifestyle for the hero building reputation of the American cowboy. The Fort Worth Stockyards became world famous.

Chalk saw opportunity at every turn of the road and with his skills, self-assurance and having accumulated a sizable amount of money, he was anxious to cash in. Wanda also had a substantial amount of money that was a plus to building a strong future. She put her money into a bank and allowed it to draw interest. It was making money but the interest rates were low.

About a month after the cattle had been delivered, Chalk and Wanda sat down on the porch and had a good talk about becoming big time cattle ranchers. They were not really sure as to what they wanted to do. The cattle business was booming and the money to be made there was good. But it could be a bad investment in years when there was too little rain and the water supply was too small. Ranching, with a single ambition in life, was a great life for an owner but it also was a lonely and isolating life in many ways.

It was now mid-summer and Wanda was considering going back into teaching. Her job at the dry goods store was honest and interesting but it was not a lifetime long career. She had many sentimental ties to Charlie. She had been her sponsor and friend and she respected her for many things. Wanda had studied, graduated from college and had a good education. She wanted to use it.

Chalk had an education in others ways. His hands on skills and his knowledge of business were always in demand. He had also been learning a lot in the field of law enforcement. As a family, they were young people on the front edge of life looking to a good but still unclear future.

Wanda went to work the next day and spent a lot of time talking to Charlie about what was on her mind. Charlie understood. She told Wanda that Carl and her had both come to Texas from Ardmore, Tennessee to find a better life. Both of them had high school training and did not want to become sharecropper cotton farmer families like their parents.

They saved a few dollars, bought a wagon, joined a wagon train and went west to Texarkana, Texas. They stayed there a year. The town was fine but the opportunities to be more independent were limited. They thought about their future and decided to go further west. They had talked to business people to Texarkana and were impressed with stories about the area just west of the hill country. They loaded their wagon and went to Fredericksburg, Texas.

The area to the south of Fredericksburg was expanding. They saw more opportunity there. They homesteaded the land that they now lived on. Early on they had invested in cattle. Carl got involved in the cattle drives and also got started in leading wagon trains to Texas. There was a thrill and real life drama to leading a wagon train. Carl had found his dream job and wanted to follow this life as long as he could. Along the way he had made a lot of friends, money and influential connections. She told Wanda to "think big and to plan big or she would never become big".

That evening, about 10 PM Chalk came home from a bad night as a deputy. He had shot a man to stop him from killing another man in a bar room brawl. The man had died. He needed a little time to cool down and get over what had happened.

Wanda saw his feelings of deep distress. She made an extra effort to fix him a bedtime snack, give him a big glass of whiskey and get him to relax. About midnight he finally went to sleep. The next morning he woke up to find a warm breakfast waiting. Before he left for work his big black dog gave him a warm lap on his face. Somehow, things were a little better.

Over breakfast, Wanda told him about her conversation with Charlie and told him he needed to think big with her. All day that idea was on both of their minds. They were both still relatively young. They were just starting their life together and needed to find a direction. They needed to make a career decision but had no clear idea as to what was out there to consider.

That night, after they got home from work, they talked. Chalk told Wanda that they needed to get away from Bandera for a few days and see some of the world that they were constantly hearing about for themselves. Wanda agreed. They went to work the next morning and told their employers that they were going to take a small vacation and go see San Antonio. After all, they had not had any honeymoon since being married and they needed some time to be by themselves. They both needed to get away from the daily routine for a while. The decision was made.

Chapter 5

A Trip That Had To Happen

Wanda wanted to go shopping in a big city. She had spent a lot of her youth in the big cities of Ohio and always liked to go to the stores, look, compare and buy nice things that were available. Clothes were her greatest joy. Chalk had spent similar time in the cities in Kentucky and along the Mississippi and Ohio rivers. He liked to see tools, wagons and fancy boots and hats. They put some money in their pockets, borrowed a small wagon from Carl to make the trip and packed a case with clothes.

The trip was begun at sun up. The trail was well worn and easy to follow. It was about 40 miles and it would be a full day trip. The trail would bring them into San Antonio on the north side of town. When they got to the edge of town they found a small Mexican restaurant and had dinner. There was a small guest home next to the restaurant where they rented a room for the night. The owner was a Mexican lady that made her living by renting rooms and baking cookies and pies. She was very helpful in learning about the town and giving them personal recommendations as to where to go.

The next morning the couple took off for town. Chalk noticed a lot of Army soldiers on horseback and saw a lot of activity as they passed an Army post named after Sam Houston. The main part of town was still about 5 miles away. The trails had changed from wagon-rutted paths to wide streets with small houses lining both sides. The homes were a mixture of wood buildings and stone structures. There were a lot of trees and a lot of flowers in every yard. Small barns and corrals behind the houses were everywhere. The horses often had fancier buildings that the residences.

The whole town was alive with busy people. Many people were dark skinned and looked to be from Mexico. This area was once a part of Mexico and the local population was still living like they had before Texas became a state. The town, for the most part, was clean. Most of the homes were well maintained.

The closer they got to the downtown section the fewer homes were seen. Business shops became numerous, as were as small restaurants and small hardware and dry gods stores. The town was a whole lot like Memphis but had a different cultural style. The colorful clothes, a lot of colored tile on the office buildings and a newly installed system of electric power lines were more obvious.

The downtown area was small but the buildings were taller and were all constructed from brick and stone. The lady at small hotel recommended that they visit the "Menger Hotel". It was supposed to be a fine place to stay. The old "Alamo" mission was right next door to the hotel and the area around these buildings full of honky-tonk bars and restaurants. One obvious feature was the large number of churches. The Hispanic people called them "Missions" and were very supportive of the Catholic religion.

The local Police worked on foot and on horseback. The central town area was well patrolled and considered safe. However, the local traffic was an unorganized flow of people, wagons and people, most being on horseback.

Chalk and Wanda got a room at the Menger Hotel. The hotel had a stable and private area to care for the horses and private wagons. The rooms were very nice and the service was as good as any. There were electric lights in the room and best of all, hot and cold running water in the bathroom. Wanda said it was a lot like being back in Cincinnati but with cowboys everywhere. There were two restaurants and a large bar in the area just off the lobby. The hotel had several security people on duty at all times to keep order. The final southern border between Texas and Mexico had been determined but occasionally somebody would walk in who was not sympathetic to Texas. If they wanted to have an argument about the situation some, loyal Texas cowboy would slug him and the security people would step in.

Chalk and Wanda went to the restaurant and had a big meal. The steak and vegetable menu was great and they were very pleased with everything. Chalk struck up a conversation with one of the security men and told him he was a part time Deputy Sheriff in Bandera.

The security guard suggested that he meet up with the local Sheriff the next day and have a conversation about their work. The Sheriff always knew more about the town than anyone so Wanda and Chalk went to meet the Sheriff. After the fact, the security officer told Chalk that the hotel was haunted. Wanda laughed and said she was not worried about ghosts.

The Sheriff, Wayne Wilson, was a tough middle-aged man. He had a real soft spot in his heart for other law officials and was very glad that Chalk had come by. He sent a runner to get his wife, Alice, so she could meet Wanda. Like any profession, talking shop was always a common subject. Wayne and Chalk discussed the law enforcement situation in both of their counties in detail.

The Sheriff brought up the situation concerning too few Judges in the state. He brought up the fact that being a Judge did not require any real legal training. He said some of the best judges were the ones that had been businessmen and had earned a reputation for being honest and fair. He also said that some Judges were as crooked as a snake and he gave them a really bad rating. He named a few. It was interesting that Judges were brought up as a topic so Chalk asked the Sheriff what he thought of the local Judges. He replied that they were often crooked and the crooks were able to buy them. He also said that it was sometimes easier to just wipe out a crook with a bullet than to try to get justice in a courtroom.

Chalk and Wanda were invited to have dinner with the Sheriff and his wife. They accepted. They had a small ranch north of

town and about 5 PM they sent a Deputy and special wagon
to bring them there. They enjoyed the evening and Wanda
was invited to meet the Sheriff's wife the next morning
and go shopping. Chalk was invited to spend a day with the
Sheriff and see the town's honest character. They planned
to meet early and spend the entire day.

Wanda and Alice met in the hotel lobby and went to a local
restaurant for breakfast. Chalk walked over to the Sheriff's
office and met Sheriff Wilson. They both got on horses and
rode all over the central town area and discussed the many
business and situations that were current.

They then rode out to the Army post, Fort Sam Houston,
and met with Colonel Rossen, who was in charge of the
Horse Calvary. Chalk told him about the wagon trip to Texas
and the Army troops that were in the wagon train. The
Colonel told him that the Army was building up its strength
in the entire western area, as it appeared there was going
to be an effort to finally neutralize several west Texas Indian
tribes.

The Colonel asked Chalk if there were any ranches in his
area raising horses. Chalk told him that there were not any
he knew of but if the Army needed horses he had a lot of
connections back in Kentucky. The Colonel told him that
the Army had a major need and if any help was available to
get good horses, he was very interested. Chalk promised
to get back with him.

They rode back to town and had lunch at a local Mexican
restaurant. Sheriff Wilson told Chalk about the railroad that
had come to town. The local stockyard was adding stock
pens hold additional cattle and facilities to take advantage
of the better transportation. There were now bridges across
the Mississippi at New Orleans and at Memphis and the trains
were bringing a lot of new business to the southwestern
part of the country.

After lunch, they rode down to the stockyard on the south
side of town. They saw several boxcars being loaded with

cattle that were going back east. The cattle were given hay and water before they were boarded and were packed into the cars for the trip. It was important that the trip not be delayed as the cattle would suffer and often become sick from this type of travel. When the cattle cars were loaded an engine was pulled up to the cars, get attached, and the whistle would sound the signal they were leaving.

Most of the people working in the stockyards were Hispanic and were skilled in handling cattle. Spanish was the language of choice and the supervisors and the visitors were only people speaking English. The men all had long hook shaped sticks that they used to prod cattle and to grab animals by the necks. They could load a cattle car in about 15 minutes.

They rode back to town and went to the Sheriff's office. His office was a small room in front of the jail. He had several deputies who were constantly coming and going. The jail cells were small foul smelling enclosures with a hole in the floor for bathroom duties. A bucket of water was normally available on the prisoner's request, to flush the hole. The jail was all weathered gray stone and had a cold and uncomfortable feeling about it.

Chalk thanked the Sheriff for his time and walked back to the hotel. Wanda had just returned and she was all bubbling with stories about the stores and places she had been. She had enjoyed her day. She had also bought several small things to take home. They ate dinner in the hotel restaurant, took a walk around the area and went to bed. It had been a long, enjoyable and busy day.

The next morning it was raining. The air was hot and the humidity made it feel a lot closer than normal. They wanted to talk about the day before so they got breakfast, checked on their horse in the hotel stable and spent the morning talking. Wanda was all excited about being in a town where things were easy to find and the selection was good. She also liked being with a lot of people who were interesting and able to talk about more than cattle, ranching and rural life.

Chalk was a good listener and took in everything she was saying. He was happy to see her so happy and to see a side of her that he had never really seen before. This was really the first time they were together in a bigger town and could be away from wagon train and ranch talk.

Wanda and Chalk both were enjoying the comforts and available conveniences available in San Antonio. The culture level in the people who were there was different from Bandera and the feeling of a strong government control was definitely present. The down side was a lot more noise and a much tighter control by the local law officers.

Wanda compared the shopping to the store in Bandera and said that Charlie needed to carry some of the items that were common in the big city stores. The approach toward merchandising was more aggressive and broader based. The use of seasonal items as sale features was a promotional idea that was working. This sales approach allowed the stores to create bigger sales volumes and generate greater profits.

Chalk discussed the trip to the Army Post and his plead from the Colonel for additional horses. It was obvious to Chalk that the military was building up resources for a potential conflict. Chalk told Wanda that they needed to keep some cattle on their ranch but also needed to expand into horses that would be desirable for the Army. His background in Kentucky and on the wagon trails had given him a broad background in horses and he was excited about the potential for this opportunity.

The comments from Sheriff Wilson about Judges and the uncertain power of jury decisions equally impressed him. His comments were particularly significant when he thought about the discussion that Carl becoming a judge. Chalk had already formed a negative opinion about big city bankers. Now he was becoming concerned about Texas Judges.

The rain stopped about an hour before dark and Wanda wanted to eat. She told Chalk she would love to have a steak and baked potato dinner. They went walking into the area west from the hotel and found a recommended steak restaurant. The food was great and the service was outstanding. So was the price. They went back to the hotel and went to bed early.

The next morning the weather was beautiful. Texas weather was never severely cold like it was in Kentucky but it could be very hot and dry when the rains were not coming. They decided they wanted to see more of the city. There were several horse drawn carriages parked in the front of the hotel. The drivers were dressed in Mexican clothing and the horses were all well groomed. Chalk asked the hotel bellman which carriage was the best one to hire. The bellman told him to wait a minute and he went to a carriage and got the driver. They returned quickly. Chalk asked him if he could give them a good city tour. The driver, named Jose, spoke good, but broken English. Chalk told him he would like to have a city tour that would take them all over the central city. He also wanted the carriage to wait for them if they wanted to stop and shop. The driver understood and agreed. His fee was $1.00 for a full day.

Wanda and Chalk climbed aboard. Jose was obviously a Mexican but he had lived in San Antonio for a long time. He told them they needed to see the old Mexico section of town first. They went toward the west. The further west they rode the more Spanish signs were seen. Many small Hispanic shops selling bakery products, clothing, religious items and fresh food and vegetables were present.

About a mile from the hotel they came up on a large government building. Jose told them that it was the County Court house. He pointed out a Judge who was just entering and said that he was a very powerful man.

There were several large parks in the area and street vendors were selling food and fruit juice from carts. Most of the people were dressed in Mexican style clothing. The women were dressed in colorful full-length dresses. Several sidewalk musicians were singing and playing traditional Mexican songs. Jose stopped and let Wanda and Chalk listen to a group that was playing an especially good song. The men were all playing and singing with a lot of gusto. Chalk gave them a nice tip.

At lunchtime Jose pulled the carriage into a courtyard located about a mile west from the busy Mexican inner city section. He parked the carriage and helped Wanda and Chalk get down from their seat. As they stood there a gentleman dressed in a formal black suit and fancy black boots came to them and said, "Welcome to our restaurant". They followed him inside. The inside was semi formal and there was a fountain just inside the door.

The floors were all covered with beautiful tile and the walls were decorated with traditional Mexican paintings. He then led them to a table that was elegantly decorated with silver tableware and beautiful dishes. The theme was obviously Mexican but this was upper class dining at it's very best.

A server also dressed in formal style, brought ice and water. A waiter then came over and asked what they would like to drink before lunch. He had a cart with iced wines, beer and fruit drinks following him. Wanda had a glass of fruit juice and Chalk had a cold beer. A large bowl of warm corn chips and a dish of hot salsa were also brought. Without ordering, the waiter brought a big green salad and a tray with several different dressing. He asked which dressing they would like and then put it on their salads.

They ate large salads and about half way through the initial course the waiter came by and told them about the special lunch for the day. It was Chicken and Cabrito relinos. He asked if this was acceptable. They quickly agreed. By the time they had finished the salads the hot plates of food were ready to be set on the table. There were also black beans, fried rice and sliced fresh avocados. The food was delicious. When they finished eating Chalk asked for the bill. The total bill was $1.55. He left $3.00. Wanda and he went beck to the carriage. Jose had eaten lunch with the cook and was already to go when they returned.

Jose asked if they were happy with the restaurant. Chalk said it was wonderful and they were pleased that he had selected this restaurant.

The carriage then went to the north side of town. There were several nice neighborhoods in the area. Many were stone homes built in the Spanish tradition. The yards had small fences around them and each yard had several flower gardens. All of them were well maintained. The flowers were blooming and the entire area was a colorful sight to see. They rode around and saw the beautiful old missions and plazas that had been there for many years.

At about 3 PM Jose pulled into a Spanish street market and suggested they might want to look around. Wanda was anxious. Shopping always appeals to a woman. There were many booths selling silver and gold jewelry. Other sellers were specializing in high fashion dresses and elegant leather goods.

There were also boot makers and saddle makers offering their services. Jose told them, "It was like being in old Mexico". Musicians were also playing soft and beautiful Spanish music. Wanda bought a few things. Chalk paid the bills and carried the packages.

At about 5 PM Jose told them that they needed to go back to the hotel soon. When the sun went down it was not safe to be in the part of town where they were. This became obvious as there were more police starting to be seen in the streets. Jose drove the carriage back to the hotel. Chalk tipped Jose and they got their packages and went to their room.

Wanda and Chalk were ready to go toward home. They wanted to see New Braunfals on the way home. They ate dinner in the hotel restaurant, went for a short walk and went to their room for the night. The next morning Chalk got early, got dressed and went down to the front desk and checked out. He asked for the bill total and the desk clerk told him it was already paid for. He asked who paid the bill and the desk clerk told him that the Sheriff's Department had covered all of his expenses. He was completely surprised.

He asked the stable keeper to hitch up his wagon and horses so he could leave. When he went back to the room Wanda was ready to go. They took their clothes and other things to the lobby. The wagon was waiting just outside. When they left they went to the Sheriff's office and looked for Sheriff Wilson. He was not in so Chalk wrote him a thank you note and left it with his deputy. He then headed north toward the edge of town. The Army post was on the way and Chalk had noticed a good-looking restaurant nearby. They stopped for breakfast. The food was basic but great. They were now ready to travel.

New Braunfels was about 30 miles to the north. The trail had been traveled so many times that it was wide and well identified.

The traffic on the road was heavy and the countryside was relatively flat. To the immediate west the eastern edge of the hill country was obvious. Several streams were flowing toward the east and the water was clear and clean. The roads in Texas were never paved or well marked. The horse and buggy traffic was almost all local and public interest to spend monies on roadwork did not really begin until the advent of the automobile.

Chapter 6

On The Way Home

New Braunfels was a booming and clean town. The population was primarily German and both languages, English and German, were spoken openly in the local business community. The town was built on the banks of the Guadalupe River. The city was building an electrical power plant on the river and had several businesses setting up shop nearby. Many of the people who lived there were recent emigrants. The Hispanic majority that was seen in San Antonio was not as common in the community.

Wanda saw several dry goods stores and wanted to shop. Chalk found a nice hotel, The Faust, and they checked in. It was late in the evening and the next order of business was a great German style meal. The restaurant was almost next door to the hotel and it was an easy walk. Red cabbage, potato pancakes, sausage and fried apples were the menu for the evening. Cold beer was also a standard part of the meal.

The next morning was cool and clear. The air was sweet smelling from all of the flowers that were blooming. The same beautiful flowers were drawing bees by the thousands to gather nectar for making honey. The town was small so they decided to walk the streets and shop when they saw a shop they wanted to visit. There were several German bakeries that served coffee and fresh baked pastries. The smell was too inviting to pass up. Breakfast was found.

After eating they walked south from a big central square. One of the first things that caught Wanda's eye was a bookstore. She had not been into a bookstore since she left Ohio. Chalk also saw a hardware store that appeared to be well stocked. They both went to see what was there and both were pleased. Wanda saw several new books about Texas and the growth of the education system. Chalk found a complete supply of blacksmith tools. Both bought what they wanted.

The blacksmith anvil weighed 400 pounds. The storekeeper said he would hold it until they drove the wagon by the next day. Wanda had 12 new books and a lot of fliers from local furniture and clothing shops.

There were several stores where they saw dress clothing and specialized household goods. These items were being shipped into the area from back east. The one thing that Wanda wanted most was some scented soap. She found several bars and had them wrapped tightly to keep the smell from going away.

That afternoon they came upon the Sheriff's office and after a short discussion between themselves, decided to go in. Chalk introduced himself and a Deputy Sheriff. The local Deputy went and found the Sheriff. Like Sheriff Wilson in San Antonio, he was most appreciative that Chalk had stopped. Sheriff Jack Cox was a younger man and had an obvious professional appearance. He had been a Colonel in the Army. After he was discharged he and his wife decided to take roots here in Texas and call it home. His office was traditional but he had several flags and documents framed and decorating the walls. His boots were well shined and his uniform was neat and clean. Wanda was impressed when he said he had grown up in Indianapolis, Indiana.

Sheriff Cox told them about the town and as always, talked about lawman subjects. Wanda was listening intently and was not a big part of the conversation. She asked him about the local schools and the teachers qualifications. Sheriff Cox said that anyone could become a teacher. However, most often were not trained in the subjects they were teaching. The Sheriff invited them to have dinner with the Sheriff and his wife at a local restaurant. The invitation was accepted and they were to meet in their hotel lobby at 6:30 PM.

Chalk and Wanda walked back to the hotel and relaxed for a while. They got dressed and were in the lobby on schedule.

Promptly on time, a carriage pulled up and the Sheriff and his wife got out. They greeted each other and went to the carriage. They all sat in the back and a driver managed the carriage duties. Sheriff Cox told them they were taking them to a small settlement on the north side of nearby town called Gruen. A local family had developed an excellent restaurant that was built just above on the riverbank. The trip was about 20 minutes and the route was through lush trees and rustic buildings. The restaurant was everything it was said to be.

Dinner was served and the conversation was healthy. This was a real joy for Wanda as the Sheriff's wife was also from Indiana and they had a lot of things in common. After dinner they went to a nearby dance hall where the local musicians were playing music. They also had plenty of liquid refreshments and everyone had a good time. By 10:30 it was dark and they drove the carriage back to the hotel. Before parting company mail addresses were exchanged. This was the beginning of a life lone friendship. Chalk and Wanda thanked their hosts for the evening and went to their room.

Wanda remembered her stop in Fredericksburg when the wagon train went through. She told chalk that New Braunfels and Fredericksburg were similar in many ways and that the German influence was obvious in both towns.

The next morning they checked out and got their wagon loaded for the trip home. They stopped by the hardware store and picked up the blacksmith tools. They stopped at a German bakery and bought some pastries to eat on the road. The trail to Bandera went through a small town called Boerne. It was about 20 miles away. Bandera was another 25 or so miles beyond. The trail was through the hill country and there were many places where the horses had to work hard just to go up the side of a long hill. By noon they were about two miles from Boerne and were hungry. When they pulled into the town they spotted a Mexican restaurant and that was great news.

After lunch they started out for home. The trail was well marked and the local streams and hills had dictated the route. The trip had been full of experiences that had made both Wanda and Chalk happy. Chalk was driving the buggy and Wanda was setting by his side. She spoke up and told Chalk that this trip was similar to a trip she and her deceased husband had enjoyed when they lived in Ohio. She went on to tell him about going to several small towns located along the Ohio river and the many fun things that were there.

For some reason Wanda opened up her memory like she had never done before and told Chalk that her parents never lined her first husband as his father had served in the Confederate Army. When they learned this they put up an immediate barrier between themselves and the young man. What they never learned was that his father was a Chaplin. He had suffered several battlefield injuries and was never in a position to do armed combat.

By about 7:00 PM they were home and they were both tired. This had been a great get away trip and they both really appreciated the chance to be alone for a while.

Chapter 7

Reality Arrives and Sets In

The next few days were relaxing. Wanda went back to the dry goods store and Chalk went to the blacksmith shop. He also went back to work as a Deputy. Their jobs were a form of security blanket and they enjoyed the good feeling from this level of economic protection. The cowboys at the ranch had kept the place in shape. The cattle herd had grown by 4 calves in a month. One of the calves was a well-built bull. The animal was marked with brown and tan colors in unusual patterns. Chalk named him "El Toro" and he became a favored bull on the ranch. Everything was going well and life was on an even and happy keel.

Wanda and Chalk talked a lot about the trip and they both agreed that they needed to do this again in the near future. It was obvious to both of them that they needed the association with more people. Both of them liked the Cox couple a lot and had a lot of things in common. Over a few months they kept in touch and became good friends. Traveling had re-opened their memories to the comforts and pleasures that are found in larger towns.

Chalk had also seen a side of Wanda that he had never experienced. He liked what he saw. Wanda was now completely happy with her situation in life and was comfortable in her ranch home. Chalk wanted to keep her happy and in the midst of educated people. Wanda saw Chalk as a happy and talented man in both the common sense matters of the world and in the field of law enforcement. They both had developed new and better opinions of each other.

In early August Wanda told Charlie that she wanted to become a teacher in the local school. They were both happy about this decision and they started making plans to transfer her work to other people in Charlie's store. The school was a small stone building with four classrooms. The classes were set up to have two grades in each room. There was a fifth room where the students would eat their meals and have meetings when appropriate.

Wanda was assigned to teach the 7th and 8th grades. This class was large, 16 students, but most of the students were girls. The boys were too busy to come to school and they normally dropped out before finishing the 10th grade. School was to start on September 12th.

Class hours were from 7:30 in the morning until 2:30 in the afternoon. There were few textbooks and the ones that were available were well worn and out of date. But, it was all that was available.

Chalk took time to send several letters to his former friends in Kentucky who raised horses. He wanted to buy some mares to breed and develop a quality line of horses. About a month after his first letter went out he got a reply from the horse farm where he had worked. The owner was glad to hear from him and said he had about 20 mares that was not racehorse grade, but he added, they were all fine horses and he would sell them cheap. He wanted to cull his stock and was anxious to do so. He would sell them for $12.00 each. Chalk would need to have them shipped at his expense.

Chalk knew a man that was now shipping cattle on the railroad in San Antonio. He went to him and asked if there was any way he could get the cost to ship 20 horses by rail from Lexington, Kentucky to San Antonio. He knew that it would be costly but a herd of horses of this quality was going to be a great investment over time. He understood the risks but was developing a "cost package' to see if it was worth it.

In a week the man returned from San Antonio and had done his homework. The railroad would haul the horses to San Antonio for $15.00 each but they would require that a groom accompany the animals to keep them fed and watered. That was going to cost an additional $100.00. The total was about $400.00 by the time he added in the feed and other required expenses. The trip was based on a 10-day schedule if everything went well.

Chalk determined that he could be able to supply quality horses to the Army in about 3 years if all went to plan. He already had a good stallion from quality stock and would put him to work as soon as the mares arrived.

Chalk put all of his plans and calculations on a piece of paper and went to see Carl. Chalk was already sold on his idea but a second opinion was always a good idea.

When Carl saw what he was planning he laughed and said that Chalk was really sticking his neck out on a long limb. But, he also said that Texas cowboys were always willing to pay a top dollar for a good cutting horse.

He thought about for a while and said, …. Damn, this will work! But he added you would need to get a separate area for the horses. Cattle and horses have different habits and sometimes they don't mix.

The next morning he sent the horse farm a telegraph message telling them that he wanted the mares and asking how he could pay for them. The banks were never his favorite institution but he knew he needed to go start a bank account.

Chalk had found a 500-acre tract on the West Side of his ranch that was available for assumption. A settler family had homesteaded the tract but they gave it up when the rancher got sick and died. His family was not willing to stay there any longer. Chalk knew the family and offered them a reasonable price to buy them out. He now had almost 600 acres and several barns and out buildings. Chalk had more than enough money to buy the land. He saw the land as a great investment.

Chalk went to "Cattleman's State Bank" and went to see the President. He told him about his need to fund the purchase of the horses in Kentucky and wanted to know what services the bank could offer. He also told him about his farm in Missouri and the legal mess that a dishonest banker had caused. The Bank President assured chalk that his Bank could wire funds to a Bank in Lexington and how this was not a major risk.

Chalk asked him about opening an account and what he suggested for a deposit amount. They agreed as to the arrangements and Chalk went to his wagon and brought in a bag of gold coins. The President was concerned about the safety of carrying such a large amount of money in his wagon. Chalk just smiled and said my pistol is a great security provider.

In about two weeks the horse farm owner sent Chalk a bill. Chalk took it to the bank President and asked that they send funds to the horse farm. The president had Chalk fill out a transfer slip and went to the telegraph and had the funds transferred to a bank in Lexington, Kentucky.

He then sent a telegraph to the horse farm owner and informed that he had a check waiting for him. The whole transaction took about 15 minutes and went smoothly. Chalk was impressed. Chalk knew he would need to pay the transportation costs when the horses arrived so he deposited additional money in the bank. He thoughts had started to change, Banks are not really that bad!

Wanda started teaching and Chalk continued his job as a Deputy Sheriff and rancher. Life became routine and every day was similar to the next. Chalk had his ranch crew set up fences on his new property so it would be ready when the horses arrived. The word got out among the local ranchers that Chalk was going into the horse business. This was great news to the local cowboys, as they always needed good working horses. The other result was that several cowboys came to chalk's ranch looking for work.

Chalk often saw Carl at the local restaurant. On one such meeting they got into a discussion about Carl's opportunity to run for a Judges job. There was still a need for local Judge and Carl had been contacted several times. Chalk told him about his conversations with the Sheriff in San Antonio. Carl took all of this in and just smiled. He had a similar opinion; Judges were not always honest, he agreed with the Sheriff.

Carl said he was going to run for the Judge's job in the next election and had been studying a lot to get himself prepared to do this job. He had been told that the local Democratic political party was going to sponsor him and he would not need to spend much of his personal money to campaign.

Chalk told him that he was glad to hear this news and would gladly support him in the election. The next election was about four months away. This was enough time to allow Carl to get his business interests in good shape so he could apply his time to doing the Judge's job. Carl's sons, Jim and John, were given almost complete responsibility to run the ranch

Wanda had spent several days working at Charlie's dry goods store before she started teaching school. They had talked about the stores in San Antonio and the bigger variety of things that they were selling. Charlie was interested and decided to see if she could add a few more things to her inventory.

Charlie and Carl had gone to San Antonio several times and she had made contact with several good wholesale sources. Over time Charlie added a lot of new items and upgraded her store with a much greater assortment of products.

On Sunday morning a fellow deputy rode out to Chalk's home and informed him that someone had rustled several longhorn cows and 5 horses from a ranch in the south part of the county. The cattle were not branded but the horses had the "55" brand on their hips. The rustlers were supposedly going south toward the Mexican border and had almost a full days travel time. The Sheriff told the Deputy to tell Chalk he was in charge of the problem and to respond accordingly.

Chalk told the Deputy to get a small group of men together and meet him at the Sheriff's office in about a half hour. Wanda heard the news and told Chalk to be careful and not put the men or himself in a dangerous situation. Chalk got dressed to ride, hugged her and headed for town. The Deputy had collected 12 men, two were also deputies and the others were local ranch owners. Chalk asked them if they were armed and ready to ride? They all said, lets go. Chalk deputized all of them to make the posse a legal force and they departed to the south.

The trail was still damp from a heavy morning dew and tracks from wildlife were all that were visible. They reached the ranch where the stock had been rustled and the owner joined the posse. He had found the trail they were using from a cut fence on the back acreage of his ranch and they all went there to start the chase. The grass was still showing hoof print damage, which indicated that the cattle had been pressured to run for some distance. In a short mile a small clearing had been trampled down and there was fresh manure on the ground. All of these tracking signs said they were moving south, but not at gallop speeds. The posse followed the trail and by nightfall they had gone several miles.

The countryside was flat and overgrown with mesquite, cactus and creosote bushes. An occasional post oak tree would be found where there were low places that could hold water. Driving cattle or horses through this type of country at night was not possible. The moon was completely covered by thick clouds. The light level was almost pitch black. Chalk told the men to bed down for the night and they would move out at daybreak. Someone found an open spot to hold up and a small campfire was built in an open area. Nighttime in the south Texas country was a dangerous place to stay out doors. The snakes and wild hogs were thick and were not to be taken lightly. A fire was supposed to keep them away and allow the men some light to keep fear down.

Daybreak saw everyone ready to ride. The men had brought beef jerky and canteens filled with water. This was simple food but not an unusual diet for a working cowboy. The set out and followed the trampled path that was before them. At about 9 o'clock they came upon a small ridge where the horizon for about 10 miles was visible. They stopped and looked south. Hondo, Texas was off to the east and the men knew that the rustlers would not go near a town. They looked toward the west and off about 7 or 8 miles one cowboy saw a small moving dust cloud. He pointed it out to the others and they all agreed it looked like cattle moving at a rather fast pace. Cattle on a drive move slow and do not cause this much dust. They sat out to catch the dust cloud.

Within an hour they had reached a point about a mile behind the dust cloud. One cowboy climbed a tree and looked into the dust. Yep, he hollered, there's the cows! He got back on the ground. Chalk drew all of the men into a circle and discussed the plan he had developed to intercept the rustlers. He wanted to separate the cattle and horses from the rustlers and then, depending on how many and what they did, take the bandits as prisoners. The cattle and horses were not to be shot, even if it was necessary to shoot the rustlers to stop the procession. After all, the cows were not at fault and cattle's rustling was illegal. Rustlers were expendable and cattle could be sold at the sale. All agreed to the plan and they loaded their guns and rode out.

The posse soon caught up to the dust cloud and took the rustlers by surprise. The rustlers saw that they were outnumbered. They were all frightened and spread out quickly going in many directions.

Most of them were young Mexican men and they were not well armed. The posse reacted quickly. Chalk pointed to a different deputy and directed him to chase a specific rustler. There were only 5 so the job was not really difficult.

The rest of the posse maneuvered the cattle and horses into a circle and calmed them down. All but one of the rustlers was cornered and surrendered. The last one tried to ride away and hide in a small clump of trees. His effort was working until he saw the Deputy pass and took a shot at him. Everyone heard the gunfire and soon the area was alive with Deputies. He continued to fire at his captors and his fire was returned in force. Finally, the shots stopped and all was quiet.

A favorite trick used by outlaws was to play dead and hope that they would leave him for dead. For this reason a group of three Deputies approached from several sides. This rustler was not going to return any fire as he was lying on the ground bleeding and on his last breath. His body was full of bullet holes. The Deputies piled stones on his body to keep the wild critters from consuming the corpse.

The captured prisoners were lined up in a procession, hands tied and horses tied into a train. Behind them the cattle and horses were lined up using makeshift halters and ropes to keep them in line. The cattle had been branded with "55" just as the rancher described. The Deputies rode in the lead, on the flanks and at the rear to make sure that the procession was moving and safely intact. Night came and the prisoners were tied to trees for the night. They had been searched and all guns, knives and metal they were carrying were removed. The deputies stood watch in shifts and the night went according to the plan. The next morning the procession moved back to the north. About an hour before dark they reached the ranch where the rustlers had invaded. The local cowboys took charge of the stock and the deputies took the prisoners to the jail in Bandera. The rancher was jubilant to get his stock back and thanked everyone.

Chalk thanked everyone for a job well done. He knew that Everyone's family was concerned that the men were ok so he told them to go home and be welcomed. Chalk had the jailer put the prisoners in separate cells and put an extra

Deputy on duty to make sure that they were secure. It was now late Tuesday and everyone was glad to be home.

Word spread quickly about the entire event. Chalk became a local hero for his quick and successful work in tracking and apprehending the rustlers. The word was out that rustling in Bandera's community was not going to work. There was never another similar event as long as Chalk was with the Sheriff's department.

Texas was growing fast and the small towns located around the bigger cities were all being affected by the continuing influx of new people. More people always led to more business. The area around the hill country was one of the hot spots in Texas. Cattle ranching, raising horses, goats and sheep were all common livestock operations. Industry was also coming to Texas. Dallas, Houston and San Antonio were experiencing factory and large retail growths. Money was being made everywhere. The negative side of the growth was the increase in crime and slick lawyers from back east that were flocking to the state.

Chalk was learning a lot and he realized that he needed to get a distinctive "Brand" for his livestock. He came up with a design that had a horseshoe, heel pointed up, with a letter G in the center. Goodwin ranch stock were all branded with this identification from then on.

About two weeks after the horse purchase deal had been completed, Chalk got a telegraph from the railroad office in San Antonio telling him his horses were in route and would be there in two days. He got several of his cowboys together and they rode to San Antonio to meet the train.

The train arrived on schedule. All of his horses were in one cattle car. The groom who had traveled with them was an older man that Chalk had known when he was working on the horse farm. The groom had taken great care of the horses and took pride in the condition of the animals. He and Chalk talked about common memories and the reunion was a treat for everyone. Chalk treated everyone to a big meal at a local Mexican restaurant.

All of the horses were unloaded and put into a holding corral. Chalk found the railroad dispatcher and paid him for the transportation services. There was an additional charge for some extra hay that had to be bought. The original supply was not adequate for the entire trip and more hay had been purchased in Louisiana. Chalk also paid the groom for his services, gave him a nice tip and bought him a ticket to get back home.

The horses rested overnight and early the next morning they were ready to start the trip to Bandera. During the overnight stay Chalk took all of his cowboys and the groom to the Menger Hotel and visited the local cowboy bars. Chalk bought the first two rounds and told them any more booze was at their expense. Chalk and his cowboys were well pleased with the horses and everyone was happy.

The horses were all healthy and the trip to the ranch was easy. When they turned the horses loose into their new home they were all frisky and glad to be unrestrained and in an open field. There was plenty of grass, fresh water and a good barn for them to sleep in.

Over half of the mares were pregnant and were not far from having colts. Chalk had been given an excellent deal from his Kentucky friend and he realized how much better these horses were that the local half mustang stock. These horses were quickly the talk of the local community and became a hot topic among local cowboys.

Chalk's cowboys soon started asking if they could buy one of the horses. Chalk had to remind everyone that the Goodwin Ranch was a breeding ranch right now and selling horses would come later. He told them they would get the first choices when this happened.

Life was now settling into a pattern and both Wanda and Chalk were living a good life. The future was positive and the comforts from a good life were starting to become available. They were now full blown Texans, and they were happy to be living here.

Becoming A Nation and Making a Real Difference

The Goodwin Ranch and It's Contributions

Book Three

Kenneth Orr

Chapter 1
Getting Started and Building a Ranch

The Goodwin Ranch, as it was now called, was a little different from most other ranches in the immediate area. But, it was also the same in many ways. There were cattle and by necessity there were horses. There were cowboys and there were the normal chores and all of the activities that go with Texas ranching. The difference was that the Goodwin Ranch had many more horses than there were cattle. The other difference was that the owner had now become associated with The United States Army as a supplier of saddle horses for the Cavalry.

It was now 1898 and the Army was still patrolling the west with soldiers were doing their patrols mounted on horses. The Army also used wagons and artillery equipment that was pulled by horses. The need for good horses was seemingly never ending. The Army had no internal programs to breed and supply their own horses but had made the decision to use suppliers like the Goodwin Ranch to fill these needs. There were many Army horse suppliers. However, most of them were still back east. Buying horses from distant suppliers was not always a convenient or timely situation for western Army Posts. The total need for horses was far greater than any one horse supplier could handle.

Chalk had begun breeding lean and healthy horses based on the supply of mares he had bought from Kentucky. He also had bought several additional horses at local auctions and from near-by ranchers who had extras. The bloodlines for a good western horse had some mixture of the mustangs that were found roaming free in the western part of Texas. The mustang horses were there as a result of the Spanish Soldiers who were once located in Mexico. Many of their horses were abandoned after battles and they soon were living in the wild and increasing in numbers. Chalk had bought several mustang studs that had been broken and were excellent stock for breeding durability into the heard.

Chalk had to quit his local blacksmithing job and to devote much more time to his horse ranching operation. However, he was still working as a Deputy Sheriff. This job had gradually grown into a full time job and was requiring much more time. As a result he had hired several cowboys and a ranch foreman to work on his ranch. Chalk was picky in hiring.

Chalk wanted hands that had broken horses for riding and who knew more about horses than they did about cattle. The ranch foreman who Chalk had hired was from San Antonio. The relationship with this man was great as he had been in the Army and was once a stable master at Fort Sam Houston. He also had been a rodeo rider and knew how to break and train first class horses. This situation allowed Chalk to do his law enforcement without worrying about the ranch.

Wanda was teaching school and had gone most of the day. Her class duties were demanding as she was trying to expand the school programs to include more meaningful subjects and attract greater numbers of students. The school was growing as more families moved into the town and all of the classes were getting larger. Finding additional qualified teachers was not easy. A lot of women wanted to teach. This was common when they had children in school.

Most of these ladies had little to no formal education themselves. The children who lived far out in the country sides had no way to get to school except to ride horses or have their mothers bring them in a buggy. Many only came a day or two a week and they wanted to take books and assignments home. Schoolbooks were in short supply and the extra work of planning homework for part-time students was a major undertaking. Wanda had her hands full.

Wanda was still someone new to her students. They were like most youngsters as they were full of mischief and were always teasing and touting one another. Wanda watched and listened so she could clearly understand the different personalities in her class. Kids growing up on a ranch and being limited in the number of outside contacts they had were a lot different from the schools she had attended in Ohio. These kids were more physical and had a lot of ideas that were based on their parents ideas. Some were well settled into a rural ranch set of values and some had customs and ideas from where their parents had come from. The total classroom attitude was positive and Wanda was working to get everyone going the same direction.

One morning, just after the class had taken a break one of the girls went up to a bigger boy and told him that she wanted to tell him a secret. Of course, a boy always was interested in what a pretty young girl wanted to say. She said she wanted to whisper it into his ear and he gladly said "OK". She got up close to his ear and he was listening intently. He was unaware that several other girls were watching from behind a tall bookshelf.

The girl got close, put one arm around the boy's waist and as he was waiting to hear her secret, she spit into his ear. The boy was immediately mad. Just as she did her trick Wanda walked by. The girl was instantly aware that she had done something very wrong, and she had been caught. The other girls who were hiding quickly disappeared and the girl had to face Wanda alone. Wanda told the boy to go wash his face and clean out his ear. He left and Wanda stood face to face with the young girl. The young girl said nothing, as she was scared and defenseless.

Wanda told the girl to go to her desk but to stay after normal school hours, she had something to say to her. The girl was quiet and did exactly as Wanda had told her to do.

At the lunch break Wanda walked down the street to a store where the girl's Mother worked. She asked her to come by the school at 3 PM and be present when she talked to her daughter. Wanda told her that there had been an incident that morning and her daughter was going to be disciplined and she wanted her Mother to be there. The Mother was Wanda's friend as they went to the same church and she was surprised to hear that her daughter was in trouble.

At 3 PM the Mother showed up and Wanda and the girl met her in the school lunchroom. Wanda explained to the girl why they were there and wanted to discuss her bad behavior. Mrs. Goodwin, as she had the students address her, also wanted to develop a plan for her punishment. He mother was shocked as what she had done. Wanda wanted the mother and the girl to both come to class together the next morning. She asked that the girl apologize to the boy while standing in the front of the class. Wanda also wanted her to apologize to her Mother and to the entire class for letting then down with her bad behavior. She had no choice but to agree. Wanda thanked the mother and they all went home.

The next morning everyone came to school and at 8 AM everyone except the girl was in their seat Wanda stood up, asked a student to lead the class in the pledge to the flag, which went well. Then the class recited the "Lord's Prayer" and Wanda called the class to order. This was all part of the normal class morning. The students knew there was something going on as the empty seat was an obvious sign that a big event was in the works.

Wanda then went to the lunchroom where the girl and her mother were waiting. They all came into the classroom together. The students were all stunned and sat quietly in their seats. Wanda told the class that the girl had something to say. The mother sat down in a chair next to Wanda's desk. Wanda sat down in her normal chair and the girl was alone at the front of the class.

She began to speak. She asked the boy she had targeted with her prank to stand up. He stood up and was surprised to be singled out. The girl told him she was sorry and asked him to forgive her. She began to cry. The boy said he would forgive her and he sat down. The girl wiped her tears away and then asked the class, her Mother and Mrs. Goodwin to also forgive her for letting them down. Everybody sad they would and the girl began crying again. He mother went to her side and they went back into the lunchroom. Wanda told the class that this matter was over and asked everyone to go on with the day's lessons. The girl soon returned to her desk and the day was back to normal.

Wanda's fellow teachers had been aware of the entire incident and congratulated her on the way she had handled everything. She became somewhat of a hero to the school and to the parents who heard of the situation. The old fashioned punishment was a paddling and additional homework. This old approach was all that had ever been used in Bandera's schools.

This pattern of life continued for three years and everything was going as per the planned schedule. One beautiful spring day Wanda came home from school and when eating dinner got deathly sick. Chalk immediately took her to see the local doctor. He examined her and asked that Chalk come into the room. He broke into a big smile and told them they were going to be parents. This was not planned but it was welcomed by both.

The impact of being parents was a new experience for everyone. The new arrival was scheduled to happen in mid-December. This was going to be an 1899 birth. There was no hospital yet in Bandera but the local doctor was qualified to perform the service. There were also several women who worked as midwives and helped women deliver babies.

Wanda completed teach school for the spring of 1899. She let the school system know she would not be back in the fall. The school was glad for her but had nobody groomed to replace her. They immediately started to look for a new teacher who was fully qualified. The search was expanded to Austin where The University of Texas had an excellent school of Education. Several spring graduates applied. Several were invited to come visit Bandera and Wanda was

147

told to pick her replacement. They were all qualified and anxious young women. Men never went into the teaching career field as they had more masculine things to follow.

At home, Chalk had his next ranch down the road carpenter add an additional room off their bedroom so the baby would have a separate room. The Mexican housekeeper was anxious to help decorate the room and to make baby clothes. Everything was on schedule as summer came.

While the new construction was going on Chalk recognized this as the right time to add a major addition to the small house he had been given by Carl. He had Wanda help him redesign the floor plan and they decided to add a large living room with a big stone fireplace. They also added a study for Wanda, an office for Chalk and an additional guest room. Construction costs were not unreasonable and they wanted the entire outside to be built from white limestone. Chalk said his name was taken from limestone and it was only proper that he and his family live in a limestone house.

In 1999 having a baby was always a big event for everyone. Wanda's lady friends and co-workers were just as excited as was Wanda. Chalk's cowboys and his fellow deputies were also excited. The other part of the joy was the smiles that were on Charlie and Carl's faces. Neither of their sons were married yet and they had semi adopted Wanda and Chalk as their own family. The mystery of being a boy or a girl was always something everyone got excited about. Also, the list of names started to be developed by everyone except Wanda and Chalk. The excitement grew higher as the delivery date drew closer.

In Bandera Carl Harmony had run for the Judge's office and had won by a landslide vote. The local people all knew him well and his opinion was always in line with the well being of the community. It would have been impossible for any other candidate to win with him running. This new responsibility was going to require a large amount of his time.

Carl's ranch was still growing and he and Charlie decided it was time to turn it over to his two sons, Jim and John. Both had found young ladies that they wanted to be their brides and in preparation had built homes on the ranch. The cattle business was great and both were happy with being Texas Ranchers. The cattle business was growing and the availability of railroad transportation had made the business more profitable.

Several large dry goods stores from San Antonio had approached Charlie about buying her store. The offers were not great but there were several and they came frequently. She told them that they needed to get serious with their offers or not to come back. Most of them never returned but two did come back.

The largest store was an independent storeowner who had similar stores in Austin and in San Antonio. He had started his business selling dry goods but had expanded into tools, hardware and ranch supplies. He also had a side business in the same operation that bought and sold hay and grain feeds.

He was an older Hispanic gentleman and had been in the area for many years. His sons and one daughter were running the individual stores and they had a reputation for being honest and good community focused people. He presented Charlie an offer to buy the store and to hire her during the transition of ownership as his local manager. His offer was much beyond any other offer and was based on front-end cash, keeping the local flavor in the business and was not a "buy out" over time.

Charlie told him that she would give the offer serious consideration and let him know in a week. She discussed the offer with Carl and they decided to counter offer with a slightly higher price and a list of guarantees that included keeping the current employees on the payroll. She got in touch with the businessman and gave him her reply. He thought about it for about an hour and said OK. The exchange of ownership was mutually scheduled to take place on July 1st.

Charlie was scheduled to stay on for 6 months and to provide a transition for the new owner's new manager. She agreed and all of the conditions and the entire contract were documented. After the deal was finalized she called all of her people into the office and told them what was going to happen. She also gave each of them an immediate cash bonus and told them they could stay on with the store if they wanted.

The meeting ended on a very positive note. Everyone was glad to have been told up front and to know his or her services had been appreciated. The scheduled date arrived and the change was made smoothly and without anyone feeling that they had been left out.

In August 1999, the local Sheriff became violently ill and the doctor told him he was not physically able to do the Sheriff's work. He told him he needed to retire immediately and to go to San Antonio to see a medical specialist. He had a serious health problem with his heart and understood that the doctor was telling him the right thing to do.

The Sheriff called Chalk into his office and told him that he was ill and was not able to go on any longer as the Sheriff. He wanted Chalk to take over and become the interim Sheriff until the next election. He knew the people in the county would respect him and that Chalk was the most qualified man in the department. Chalk knew he had little choice in the matter but agreed to the request. This was a major decision but it was obviously one that would affect Chalk's family and how they looked at life. Being a Sheriff was not only a position of high responsibility but it was a dangerous and demanding job.

Chalk called Carl over to the Sheriff's office and told him what was happening. Carl was shocked. The Sheriff had been his close friend for many years and his health had never been an issue. The Sheriff wanted Carl to swear

Chalk in as the new Sheriff effective as of that day. Chalk would need to run for the office in the next election if he wanted to continue. In reality, there were no other qualified candidates in the county to oppose him. Chalk knew the responsibility he was about to be given. He also understood the trust that everyone was placing in him and the value of his reputation.

Chalk wanted to have Wanda, the Sheriff's wife and Carl and Charlie present when the actual exchange of office was happening. A meeting was scheduled for the late afternoon and a public notice was posted on the courthouse door. The word of the change spread quickly all along the main street of Bandera. When the time arrived everyone was present, as were several of the local business owners and citizens. Judge Harmony opened the proceedings and said a few words of thank you to the retiring Sheriff. Then he asked Wanda to hold a bible and Chalk placed his right hand on the bible as he took the oath of office. The swearing in ceremony took about 5 minutes and it was quickly over. The Sheriff pinned his badge on Chalk and wished him well in wearing it.

When the ceremony was over the outgoing Sheriff and his wife shook everybody's hand and went to their buggy. They went home and were now private citizens for the first time in many years. Carl and Charlie invited Wanda and Chalk to dinner. They went to a restaurant and had a great meal. Everyone then went home. A new level of responsibility had immediately come over everyone.

Chapter 2
Adjusting To Meet Change and Responsibility

1899 was a year where a lot of changes were being made. The new status for Chalk, Wanda, Carl and Charlie in Bandera was only a small part of the new bigger picture. The United States and especially the state of Texas were growing at an increasingly rapid pace. Texas was becoming a key part of the United States and was well positioned for entering a new century.

In Ohio there were a couple of young men working with a new machine that was hopefully going to be able to fly. In Michigan and Indiana there were several small companies trying to develop machines that would travel over the roads under it's own power. There were also many new factories working to build all kinds of new machines that would be powered by steam and gasoline power. Gasoline was becoming a fuel that was in demand as the internal combustion engines being used had to have large amounts to keep them running. Oil, kerosene and other by-product from petroleum were also growing in demand.

In east Texas several new oil fields had been discovered. The rush to find more oil was becoming a near panic. Money was being made by the bushel and people in the right position were becoming very wealthy almost overnight. The influx of new people in Texas continued to increase. It was similar to the gold rush to California in 1849 where everyone wanted to become rich overnight. The railroad had built rail lines across central and south Texas that opened up several new western areas for development. The day of the wagon trains was over.

Chalk was adjusting to his new job as the County Sheriff. He was also watching Wanda get ready to take on motherhood.

The situation where Judge Harmony was presiding over the county court gave Chalk a feeling that there was real sense of fairness and honesty available to settle legal matters. He knew that the reputation for County Judges was not lily white in Texas but he respected the fact that Judge Harmony was going to try to do an honest and fair job when he was called to make hard decisions.

Chalk had 6 deputies in the Sheriff's department. There was a jailer, three patrol level officers and two duty sergeants, The force was mostly older men but there was one patrol officer who was young, and he was also a hothead. Chalk called everyone into his office, one at a time, and explained how he intended to run the department. Everyone but the young Deputy had no problems with the change. The young man was not happy with the change in leadership. Chalk told him that things were going to be run one way, not left up to the individual officers and this made him unhappy. He had joined the department about a year earlier and was becoming a recognized source of trouble. Chalk suggested that he take a leave for a couple of weeks and consider what he had been told. He got extremely defensive and said all that Chalk was doing was forcing him out. Chalk saw that this relationship was not going to improve and took the opportunity to tell him that he was fired. Chalk told him that he needed to turn in his badge and sidearm. He gave Chalk his badge and issued sidearm and left Chalks office in a huff.

Chalk had an immediate opening in the department but the officers who were still there were happy about the way he had handled the entire transition.

Chalk told everyone that there were several good men in the community who would make good officers and he wanted to fill the opening and hire one additional officer. It did not take long before the line at the front door of the jail was bringing in a lot of new blood for consideration as police officers.

Bandera, like most small towns in rural Texas did not yet have a separate city and county police department. The Sheriff had jurisdiction over the entire county and all of the towns and communities within the county. This was a large responsibility as the county was growing and the small towns were numerous.

Chalk recognized the need to build strong relationships with the law officers in neighboring counties. He took a day a week and went to visit each of the adjoining county Sheriffs and build a personal and positive working atmosphere. Carl saw what he was doing and praised him for his wisdom in how he was starting out. He put his two duty sergeants in charge of 12-hour shifts and told them that he was always on call if needed. These men were older and knew the ropes. They were also firm believers in the way things were being run. Within a month the department had built a stronger, more positive reputation and was staffed to full strength. Chalk was off to a great start and he was enjoying his work.

In November a cowboy from a ranch in the south part of the county came to town to party. He got drunk, got into a fight over a girl and killed another cowboy. He then cut him up with a big knife. The deputy that responded to the situation arrested the drunken man and put him in jail. The next morning another man from the ranch where he had been working came to the sheriff's office and wanted to bail him out. Chalk told him that an order from the Judge would be the only way he could be set free. The man went to see Judge Harmony and he refused to set a bail, as this was a very serious murder crime. The man became very upset and stormed out of the Judges chambers. He threatened to shoot someone if this decision was not changed.

The Judge went over to the jail and told Chalk about the man's statement and told him to arrest him on sight. Chalk was aware that this man, Carlos Ruiz, was a member of the Hispanic community and he was considered a gang leader in the local area.

The man left town but Chalk knew that he would be back. He probably was going to have a large group of men with him and try to force the accused man's release. This group of men had a history of being troublemakers and was well known for living on the edge and often outside of the law. The result was that Chalk suggested transferring the prisoner to San Antonio where there was much stronger jail and Sheriff's department. Chalk got in touch with the San Antonio Sheriff and he agreed to house the prisoner there until the trial was held. Chalk kept his plan quiet from everyone except his officers. It got dark about 7PM that night. As soon as the town shut down for the night Chalk had a covered wagon pulled around behind the jail. The prisoner was gagged, put in handcuffs and leg shackles and loaded into the back of the wagon.

He was then cuffed to the wagon so he could not escape. His eyes were covered to keep him unaware of where he was going. Two regular Deputies and four temporary deputies with weapons were escorting the wagon to San Antonio. They left as soon as the darkness was a good cover and made the trip without any incidents.

The next morning Carlos Ruiz and about 20 additional men showed up in front of the jail. Carlos went in and demanded that the prisoner be released to him at once. The jailer told him that he was not there. Carlos was furious and said that the law was rigged to get his men. He stormed out and went over to the Judges office. He demanded to know where the prisoner had been taken. When he was told San Antonio Carlos knew that he could not bully his way around in that town. He went back to his horse, gathered his men and rode away. The jailer knew that Carlos was supposed to be arrested on sight but chose not to do so as he was severely outnumbered.

Chalk went to see Carl and wanted to have the trial as soon as possible. The county prosecutor was called in and a trial date was set, in San Antonio, for three weeks away. The information was posted on the courthouse information board.

The next day a Lawyer, who Carlos had hired, contacted the court and informed them that he was representing the prisoner. He wanted all of the records that were available concerning the case. They were provided for his review. He was told not to take any and two deputies supervised his review. It was obvious to the people in the courthouse that this Lawyer was not to be trusted when he attempted to steal a couple documents. He was ushered out and told not to return.

The trail date arrived and Judge Harmony was on the bench at the San Antonio courthouse. A local Judge who was present supported him because the actual crime was committed in a location other than San Antonio. A jury of local San Antonio people, with 5 being Hispanic, was selected. The County prosecutor presented the charges and outlined the history of the entire case. The defendant's Lawyer then got up and made some ridiculous accusations that were not remotely close to the truth. It was obvious that he was fabricating conditions to better serve his client.

After two days of witnesses and lawyer bantering, the case went to the Jury. The Judges both told the jury to measure the facts and that if the verdict was guilty the penalty could be either hanging or life in prison.

Carlos Ruiz and approximately 30 other Hispanic men gathered outside the courthouse and with noise and jesters made their presence known. Carlos was vocal about the charges and accused the legal system of lynching his friend. The local Sheriff sent a detachment of deputies to keep the group under control and not allow local citizens to be injured. He personally told Carlos that he had a warrant for his arrest in hand from Bandera and would use it if any unrest was started.

The jury deliberated for about three hours and sent word to the Judge that they had reached a verdict. The courtroom was put into order and the prisoner was brought in. The Court Bailiff read the verdict, "Guilty as Charged". The Judge sent the jury back into deliberation room to recommend a sentence.

They returned in twenty minutes and recommended death by hanging. The Judge read the penalty. The courtroom went quiet. Several deputies led the doomed man away and the courtroom was quickly cleared.

Outside, Ruiz was livid. He knew that there was no way to change the decision and this was not a good place to start a riot. The Sheriff had his men outnumbered and out armed. He and his men mounted up on their horses and quietly rode away. Ruiz had just seen that the legal system in Bandera had teeth and throwing his weight around was not going to be tolerated any longer.

The prisoner was hung at dawn the next morning. His remains were buried in a pauper's grave in San Antonio. Back home in Bandera the local citizens were pleased with outcome of the entire situation.

Everyone in the south part of the county had been concerned for a long time about the way the gang had bullied their way around. They now had received a clear message that there was not going to be any room for this kind of behavior anymore. Chalk was concerned about potential future problems from this group of men but they never happened.

Chapter 3
Personal Changes and Adjustments

Wanda was nearing the time of giving birth. In December she was concerned that the event could happen at any minute. To provide a piece of mind, she hired a midwife to stay with her full time until the birth occurred. Chalk was gone a lot but he made as much time with her happen as he could. The three months prior to the scheduled birth were happy times for Wanda. She was given several baby showers and parties every couple of weeks. These events were all building up to an arrival of the baby that would top every other event.

In late December, at about 5PM in the evening, Wanda knew it was time. She called the midwife to her room and had her send a cowboy to get the local Doctor and Chalk. Chalk was still at work and luckily; he was in the office when the cowboy arrived.

He got home about 7:30 PM. When he went into the house he heard a baby crying. He knew that he was too late but he immediately went to Wanda's side. She was still being cleaned up from the delivery. She and the baby were just fine. When she saw Chalk she smiled with pride. The baby was wrapped up in a small blanket and was being held by the midwife.

Chalk was also smiling. He sat down on a small stool next to the bed. He was hoping for a boy but he never told Wanda he had such wishes. Wanda told him he was the father of a healthy blue-eyed girl. Wanda was very happy and told Chalk he could name her. He immediately smiled and told Wanda that he was thrilled and happy to be her father.

Chalk was always proud of his mother Irene and the care and concerns she had given him. He also was proud of his wife and was torn as what name to give his baby girl. The Goodwin family, beyond Chalks immediate family was never close and there were no names that had been positive from that side of the family. Wanda was close to her Mother whose name was Jane. She never wanted to select her name for a child. The bottom line was clear, there was not any reason to use an old family name. Carl and Charlie were the closest friends they had and their names were also discussed.

They sat there for about 20 minutes and Chalk spoke up. Let's name her Barbara. That name is all new to our family and this little girl deserves a new name. Wanda agreed and the name was written on the birth record.

Barbara had a small amount of dark hair and her skin was almost pink. She weighed about 8 pounds. The blanket was wrapped tightly around Barbara but her tiny hands were near the edge of the cloth. Chalk looked at her tiny figures and realized just how precious and special a little girl can be. She had great lungs and was using them to let everyone know she was there. She was obviously hungry and ready to begin her new life.

Chalk was hungry and the Hispanic housekeeper, Maria, had fixed some great Mexican food. Wanda drank some fresh milk and had a small dish of mashed potatoes and a small dish of refried beans. The baby had a small bottle of milk and some cool water.

The first night of Barbara's life was an event for everyone. Chalk could not get his mind off the fact that he was now a father and that he had a new responsibility in life. Wanda wanted to hold her baby next to her and just enjoy the moment. The word of Barbara's arrival spread quickly on the ranch. One of the cowboys rode over to Carl's house and told them about the new baby. From there, the whole community soon knew about baby Barbara's arrival.

The Sheriff's department soon found out about the birth and planned a small party for Chalk when he came back to work. They cut out pink paper storks and hung them all around his office. Then they hung a long banner on the front of the jail saying they had a new local resident to protect.

Within a month life at the Goodwin Ranch settled down and started to become routine. The house staff was doing most of the housework. The baby's care was strictly Wanda's responsibility. Chalk's job was back to normal but his time was becoming so occupied that he saw the need to add an additional deputy just to keep the local contacts satisfied with daily business.

The local business owners all wanted to be involved with the law enforcement department. They were all experiencing rapid growth and almost daily someone had questions and situations that needed attention. The most common problems were petty stealing and family problems. Occasionally somebody would get drunk and want to cause trouble. All of these situations were minor but they all needed to be resolved.

Chalk knew that his strength came from the local people and he focused on keeping them happy and satisfied with the local law enforcement office. Four of the Sheriff's department's staff was Hispanic. Chalk was still learning to speak Spanish and the bridge they provided for him and to the community was very positive.

Chapter 4
Horses and Cattle

The Goodwin Ranch was growing fast. There were over 1000 head of cattle on the ranch and the horse operation was now counting over 600 head. Every month Chalk was selling off about 50 cows but the size of the heard kept on growing. Horses were another story. The care for a good military horse requires more time and work that raising cattle. The first requirement was breaking the animal to carry a rider. After that, the horse needs to be maintained in a controlled environment or they can revert to a stubborn and uncontrolled animal. Horses need to be kept in barns and controlled in a training program. This takes a lot more good cowboys.

Every month Chalk's ranch foreman would select approximately 30 horses that are candidates to be sold. Each of the selected horses was assigned to a handler that would saddle the animal, ride him every day and train the horse to meet specific handling requirements. Some horses were better than others were and these animals were sorted as select stock. The best horses were always in demand and always brought higher prices. The local cowboys always wanted to buy the selected horses and sometimes they offered more than the asking price for these horses.

The Army had strict requirements but with the right training a basically good horse would qualify. The monthly sale rate of 30 animals was normally sold 5 or 6 to local cowboys and the balance to the Army. Within two years, the Goodwin Ranch reputation was well established and there were waiting lists for good horses. The size of the ranch herd continued to grow and the targeted size was to grow the herd to no more than 800 horses and to sell approximately 50 horses a month.

Fort Sam Houston had expanded their order to buy every horse that was available. In addition they had soldiers assigned to take delivery at the ranch when horses were delivered. The military efforts for keeping the Indian problems under control in the west were diminishing. However, the Army was anxious to add more horses due to a pending involvement in a war that was brewing in Europe.

The Army had learned that a soldier and his horse need to be completely at ease with each other. The result was that each soldier was assigned his own personal horse. This became a standard and productive pattern for the Army. The developing relationship between the soldier and the horse was important as this mutual relationship determined the quality of the Army efforts. Combat operations would often spook horses. A horse that knew his rider well would do much better in such situations.

In November of 1901 a man from Kentucky came by the ranch and made arrangements to see Chalk. His visit was unannounced. He was a businessman and his father was a racehorse breeder in Lexington, Kentucky. The man was fully aware of the horse operation for Fort Sam Houston that Chalk was running. The man, Mr. Berea, was supposedly looking to start a horse breeding operation in Texas to supply horses to the horse racing market. The dollars being spent for breeding and supplying good racehorses were substantial.

Mr. Berea reflected that the county fair horse racing circuit was growing rapidly and every small town with fairgrounds had a small racetrack. The public was always willing to attend these races and betting was a big and very profitable profitable business.

Mr. Berea had once worked for the same horse farm in Lexington that Chalk had once worked for. Chalk's current reputation for raising high quality horses was well known in Lexington horse circles. It was also known that Chalk had developed a crew of well-qualified cowboys, who understood how to break, train and get the most from a basically sound horse.

He offered Chalk a business opportunity to develop a strictly racehorse breeding operation in Texas. The shorter cold weather season and plentiful quality pastures were very desirable. If the right management and people were made available to raise racing horses Mr. Berea stressed that this would be a very profitable business.

Mr. Berea had a check for $100,000 in his possession that he would deposit in Chalks account if they could come to an agreement. The Kentucky Farm would also supply 35 breeding mares to start the operation and would agree to split some of the profits down the middle. The Texas operation would be targeted to supply approximately 50 horses per year. Chalk would be responsible to buy the land, supply the personnel and oversee the operation. The life of the contract would be 10 years at which time everything, land buildings and remaining horses would all belong to Chalk. Chalk asked for a week to respond to the offer.

Chalk knew that this additional responsibility would put a strain on his time and on the staff he had built at the horse ranch operation. He also knew that this opportunity was very lucrative and with the demand for Army horses could sell any horses that were not sold to racehorse people.

Chalk called his ranch foreman into his office and told him about the offer he was being presented. The foreman was excited that their reputation was so well known and was proud to be given consideration in making the decision as what to do.

He told Chalk he had two friends in west Texas who were just getting out of the Army that could be of value in supporting such an operation. One of them was a career Army horse trainer and was well qualified to groom and develop racehorses.

There was a large parcel of land out by the pipestone community that would be ideal for such an operation. At the current time this property was a cattle operation. There were already several good barns and the land was rich and covered with good Bermuda grasses. This was property was going to cost about $25,000 to buy and get set up properly to do the job. The current owner was anxious to sell and wanted to retire from the cattle business. Chalk went to see his long time friend Carl and asked for his advice. Carl suggested that he get all of the numbers together and then come back.

Chalk rode out to the "Pipestone Creek" ranch and met with the owner. He had no debt and wanted to sell everything in one package, cattle, land and all improvements. He currently had a herd of about 200 longhorn cattle and they were all in good shape. There were also 300 Boer goats that were included with the deal. The ranch was approximately 750 acres in size. There were three stock tanks, two small barns, a house and a creek that flowed year round.

Chalk asked the ranch foreman to contact the friend that was getting out of the Army and have him come visit Bandera. His friend, Mr. Scott, arrived in two days and he sat down with Chalk. Chalk asked him a lot of questions and was impressed with his answers. He then took him out to the ranch and asked him to show him what he could do with a particularly rank horse. Mr. Scott got on the horse and within 10 minutes he was riding him with no apparent problems. It was obvious, he knew how to handle horses. Chalk told him he wanted to hire him, even if the racehorse deal was not finalized. He was still growing his horse ranch and a man with these skills was too good to pass up.

The following Saturday Chalk took all of the information he had gathered and went to see Carl. Carl was always a slow to come to decision person. This approach had paid off in his many business deals and he encouraged Chalk to take his time. Time was not so important that he needed to make a decision just to meet a calendar date.

The data was financially positive to every test. The only unknown part of the decision was the exact relationship that would exist between Chalk and the business people in Kentucky. The explanation as to what the people in Kentucky expected to get out of this was still not clear. All Chalk had to make judgment around were the words of Mr. Berea.

Chalk asked Mr. Berea if the people in Kentucky would be willing to meet with him. His job as the Sheriff limited the amount of time he could be away from town. Chalk wanted to proceed further if this entire deal was really what it appeared to be.

There was something behind the whole deal that just didn't fit. He told Wanda that he was not negative to the opportunity but had less than a complete commitment in his heart. Mr. Berea checked on a railroad ticket to Kentucky and found out that it would take about two to three days to make the trip, each way. Mr. Berea came back with an answer that his business people were available at any time and would be glad to meet with Chalk.

Chalk told his deputies that he would be gone for a little over a week and planned the trip. He and Mr. Berea would ride horses to San Antonio and catch a train to St. Louis. From there he would go to Louisville and on a third train go to Lexington.

Mr. Berea was going to travel with him and offered to pay his train fair both ways. On Thursday, they set out to ride to San Antonio. Chalk would leave the horses at the Sheriff's livery barn until he got back.

Chalk had never ridden on a train. He was surprised at the distance a train could cover in a relatively short time. The passenger cars, two of them, were at the front of eight freight cars. The steam engine was noisy and the black coal smoke would filter into the closed passenger cars when the wind was from the front direction. The railroad car was basically strong but it lacked a tight seal against the outside weather. The engine was powered by steam. About every two hours the train had to stop and take on more coal and water. These stops took about 15 minutes each but they were welcome pauses in the noise and constant rocking motion in the passenger cars.

The passenger car had seats placed in rows of two on each side of a central aisle. The windows were wood as was the construction of the car. Baggage was stored in a bin above the seats.

A small coal fired stove was at the front of the car and the porter would build a small fire to keep the interior warm. When it got dark the Porter would light several kerosene lamps and hang them on hooks in the ceiling. The light was poor but it was better than riding in complete darkness.

The train would stop at almost every small town that it passed through and people would get on or off. The freight cars were also added or left when the material inside had reached the designated depot. This activity took a lot of time but the travel time on the rails was still extremely fast as compared to any other available method. Sleeping in the passenger seat was not comfortable. Sleep came in small naps between stops and noise from other sources, especially crying children. The Porter told Chalk that some passenger cars had small compartments where the seats folded down to make beds. This train did not have such accommodations. Occasionally the train would be put on a siding to allow another train going the other direction to pass. These stops were the best time to sleep as they were less noisy and usually for longer periods.

The train finally arrived in St. Louis and everyone got off. The terminal building was practically new and there were always a great many trains coming and going. Chalk's next scheduled train was scheduled to leave in about two hours. Chalk took the opportunity to go to a restaurant near the station and get a good meal. Mr. Berea insisted on paying the bill.

It was Sunday night and their train was leaving about 10 PM. They boarded and found seats near the stove, as the weather was getting cold. They tried to sleep but the noise from the clicking of the wheels on the track kept them from getting much of sleep. The porter would come through every couple of hours selling hot coffee in big paper cups and cold sandwiches.

The next morning the train arrived in Louisville and the connecting train to Kentucky train was almost ready to leave. The made the switch quickly and within 5 hours they arrived in Lexington. When they got off Mr. Berea spotted his boss, Mr. Reynolds, waiting on the platform. He quickly saw Mr. Berea. Chalk was glad to see him and they all exchanged welcomes and got into a horse drawn coach. The coach driver took everyone directly to the horse farm.

The road was muddy, as it had rained the past two days. Mr. Reynolds asked Chalk how long he could stay and told him that they had a room ready for him to use while in the area. The old stacked rock fences and the fancy horse barns along the road reminded Chalk of his earlier life and brought back many pleasant memories. The large fields were all well maintained and several horses were out grazing of the late fall grass. These were good memories and the fact that time had passed seemed to be of little concern. Things were certainly different, but they were also just the same.

The coach arrived at the main house and a black servant met them. He was very gracious and made sure that everyone was comfortable. He immediately offered hot coffee and a snack. This hit the spot with everyone. Mr. Reynolds told Chalk he was glad he had come and that they needed to spend some time in closed discussions that afternoon and evening. Chalk went to his room, took a warm bath, put on a fresh set of clothes and returned to the main room. Mr. Reynolds was there and they went into a small office by themselves.

Chalk opened the conversation by asking what was the real reason or intent to have a horse farm operation in Texas? Mr. Reynolds was quick to recognize that Chalk was not sure as to what objective was really driving the decision. He asked Chalk if he could keep several things to himself and there were reason to do so concerning this deal. Chalk agreed and Mr. Reynolds brought out a paper that was headed up with identification as being a Document from the Government of the United States. Chalk read the statement about keeping things secret and agreed to sign the document. Then Mr. Reynolds took several additional documents from a small safe and began to talk.

Mr. Reynolds told Chalk that he was actually an officer, a Captain, in the U.S. Army and had been given his commission when he was a member of the Cavalry. His home post had been Fort Knox, which is located about 50 miles south from Louisville. His father had also been soldier for the Northern Army in the Civil war. His father and he had built the horse farm over many years and were well recognized as experts in the racehorse breeding business. His horse farm was selling racehorses but was also active in supporting the Army's needs.

He then asked Chalk about his horse operations and wanted to know a lot of things about his personal life. He was surprised to learn that Chalk was the County Sheriff and that he had built a strong business from both Cattle and Horses.

Chalk told him about locating the available land out by the pipestone community. He told him that it was ideal if he were to plan an expansion of the horse operation. He also told him about the need to see where all of this would end up at the end of the proposed ten-year operation. After all, everybody in business has got to make money or they would not be around very long.

Mr. Reynolds then told Chalk that the nation was aggressively building up several of its key Military resources, as there was a war in Europe. Quality horses were considered a basic Army requirement. Everyone feared that The United States was going to become drawn into this conflict. The need to have a large inventory of healthy and trained Cavalry horses ready if they were needed. The military wanted to be more than one group of horse suppliers ready when and if that need ever comes. The Senior officers at Fort Knox had contacted him and wanted to know what he could do to assist in this effort.

The front door product of racehorses was a good cover for a build up but it was not anticipated that this effort would happen in Lexington. Chalk's earlier purchase of mares from this area was remembered. Based on this information Mr. Berea's trip to see Chalk was undertaken.

Project funding for this operation was actually coming from the U.S. Government. At the end of the project any land, facilities and horses that were still remaining would become the property of the horse contractor. The Government had no intention of getting into the horse ranching business.

Mr. Reynolds was also providing some of the front end funding for the project. He wanted to realize $14.00 per horse of revenue for the first 500 horses that came from this operation. He said this would cover the initial expenses that he was going invest. Based on this he was prepared to locate and buy an initial herd of good Kentucky and Tennessee breed mares and pay to transport them to Texas.

Mr. Reynolds told Chalk that he would make sure that the horse delivery could be handled using facilities at or near Fort Sam Houston in San Antonio. He also stated that the Army would be receptive to accepting horses from Chalk's operation and dispensing horses to the Army's other posts from there.

Over time Fort Sam Houston had become a major Army base and was an obvious contact location should this plan be incorporated. Chalk asked for an hour to set down and think this through. It was obviously this situation was much more important that it had appeared to be on the surface. The profit motive must still important. However, it was also important to consider that the future of the Nation's Army was potentially involved with the outcome of this decision.

Chalk had thought the whole situation through and knew he was going to be pressured by Mr. Reynolds to accept this business proposition. He also knew the decision was not a personal profit alone. This was a matter that had far greater impacts for the future. In perspective, there was also a lot of money to be made if this contract was agreed to and executed.

Chalk went back to the big room and told Mr. Reynolds that they needed to talk. They went into his private office. Chalk told him that he would work with him to set up and run a volume horse breeding and training operation and would be glad to serve his country in this role.

Mr. Reynolds asked Chalk to go with him the next morning to Louisville and on to Fort Knox and meet the Colonel who was in charge of the project. Chalk agreed.

The next morning they got up, ate a big breakfast and had the driver take them to the train station. Chalk saw a jewelry store next to the train station and went in. He bought Wanda a necklace that had a small silver horse on a fine silver chain. He bought Barbara some hard stick candy and had it wrapped up in a simple white box. In about an hour they boarded a train going to Louisville. Mr. Berea went to the train station with them and waived goodbye as the train pulled away. When they arrived in Louisville they boarded a second train that was going south toward Nashville, Tennessee. After about an hour train ride they arrived at the small town of Elizabethtown, Kentucky. There was an Army coach and driver waiting when the train pulled into the station. The driver identified himself and his high priority passengers were driven quickly to the front gate at Fort Knox and were joined by an escort who took them directly to see Colonel Allen.

Colonel Allen met them at his office and they were given his full attention. He told Chalk that this operation was very confidential and must not be discussed with anyone outside of the room, even his wife back in Texas. Chalk understood and agreed. Colonel Allen asked Chalk about his history working with horses and wanted to understand how his current ranch operation in Texas was doing. Chalk explained everything in great detail and made sure his capabilities were well understood. He was also cautious not to overstate anything, as he did not want to leave a false impression.

The Colonel then outlined the impact of the program to the Army and told him that they wanted to have a horse population of approximately 5000 by 1908. The Goodwin Ranch could become an important contributor to this objective. The Army would fund him immediately with a $100,000 check written against the Lexington horse ranch. Chalk would be paid this front-end money as an investment for the development of a ranch to provide horses. If Chalk fulfilled the contract this front-end money would be considered as earned. The sale cost charged to the government for horses would not deduct any monies from this front-end advance. The actual sale price for horses would be at fair market value with no deductions for any Government discounts. It was extremely important that the Government not be identified as the funding organization. Mr. Reynolds as a recognized horse breeder was to be the front organization would keep the real source of the funds undercover.

The political leaders were concerned that any obvious military buildup would cause more tensions between our government and the European war leaders.

Colonial Allen agreed to have horses delivered to Fort Sam Houston in San Antonio, Texas and would make the arrangements with the proper officers. He also agreed that Chalk was to have complete authority as to how to develop his operation and there would be no government interference in his decisions so long as he made deliveries. Colonel Allen had gained a high level of confidence in Chalk and knew that anything further that he might offer to seal the deal would not be significant.

Everybody agreed to the deal with Chalk saying he would try to meet the objectives but everyone must understand that weather, sickness and other events could have an effect on the outcome. A contract outlining the general program was drafted and signed by everyone. Chalks contract to take home was written to reflect the horse farm as the customer, not the US Military. Colonial Allen opened his cabinet and took out a bottle of Kentucky's best bourbon. Everyone had a drink and said, "let's go!"

Colonial Allen was obviously impressed with Chalk's experience and knowledge about horses. He listened intently and let Chalk tell him about what was going to be required to develop a first class horse breeding operation. Chalk covered every possible detail and made the Colonel comfortable that he was capable of meeting his requirements. For a man that had little formal education and had become a business owner, Sheriff and savvy negotiator, Chalk was held in high regards. Colonial Allen recognized that Chalk had given a lot of credit to his relationship with Carl Harmony, who he talked about often, for his success and saw that he was not just bragging.

Chalk and Mr. Reynolds went back to Louisville on a local passenger train. The trip was slow and because of the nature of their business they could not discuss what was really on their mind. Both men were tired but relaxed in the way they enjoyed from having reached a successful business arrangement. Chalk noticed that Mr. Reynolds and the Colonel both were wearing rings with the same design cast into the crown. He mentioned the ring and Mr. Reynolds told him that the Colonel and He were both Masons. The rings were symbols that were special to them. He asked Chalk what he knew about the Masonic Order and told him he had very little knowledge other than that it was known as a secret or private organization. Mr. Reynolds told him that it was an organization that was centuries old and was based on the belief in God and the premise that freedom, honor and personal discipline were at it's core.

He also told Chalk that every man that signed the American Declaration of Independence was a Mason. Chalk was impressed and told Mr. Reynolds that he was impressed with his dedication to such an honorable group of men. He also complimented the Colonel as a man who had character and was obviously dedicated to his country.

Chalk had about a twenty three-hour wait for the train going back to St. Louis. He found a comfortable hotel near the train station, spent the night and caught a train going to San Antonio at 8:30 the next morning. That train was slower than the one that came north. There were more passenger cars and the people traveling to the west were primarily families with a lot of baggage.

The second train arrived in San Antonio at about 10PM. It was cold outside and Chalk was hungry and tired. He went to the Manger Hotel and got a quick sandwich, a stiff drink and a room for the night. The next morning he stopped by the Sheriff's office and got his horse. The trip home was slow as the road was muddy and had several low water crossings that were flooded from a local storm. He got home just as darkness was falling. Wanda and Baby Barbara were glad to see him. They had missed him and he had missed them too. Chalk gave Wanda the necklace he had bought up north and she was very pleased. Barbara ripped the package of hard candy open and she immediate stuck a piece in her mouth.

The next morning Chalk went to the Sheriff's office and greeted all of his staff. The time he had been gone was not eventful and everything was in good order. Chalk checked on who had been put in jail and saw that a man from New Mexico had been arrested. He had got drunk and started a fight in the local saloon. Chalk told the jailer to see if he had sobered up. Chalk had him brought to his office and told him he was turning him loose with a warning that he had been given a chance, "don't get drunk and pick a fight again in Bandera".

The county court was in session and Judge Harmony was hearing several cases. Chalk wanted to tell him he was going to expand his horse business. He also wanted to see if he had any extra cowboys at his ranch. He finally got to see him about 5PM. The next day he went to the bank and deposited his big check. He went to the bank president, as he did not want some mouthy teller to spread the word that he had made such a large deposit. Chalk still did not like doing business with banks but he had no choice in this matter. The system for handling money was too well imbedded into the economy to buck.

From there he went to the ranch at "Pipestone Ranch" and closed the deal. He got all of the land, buildings and cattle that were on the property. While traveling on the train he had decided to take the cattle that would come from the pipestone ranch and combine them with his current herd at the Goodwin Ranch in Bandera. He would then move all of the horses he currently had to the new ranch and keep the two operations separate. He already had a contract with Fort Sam Houston to deliver horses so any additional horses delivered would appear to be an expansion to the current contract.

There were 3 cowboys currently working at the pipestone ranch. Chalk only wanted to keep one of them. The other two men were known drunks and had been in his jail several times. Chalk had a good handle on most of the troublemakers in the county. This was a real positive when you were hiring people.

Chalk called all of his ranch hands together and had a weekend bar-b-que and business meeting at his ranch. He told them he was going to expand his horse operations and that some of the better the horses would be sold to the racehorse industry. He also stressed that they would still keep supplying all of the available horses to the Army.

He realigned his people and developed a special 'management team". Chalk put one man in charge of each of the two ranches. The existing ranch would be know as the Goodwin One and the new ranch was named the Goodwin Two. He then outlined a plan to move the cattle and horses to their new locations. He outlined a broad approach plan for the new organization and left the final details up to the Ranch managers. Chalk requested a set of plans to do this as quickly as possible.

It was getting near Christmas and Chalk and Wanda gave every cowboy a shiny $20 gold coin. He was good to his people and they all were supportive to him and to the ranch operations.

Chalk went about his job as Sheriff and saw that his total workload was becoming heavier and more demanding for his time. He had a lot on his mind and a lot to do everyday, but he had grown into responsibility with a capability of being able to handle it. He also had a personal, self-imposed, standard that he wanted to do everything he did well. Poor performance was not acceptable from himself or from his people. His people all understood this unwritten but obvious message.

A telegram arrived in early December informing Chalk that approximately 100 mares would be arriving in San Antonio in mid January. There would be a second shipment in February or early March and it was estimated to be about the same size. He gave this information to his ranch foremen at the Goodwin Two ranch and told them that they needed to be ready to accept these horses. He also stressed that they need to also be ready to accept even more horses in the near future.

Everyone knew that Chalk had worked some sort of big deal to raise horses but they had no idea as to the financial impact that was involved. The bank was also very interested, as the size of his deposit was substantially more than most checks that they had ever handled. The bottom line was a positive and a large plus for Chalks reputation as a businessman.

Chalk recognized that all of this activity had to be managed and that he lacked the time and skills to do all that was going to be required. To overcome this situation he found a lady in San Antonio that was an accountant and had owned her own business. She was in her late 50's, had lost her husband about 4 year ago. She started a small retail business and after it grew to prominence she sold it for a nice profit. She was a stable and mature businessperson. Her name was Becky Brock. He hired her and she moved to Bandera. Chalk set up a small office for her in the bunkhouse and told her that he would have her a new office in town as soon as he could have one built.

"Mrs. Becky" was responsible to keep records on all the animals, keep the bankbook balanced, do payrolls and report the status on everything being purchased to Chalk every two weeks. The final decision on all spending was still remaining with Chalk. He was not ready to turn loose of too much until he knew how things were working out.

The ranching operation was growing and handling all of the business associated with the daily transactions was a big job. Chalk built a small three-room office building for his ranch office in the downtown area of Bandera and set up ranch management from this business office. Mrs. Brock was put in charge of the office and she was good at keeping records and business situations under a firm and honest control.

Chapter 5
Reality and Honor

In January 1902, the weather turned extremely cold. The Goodwin Ranch was busy rounding up both horses and cattle to keep them from freezing. The cowboys were all busy with the construction of new barns and with moving all of the cattle and horses to their new locations. The cold weather was not welcome. About the 15th of the month a message came into the telegraph office that the first shipment of horses from Kentucky would be in San Antonio on the 20th. This was not a good time to add more stock, but it was not something that could be changed.

The ranch foremen, Mr. Scott, for the Goodwin Two ranch borrowed 3 cowboys from a neighbor and had them help take care of the daily winter-feeding and chores. There were now over 190 horses in the herd and it was a lot of daily work. He and 5 of his best horse handlers went to San Antonio to meet the train. Chalk also went but was about two hours later as he had to do some special work as the Sheriff. All of the cowboys had nicknamed Mr. Scott as Sarge. It stuck.

Winter in San Antonio is not bitter like it can be further up north. But, it can be cold, raw and very windy. The cold air can make one feel like they are freezing. The train arrived and the weather was really nasty. A slow drizzle was in the air and the chill from all of the cold air and moisture was bone chilling. The unloading operation was slow. There were 67 horses on the train. The groom that had traveled with them had kept them well fed and they were cold but arrived in good condition. The groom told the foreman that there were more horses planned but the railroad did not have enough cattle cars to haul them. The unloading was finished about an hour before the sun went down. Sarge put rope halters on all of the horses and linked them together in-groups of 5 or 6 animals.

177

They were then taken to a local livery barn where there was plenty of room to bed them down for the night. The holding pin they were in was normally used to hold cattle that were being shipped to market. The people at the stockyard were responsive to the horses needs and the support services they provided were good. The horses were all travel weary and needed some rest and food before they were to be driven to Bandera.

The groom had a ticket to return to Kentucky. He said he planned to be back the next month to deliver more horses. His train left town early in the morning.

The cowboys and the horses started their trip to Bandera. There were several horses with each group of horses and everything went well. When they arrived all of the animals were put in barns. The next morning each had a number branded on his left rear hip. The numbering system was designed to have a "G" followed by a number. The letters and numbers were small and only covered a small skin area. This was a common method to keep track of animals and it was only a small temporary pain. Mrs. Brock used this information to set up a record for every horse in the herd.

After the other horses were branded they were taken to a new location and each horse had a paper file set up. Accurate records of the breeding and any special expenses were given to each horse. There were also rated as to what the cowboys thought about the animal's capability. The last of the cattle were finally moved to the original Goodwin Ranch. Things started to become daily business and the life style became somewhat predictable.

Chalk's Sheriff's job was busier than ever. He was now being asked to make public appearances and to speak to different groups all over the area. His department had become recognized as one of the better-run legal offices in the area and as a result his popularity and reputation as an effective lawman and businessman was growing.

In March additional horses arrived and the same routine was followed to get them to the ranch. The Texas weather was now warming up and the grasses in the pastures was turning green. This was good news as the cowboys could spend their time doing jobs other than feeding hay and finding lost strays. When the final group of mares arrived there were 95 new animals. Several were pregnant and were going to drop folds in the spring. The horse herd had now increased to 388 animals strong.

The entire area around Bandera was growing. The local people had formed a co-operative power company and were working with a group in Johnson City to make electricity available to the town. There were a few private steam powered generators on small farms but electricity for the general public was something that was badly needed.

The same group also was working with a small company from San Antonio to get telephone lines run to the town. Progress was slow in coming to towns west of San Antonio but it was gradually happening. The best fallout of the whole situation was the improvements in communication and lifestyles.

Chalk had hired a young man to work fulltime on the ranch as a carpenter and general repairman. "Elwood" was from St. Louis and had come west to find work and make his stake in life. Back in St. Louis he had been working for a company that built wagons. His job was making wheels. His skills were developed far beyond anyone in the Bandera area in repairing wheels. The Goodwin Ranch had several wagons and keeping good wheels on a wagon was a constant effort. If the bearing got dry, it wore quickly and the wheel would become loose. Ruts and chuckholes were constantly breaking spokes or tearing up the steel tire on the outside of the wheel. There was always a lot of work to be done.

In the small community of Bandera the word spread quickly that there was a good wheelwright working at the ranch. In a short time the neighboring ranchers were bringing busted wheels to the Goodwin Ranch to see if they could get them fixed. Chalk saw what was happening and recognized the opportunity that was at hand. Chalk went to Elwood and asked him if he would like to go into business in Bandera and fix wheels for the community. Chalk offered to set him up in a building and help him get enough tools and supplies to get started. Elwood jumped at the offer and told Chalk he would repay him for his investment as soon as he made enough money. He also promised to give priority to any wheel from Chalks ranches.

Chalk and Elwood went to town and found a small building that was for sale. It was behind the blacksmith shop and had a lot of room inside. It was just what was needed and Chalk made arrangements for the purchase. Elwood named it "The Broken Spoke". Within a month he was open for business and doing well.

Wanda had found several lady friends who also had small children and her days were busy with home-making and childcare activities. The local school was growing faster than ever and the teachers were finally coming from backgrounds where they had basic professional education. Wanda kept in touch with her old friends and often would provide advice and assistance in daily school matters.

It was now possible to say that the Goodwin reputation was established and it was good. Wanda and Chalk were happy and they were always glad to be good neighbors to the local people they had made into good friends.

Judge Harmony, as Carl was now commonly being addressed was doing well and his sons were managing the cattle ranch as a profitable operation. Time to relax was always at a premium but it somehow was always available when it was needed. The summer ranch parties and the fall hunting ventures were always popular with the men. The women had their sewing circle and "Hen Parties" and kept themselves busy and relatively happy. Cooking was another past time. The Hispanic ladies and the immigrant ladies often learned from each other and the food they cooked was unique and delicious.

In November of 1904 the Goodwin Ranch business office received an urgent call from the people in Kentucky asking how many horses could be made available in the next 60 days. Mrs. Brock got in touch with chalk immediately and gave him the message. Chalk knew the message was really from the Army but the horse ranch was still acting as the go between. Up until them they were delivering approximately 30 to 40 horses per month to Fort Sam Houston. Chalk had wanted to build the herd up to a stronger breeding base by not selling every horse that was really available. Chalk now had a telephone in his home and in the ranch office and he called Mr. Reynolds in Lexington.

The conversation was, by necessity, guarded but got to the point. The need was immediate for more good horses and the "customer" was most interested in an answer as soon as possible.

The Goodwin Two herd was now over 500 head and Chalk and his foreman made a determination that they could ship 250 animals if necessary. Sarge was anxious, as this would seriously reduce the future heard development rate. Chalk told him that that was not as important as making a big shipment. The answer was called into Kentucky. Chalk waited for a reply.

Early the next morning the phone rang and it was Mr. Reynolds. He asked if the Army could start picking up 50 horses every two weeks until the 250 quantities was reached. He said that the need to keep the details of the business deal a secret was over as the Army was openly building up a force fearing the nation would be required to go to war. Chalk asked for an hour to discuss the situation with his people.

All of the ranch hands at the horse ranch were called in and Chalk told them the real story about the Army deal and the current situation. Everyone was shocked but they were all supportive to meet the Army's needs. Several of the ranch hands were former soldiers and they were fully aware of the need for good horses in the Army. They said they could have

50 good horses ready in a week and then would work to get similar quantities ready meet the requirements. Chalk called Mr. Reynolds back. They talked for several minutes and it was decided that the Army troops from Fort Sam Houston would come to the ranch and take delivery there. The plan was agreed to and everybody was informed as to the needed events.

Chalk told Judge Harmony what was happening and he was completely surprised. Wanda was equally surprised when she was told. The impact of Texas horse ranching and the connection to the military effort was being recognized. The responsibility for national interests, not just local concerns, was coming into play. The business atmosphere was almost too charged to react as if things were normal Texas issues any longer.

The following morning a call came into the Sheriff's office for Chalk. He took the call in his office. It was Colonel Allen from Fort Knox. He thanked Chalk for his efforts and told him he wanted to officially recruit him as a Commissioned officer in the Army. He added that he would award him with the rank of a First Lieutenant. He said this official Army position would allow him several privileges and clearances to do a better job for the Army. Chalk was surprised and explained that his job as a Sheriff, as a ranch owner and as a businessman was also considerations he would need to evaluate. The Colonel told him that he would help him adjust his personal life but his services were badly needed and his answer to the offer would be a positive step toward the nations needs.

Colonial Allen told him that Officers commissions were normally awarded for demonstrated leadership skills and for urgent needs that sometimes happen on the battlefield. Chalk thought about what was happening and realized that this was much more than a request, it was almost a mandate.

Colonel Allen told him that once he had accepted the Commission he should report to Fort Sam Houston to get a uniform, receive his basic overview of an officer's training and to be briefed as to his projects status.

He told him his military assignment would be to oversee the raising of horses and to work closely as an Army Officer to making the horse cavalry a stronger Army Division. Chalk was not given an opportunity to refuse. He tried to ask why he was selected but the Colonial told him that he was the only choice and his services were required. He was now going to become an Army Officer.

Life just became a lot more complicated. Chalk went home, discussed the whole situation with Wanda and they jointly came to one common decision. The call from the military was a national issue and there was only one way to respond. That was to give it your best and allow the other thing in life that can be done by others to go forward. He decided to agree to this opportunity.

Chalk considered his job as the County Sheriff. He knew he would not be able to continue in this position and also do his Army job. It was obvious, he needed to find a new Sheriff. He knew that the best choices would be from the men that were currently in his department. He chose to select the best one, appoint him as the Sheriff and resign his office. The national need for horses and for working with the Army was a much more important responsibility. He was obviously upset with some of the impacts of the situation but he was honored that he had been selected and delegated so much responsibility.

He sat down in his kitchen at home and rated all of his deputies as to the most capable and the most honest. One name came up several times. Chalk got on his horse, got a fresh bottle of good whiskey and rode over to see Judge Harmony. He told Wanda that this was a man's time to talk and he needed to go alone. She understood completely.

When Chalk arrived he was unexpected. The Judge knew something important was on his mind. Charlie saw Chalk carrying the bottle of whiskey and got two glasses. Chalk and Carl went out on the front porch and sat down. The air was still and cool but the whiskey took the worst of the chill off the coolness.

Chalk asked Carl if he thought He had done a good job at becoming a man? He had never forgotten that he was just a young kid half-breed from rural Kentucky when Carl first met him. He knew that everything he had achieved was in part with Carl's help and support. Chalk knew he had grown to a level in life he had never imagined or planned to see. He was humble and the tears were coming down his cheeks.

Carl asked him to tell him what was going on and Chalk told him about the call from Kentucky. He also told him that he had to leave the Sheriff's job so he could become more involved with the Army's needs. He told him about the Officer's Commission he had been offered. After the whole situation sunk in with Carl he started to see a man who was confused and hunting for some hard to find answers. For the first time in his life he was being asked to leave a job he truly loved and his men all had the same respect for him.

Carl also knew that the ranching operation was stable but leaving it in the hands of others was not something he had ever considered. He also was about to enter a life that was demanding and he was not sure what to expect or what to plan on for his immediate future. He was equally concerned about his family and knowing he would be gone from home a lot.

Charlie had been listening from the window and she came out and put her arms around him and told him he would do the right thing, he always had. She added that she and Carl were very proud for him. She reminded him of the conversation she had with Wanda several years earlier when she told her to "think big to become big." She said it was time to recognize what was really needed and to stand up to the challenge full force. After about three good stiff shots of whiskey and a little time, reality seemed to become more acceptable.

Chalk asked Carl for his opinion on the man he had selected to take his place as Sheriff. Carl agreed that this man was the best choice and added his approvals. Chalk rode his horse home on the dusty trail that he had traveled so many times before. This time it seemed different. The dust and the night bugs making their familiar sounds were more spectacular than ever before. Chalk was now almost 40 years old and life had never been so complicated.

Early the next morning Chalk got up early, put on his best Sheriff's uniform, shined his boots and went to work early. He had selected a deputy named Leon Price to take his place and he called him into his office as soon as he arrived. Chalk told him what was happening and asked him if he would take his place. Deputy Price was gratified when he was told about his the selection and said yes. Chalk then called all of the deputies that were on duty into a room and announced the change. Everyone was shocked but happy for Chalk.

They were all supportive of his choice for a replacement. Judge Harmony conveniently showed up at 10 AM and the new Sheriff was sworn into office.

Citizen Goodwin then went to the ranch business office and called all of his ranch foremen and key people to attend a special meeting. He told them what was happening and asked that they support the Army and his assignment as well as they had in the past. Everyone was happy for Chalk but they knew he was in for a lot of hard work in the very near future. They also saw a greater responsibility for each of them.

During dinner that evening the telephone rang and the call was long distance and was for Chalk. It was Mr. Reynolds from Kentucky. He asked Chalk if he could talk for a few minutes. Chalk took the call in a private room. Mr. Reynolds wanted to congratulate Chalk for being selected to head up the horse procurement and assignment program and to enlighten him of several changes that were coming in the Army. Chalk listened with an undivided attention.

The Army was in the middle of a massive reorganization and was trying to get ready to fight a war in the very near future. The companies in Detroit that were starting to market automobiles had also begun to develop a new vehicle called a Tank. They were also developing "trucks" to carry freight.

Tanks were being designed rapidly. These were being designed to have armor all around the combat troops and had a cannon mounted on the top. A gasoline engine inside the tank was developing vehicle power. A special set of wheels and a set of mud gripping tracks would enable the Tank to cross all kinds of terrain. Fort Knox had been designated as the development base for these vehicles. Tanks were still not tested and they were not yet ready to take any assignment in a battle zone.

This was causing a major change in the way the Army was looking at horse soldiers. The result was that the entire horse Brigade stationed at Fort Knox was being transferred to Fort Sam Houston in San Antonio. Colonial Allen had just been promoted to the rank of General and was being transferred to Texas to manage the entire horse soldier operation. Mr. Reynolds let a secret out of the box. The selection of Chalk to be an Officer was a planned move by the General. He had developed a deep trust in Chalk when they were in Kentucky and wanted to have his help in making this transfer and Fort Sam Houston operation successful. He also saw a leadership talent in Chalk that was badly missing in current personnel.

He also told Chalk that the new flying machine that had been developed in Dayton, Ohio was going to be funded for development and Texas had been selected as a pilot training location. San Antonio was the site so that the weather was not as significant factor in training operations.

Mr. Reynolds told Chalk that he thought he would do well in the Army and his initial assignment might become expanded as the changes were incorporated. Chalk thanked him for the call and told him he appreciated the insider information as to what to expect.

Chapter 6
A New Way To face Life

The Goodwin household was surprised by all of the information that Mr. Reynolds had given to Chalk. It was Thursday and Chalk had scheduled his arrival in San Antonio for the following Monday morning. He knew he wanted to serve his country but not being at home all of the time was a serious unplanned situation. Wanda was very supportive and had a good grip on the home. Barbara was now in pre-school and was not sure what was going on. Chalk knew she was going to miss him as they always spent a lot of time together. He was also going to miss her and Wanda.

The ranch operations were in good hands but his leadership had been a key part of keeping things going smoothly. The information he had received about the Army's shakeup was not all fitting together and he was anxious to see what this new status would really mean. The cattle operation at the Goodwin One operation had grown to a substantial size. The original heard of whiteface and charlois cattle had doubled in size. The longhorn cattle that came from pipestone were also multiplying rapidly and the market for cattle in general was strong.

The pipestone ranch, when purchased, had a substantial herd of goats. Chalk sold part of the herd at the local auction. The remainder was brought to the Goodwin One ranch to graze on the several hilly sections. Cattle were not commonly seen on steep hilly areas and the goats would keep the undergrowth down. This would reduce some of the fire danger in dry seasons. Goats were also a great source for meat. The Hispanic culture had many delicious dished based on "cabrito" as the main ingredient.

On Sunday morning everyone got up, had a big breakfast, dressed up in their good clothes and went to church. The Minister had learned of Chalk's new status and knew he might be out of town a lot while he supported the Army.

After the services he made a special effort to get to Chalk and his family. He told everyone that all of the church people would be behind him and his would make sure his family was well and happy. He said what ever Chalk was asked to do he need not worry about home situations. They all thanked him and went home to a big meal.

About 2:PM he changed into riding clothes and packed a small case with clean clothes for a couple of days. He hugged everyone and rode off toward San Antonio. The day was clear and the trip was easy. He had made it so many times before that the landmarks were now very familiar.

When he arrived in town he got a room at the Manger Hotel, had a good meal and went to bed. He had a hard time going to sleep as his mind was still going full speed. He finally went to sleep and was awakened at 5AM by his alarm clock. He took a bath, shaved and put on his best clothes. He made sure his boots were clean and shiny and started the short ride to Fort Sam Houston.

Upon arrival he went to the gate guard and told him whom he was and added that he was to report to the Commander of the Horse Calvary. The guard had been alerted and got an escort to take him to the right location. He saw several horses bearing the Goodwin Ranch brand being ridden as he crossed the base and took pride in the fact that his work had been meaningful.

The Commanders office was quartered in a building that looked more like a home than a military office. The white limestone exterior was well landscaped and every window was draped in elegant curtains. Everything was well maintained and reflected a constant effort from the base maintenance personnel. The lower level was his private office. The upper floor of the building was his home. The ground floor was outfitted with simple but nice furnishings and it reflected all of the protocol associated with a military office area. Much of the furniture was made from Texas mesquite lumber. The deep brown color stood out sharply against the white walls and the red tile floors.

When he entered the front door a soldier took him into a waiting room while he announced his arrival. In about 5 minutes a large man who was wearing the stars of a General came through a door and greeted him with a healthy handshake. They went into his office and sat down at a small table. The General's name was Charles Polk. He told Chalk that he had been highly recommended by General Allen and soon would be seeing him. He explained that the Army was in the middle of a buildup of forces. There was a lot of change being introduced to have the best people in the right places.

The General told Chalk that he would be assigned to the Fort Sam Houston base but was expected to spend most of his time at home and on the road developing horse suppliers. The Goodwin Ranch horse operation was singled out as an outstanding contributor and his past efforts were recognized. He would be assigned a small group of soldiers who would be located at the Fort and they would be responsible to receive and care for new arrivals at the horse stable. Horses that were being assigned to the Calvary troops were normally sent with them when they were sent to other bases. Some horses were also being sent to other bases as the pool of horses at "Fort Sam" was for a much bigger coverage.

Some travel was going to be as required. His first trip would probably be to Fort Knox to assist with the transfer of the horse Calvary at that base to Texas.

The was also a major horse Calvary Garrison located at Fort Clark, Texas which was about 120 miles west of San Antonio. This base was special, as many of the soldiers were Black men. The General referred to them as "Buffalo Soldiers". He added, these men are great fighters if they are serving under good leadership. They respect authority and give everything they have to please their leaders. Chalk would also be responsible to manage newly arrived horses that were at that location. He would also have several soldiers located at that base who were responsible to him.

The General called in his aide and two other officers who were in his building and asked them to witness the swearing in ceremony for Chalk. The aide gave the General a copy of the oath to read. Chalk was asked to stand at attention next to an American flag and respond as asked. The entire oath ceremony took about two minutes. Everyone shook his hand and welcomed him into the Army.

The aide then took Chalk to the base supply store where he was issued a uniform, spare uniforms, a side arm and all of the boots, shoes and other personal items that a First Lieutenant normally needed. It was almost noon and the aide took Chalk to the officer's mess for a good meal. Just before the meal, the aid called the group in the mess hall to attention and introduced Chalk as the new Officer who had just been commissioned by the base Commander.

Everyone applauded him and expressed their approval of his joining the Army.

An office for Chalk, who was now being addressed as Lieutenant Goodwin, had been made ready in one of the stone building next to the horse barns. There was a private bathroom and a small bedroom in the rear. This was for his use when he was on base. An orderly came by and helped Chalk understand what to expect and how to wear his uniform. The Army has many traditions and protocols and they were all new to Chalk. The orderly attempted to explain some of this to him.

At about 4:30 a knock came on the door. It was General Allen from Kentucky. He had just arrived by train and was anxious to meet with Chalk. Both of these men were new to the base so they decided to get the Officer of the Day to give them a quick post tour. Who could refuse a General?

The tour was an hour's ride in a comfortable horse drawn buggy. The driver was a senior Sergeant who had been on the base for several years. He was a good source for all kinds of insider base information. After the tour they went to the mess hall and had dinner. Being in the company of a

General drew a lot of attention to Chalk and he had to adjust to the fact that rank in the military was a whole new world of formality. Chalk was frankly humbles and impressed with his new status.

Chalk was going to be required to stay at the base for about 10 days and go through an Officer's orientation program. He also had to get his uniform tailored and his rank identification stitched on. About 9PM the two men parted and Chalk went to bed. His bunk was not as comfortable as his bed at home but it was welcome.

The next morning at 6AM he heard the bugler sound the wake up call. He put on clean civilian clothes and went to the mess hall for breakfast. The General's aide had made arrangements for a seamstress to come by at 9AM, measure his uniform, make the necessary alterations and attach all of the rank identification. The seamstress, a young male soldier, showed up on schedule and the uniform fit was perfected. Chalk put on his uniform and started to feel and look like a member of the Army. Two additional sets of uniforms were also tailored and Chalk hung up his civilian clothes.

Orientation was scheduled to begin at 1PM. The class was in a big classroom area and there were 4 other men going through the same class. Chalk learned what an Officer was expected to do and mastered the art of saluting. He also learned what the chain of command means and what was expected of an officer on the base and in public.

The class lasted the rest of the week and was over at 5PM on Friday. General Allen asked Chalk to stay on base for this weekend so he could have some time to work out the specifics of his assignment.

One of the surprises that came along was the issuing of a military saddle and the offer to give him an Army provided horse. What was comical was the fact that the horse they offered was one from the Goodwin Ranch. Chalk said he would rather use his personal horse for now. He put his new saddle on his own horse. He liked the military saddle and took pride in the shine on his new boots. They were all made from the best leather.

Friday night General Allen and Chalk went to dinner and then went to a small office to talk. General Allen explained that he had a lot of time looking for a man that he could trust and he knew would make the right decisions concerning horses. He knew he had found the right man when he met Chalk. The Army had gone through several young men before and all of them had not worked out. The most common problem was no experience and no patience. Chalk appeared to be more than qualified and he was already in Texas. The fit was perfect for Chalk.

He wanted Chalk to serve for at least four years and to become qualified for many benefits that were available to Officers who were on duty for at least that long. He also told him that additional rank would come quickly as the need for more senior Officers was common in all of the Army, especially in Texas. Chalk listened and took everything in.

He told Chalk he needed to stay on base all of the next week and meet his men. He would be free to go home on the next weekend and would be able to determine where to spend his time from there. He wanted Chalk to go to Fort Clark within a month and see what was happening there. The General was concerned as he had a Captain out there that was not dependable. He had asked for several reports concerning both men and equipment and the replies he had received were not complete and were confused. He was very unsure of what was happening and how well the base was being manned.

On Saturday morning Chalk called Wanda and filled her in on his week. She was glad to hear from him. The rest of Saturday was spent looking over paperwork he had been given in class and getting settled in his quarters. Army life was all new to him and he was anxious to learn. The experience with the Army detachment traveling with the wagon train to Texas from Memphis had already given him some feel for the life of a military man. He realized that all he had seen was the basic and soldier side of duty. There was so much more yet to be experienced.

On Sunday he went to church in the base chapel. There were two scheduled services. The first service was for Catholic troops. The second was for Protestants. The San Antonio area had been predominantly a Catholic community for a long time. Many of the soldiers at the base were Hispanic and of the Catholic faith. This was by far, the largest attended service. Chalk attended the second service.

The next week passed quickly. Monday morning the General took Chalk to meet his men. There were four fellows in his organization. Chalk greeted each with a big handshake and asked the senior Sergeant to show him around. The three older men had been in the Army for several years and were seasoned horsemen. The forth man was a new enlistee who was still learning the ropes. The tour went into the horse barn where each horse was quartered in a small stall. The area was clean and the animals all were well fed and groomed. The tack area was also well maintained. A blacksmith's area was in one smaller building. Horses were brought here to have new shoes installed and to be branded.

The discussion of new horse arrivals brought up the recording system used for qualifying a horse and accepting the animal into the stable. Prior to acceptance they were kept in a covered corral. Each horse had to be examined by a Veterinarian prior to being assigned a stall. Once examined, a report was completed on each horse that was the beginning document for his service career. Chalk looked over the document and saw what he considered to be a very meaningful examination.

One item he saw concerned him. There was no real examination of the horseshoes as the animal was received. They examined the feet of split hoofs but shoes were not called out. This was apparently left up to the grooms to take care of. He suggested that this item be added. The men all agreed.

The conversation between everyone soon revealed to the men that Chalk was the owner of the Goodwin Ranch horse operation and many of the horses in the stable had come from his ranch. This immediately built a positive bond between the entire detachment that was based upon professional respect. Chalk's initial contact with his men was off to a great start.

It was now lunchtime and Chalk invited all of the men in his command to be his guests for a Mexican meal at a small restaurant just outside the base gate. General Allen was invited and also went along. Lunchroom conversations were open, happy and positive. After the meal everyone went back to the duty area. The afternoon had been scheduled for additional classroom work for Chalk so he went to the base school facility. Chalk quickly saw that General Allen was not a man to use rank to impress people. He wanted to be on an open level with his assigned troops and expected them to be open to him about what they were thinking. Chalk liked this a lot.

General Allen asked Chalk to check with him on Friday when school was over and he would help him determine what was going to be his next step as an Officer.

School was interesting. The instructor was an older man who had been in the Army for over 20 years. He started with a history of what the Army has done since the Civil War and the impact that resulting from military efforts. He stressed the point that many of the countries in Europe were seemingly always at war with each other and the result had been centuries of slow growth, mistrust and savage hostilities. He also compared the United States to Europe by recognizing that each of the individual States in America was a locally governed body but the all contributed men and financial support to a military organization that bound them into one strong country.

He then went on and discussed how the military had funded many projects that developed the tools and equipment that were a basic part of the national strength. He underscored the current projects where the new flying machine in Ohio was being funded to become a military tool. He then discussed the development of gasoline-powered trucks, tanks and automobiles.

On a broader scope he discussed the Army Corp of Engineers and how their efforts were bringing electric power, better river navigation and flood protection to many areas of the country. By now Chalk was all ears and very excited. The discussion about flood control hit home with Chalk. His riverboat experience had given him a deep knowledge about floods on major rivers. The need to gain a better control of the river flow and pool depth was critical to river transportation.

The first two days of class were focused on history. The next three days were more focused on the role of an Officer's leadership. The instructor stressed that anybody could be a manager. All that was required was for a person to be put in charge. He then gave several examples of how just being in charge did not assure that any improvements or major strides toward goals would happen. The instructor told actual stories of people being put in charge who had no leadership skills. The results were often tragic.

After everyone was made comfortable with the role of Military management. The instructor expanded the conversation and brought in the role and necessity for leadership. There were many examples placed in the discussion concerning why many things had been successful and why many other projects had failed. The subjects of money, timing and manpower were all evaluated under each discussed project. In every instance the presence of effective leadership, or the lack of, was soon recognized as the one key element to success, or failure.

A great deal of discussion was held about early military history. The instructor pointed out the American civil war was the first war in the history of the world that was fought with soldiers on both sided that had good basic educations. This was only 50 years ago and the role of education was a big part of the military's training programs.

At the end of the 4th day an hour was devoted to understanding how to know when and how to take risks. The instructor gave several examples of risks that were not difficult, almost always would be successful and was easy to take. He also identified risks that were much more subject to failure and how to determine what to do when these decisions were required. This discussion got everyone to think seriously about their responsibility as an Officer. Being responsible was much more than just managing troops and projects. It was making sure that the right results was realized and that the lives, assets and reputations of everyone were also protected.

The last day of class required each class member to stand up and explain what they had enjoyed most and got the most good from in the course. Everyone was impressed with the role they need to follow as an Officer and the need to continue to learn more about leadership.

On Friday, after class, General Allen asked Chalk to stay home a week and absorb all of the information he had been given. He had the phone number at the Goodwin Ranch and told Chalk that he would call him if anything important happened. Chalk had been given several manuals that he needed to read and get ready for a trip to west Texas. He wanted to make this trip with the right level of Army professionalism. Chalk was excited and humbled by having so much responsibility authority so soon.

At 5PM Chalk, changed into clothing comfortable for riding a horse and went to the stable. His new military saddle was already on the horse's back and his soldiers had found him a saddlebag to hold his personal things. He told them to look for him to be back in a few days and wished them well. The senior sergeant was put in command while he was gone.

His suitcase and a gift package for both Barbara and Wanda were strapped onto the top of the saddlebag.

He rode home and when his horse entered the long driveway to his house Wanda saw him coming. His new Army uniform was a little dusty but she was so proud of her husband. Little Barbara saw him soon after he got to the house. She ran and grabbed him by the leg and cried tears of happiness. Daddy was home.

Serving Our Nation and Maintaining a Family

Chalk Goodwin
Book 4 of 4

Kenneth Orr

Chapter 1
A Lifestyle of Adjustments

The Goodwin Ranch was still Chalk's home. Going home was always his greatest joy. The first weekend Chalk went home he spent all of his free time with Wanda and baby Barbara. They had missed Chalk and he had missed them. This was time to be a family and to just relax and get some of the tensions from being away relaxed. After all, this was the first time Chalk had been away for such a long time and he knew that the future was going to be much more of the same.

On Sunday they all dressed up and went to Church. Chalk wore his civilian clothes and wanted to keep a low local profile about being in the Army. After the services they went straight home. The housekeeper had a big delicious meal waiting on the table. Everyone ate a full meal and enjoyed each other's company. In the afternoon they put on relaxed feelings clothes and got out the ranch wagon. Pipestone was not far away but was a very relaxing ride. The weather was beautiful and the ride was relaxing and fun for everyone.

Barbara rode up on the front seat between her Mom and Dad. They just rode and talked for a long time. Wanda watched as Barbara reconnected with her Dad. He had lost his daily conversations with her while he had been away. Just being together was good enough.

Monday morning Chalk got up, dressed in his cowboy clothes, and had a big breakfast with Wanda and Barbara. The ranch foreman had the wagon waiting outside and He went to the ranch office in Bandera. When he walked in everybody, all three of them, stood up and clapped. Chalk smiled and hugged each of them. He went to his desk and started to go through his mail. Mrs. Brock had sorted the junk and normal bills out of the stack. Her work was always focused to keeping Chalk's work refined to just the necessary and urgent issues.

She had a list of pending ranching issues that needed Chalk's judgment and approvals. There were several requests for purchases, which were primarily from the Goodwin Two ranch. The ranches had survived but it was clear that not having Chalk around was not comfortable.

Mrs. Brock had a current bank statement and the accounting data to support all of the current bank transactions. She had the small cash box all sorted out and made sure that the dollars were all accounted for. All of the ranch financial issues were in obvious good shape. A neighboring rancher had contacted Mrs. Brock concerning the cattle operation at the Goodwin One.

He wanted to sell them his cattle. The owner had recently suffered a heart attack and wanted to get out of the cattle business. There were over 100 longhorns in the herd and most of them were ready to go to the "sale" barn. Chalk knew the owner and was always on a friendly relationship with the man. He called him on the phone and asked him when would be a good time to come out to his place and visit with him. The made an appointment for Wednesday.

Chalk had lunch with Mrs. Brock and discussed the fact that he was going to be away more often than he had anticipated. He wanted her to become his senior business manager. He wanted her to be comfortable when she needed to make important immediate decisions. He told her that he was comfortable with her judgment ability and let her know this first hand. He also gave her a nice increase in pay.

In the afternoon Chalk rode out to the Goodwin Two ranch and called the entire ranch people together. He bragged on them about everything he had seen at the military base and relayed the positive attitude that everyone at "Fort Sam" had toward their "Goodwin Ranch" horses.

There were a lot of questions from the cowboys and other workers. Chalk gave everyone time to speak and answered each question to the best of his knowledge. Chalk then took his ranch leadership role and began to outline a plan he had developed for the future of the ranch.

First, he wanted to build a larger stable area where there were stalls for at lease 100 horses, potentially a lot more. He drew a crude sketch on a large paper pad defining the outline and general shape of the ranch. He added notes to the outside of the design for proposed changes. He also wanted to build an exercise track where horses about to be delivered could be ridden approximately 5 miles every other day.

This entire facility was going to be similar to the one at Fort Sam Houston. He wanted to get started as soon as it was practical. In addition he wanted to add a nice but basic residence building near the stable area. The purpose for this structure was to provide housing for up to three or four assigned Calvary soldiers. The Army was going to take a very close support role on the ranch.

His plan was to have Military personnel on site to help do the final training for Army horses. He had observed that all of the horses, soon after delivery, were given specialized military training in how to stand in formations, be in a march column and conditioned to not react when gunfire was present.

He had discussed training horses with this skill with General Allen. The General said the Army would pay more for horses that had these skills. He had left the "how" part of this proposal up to Chalk. Chalk was beginning to delegate much of the tasks at the ranch to his people. They were all being given more responsibilities and duties. This made them feel more important and proud.

The ranch foreman, Sarge, had been at Fort Clark and already knew a lot about where Chalk was heading. He was also excited that they would consider doing some of the basic training for every horse. The presence of soldiers on the ranch would also add a point of quality control to the ranch operation that would be unique.

After the meeting the ranch cook served a big meal, which everyone enjoyed. Chalk went home and spent the evening with his family. His first working day home was different from his old style. For the first time Chalk was acting more like a seasoned leader and less like a manager. He was learning skills that were going to be valuable to him and to his people for the rest of his life.

Tuesday morning Chalk went directly from home to the Goodwin One main building. The foreman had requested for all ranch hands to be assembled in the main eating area. Chalk went through the same basis discussions with them as he had at the Goodwin Two the prior day. His explanation about the new construction at the Goodwin Two was based on the needs of the Army customer. Chalk had a concern that the men working the cattle ranch might feel left out from the planned efforts. He had developed a plan to overcome this concern.

When the first part of his discussion was completed Chalk asked everyone at the same time, "How many more cattle can our ranch support"? Everyone looked at him and was confused as what his question meant. He smiled and said, "Just tell me how many more cattle this ranch and our grass crop will carry and still be comfortable"?

Everybody looked toward the foreman and waited to see if he was going to respond. The foreman scratched his head and looked at everyone in the room. He said we could handle about 100 or perhaps a few more head with the grass and hay we can grow, and that's a real tight upper limit. Chalk listened and smiled.

He then looked at everybody in the room and asked, "Do you all support this statement"? One old cowboy stood up and said, "If the boss says we can do it, yep, we can do it". Everybody cheered his answer.

Chalk then told everybody that there was a good herd for sale at a nearby ranch and they were all supposed to be first class Texas Longhorns. He also said that if he bought these cattle there could be several good cowboys looking for work. He asked, "Do we need more help if we get these cattle"? The foreman stood up quickly and said he already wanted to discuss hiring two more good men. The additional cattle would add to the already tight workload.

One of the cowboys asked which ranch was selling their cattle? Chalk told the group who the owner was and why he was selling out. Several of the cowboys knew the ranch and were surprised. This was a good ranch and the cattle were always well maintained. The cowboys were anxious and excited that they might have Texas Longhorns on The ranch. They were easy to work and had a unique and impressive historical status in Texas. He told them he was going to meet with the owner the next day and needed to have his people behind him before he decided to buy any additional cattle.

Chalk's ranch house was located near the front gate of the Goodwin One and everyone knew that everything on this ranch was very special to Wanda and Chalk. Cattle were still a big part of his life. He loved his ranch and took a lot of pride in keeping it presentable.

Chalk had become good friends with the local saloon owner. His Sheriff's job had brought them together often and each had a deep respect for the other. The saloon owner bought his whiskey in wooden casks. They were shipped in from the distilleries and always were safer than trying to ship glass bottles. The saloon owner would remove the bung plug from the cask and insert a small wooden tap to fill glass bottles. The valve on the tap would serve to control the flow and keep the whiskey that was still in the cask fresh. The empty casks were then discarded. Back when Chalk was the Sheriff he had requested that he be allowed to have several of the old casks to make flower boxes along the front of his ranch entry. The owner gladly agreed. The inventory of used casks would build up and the owner would tell Chalk to bring his wagon by and he would load them for him.

This was a good arrangement for two reasons. The cowboys found out that sometimes there was still some whiskey left in the cask. They would be careful to empty every drop into a jug when Chalk brought the casks home. The empty casks were then adapted to hold flowers and placed next to the path to the ranch house. When Chalk came home the cowboys always made sure that the flowers were in good shape and that there was room for some additional casks. While Chalk was home the flowers were always maintained extra well. The standard joke on the ranch was that "they needed more flower pots".

Tuesday afternoon Chalk called Carl and asked him if he was busy. Carl was going to hold court all day on Wednesday and had the rest of Tuesday available. Chalk said he was coming over. Chalk loaded Wanda and Barbara into their buggy and the went to see Carl and Charlie. Carl was very interested in what had been happening to Chalk and they had a great reunion.

Chalk took his new military pistol over to show Carl. Both were gun nuts and a new gun was always a real good experience. He was proud of it and wore it on his hip.

Chalk told Carl about the impending cattle deal and asked him if he thought that his sons might want to share in some of the cattle. Chalk knew he had all of his folks behind him but he also knew that he was running out of good grass land and if the weather should turn dry some cattle would either need to be sold or he would be required to buy a lot of hay. This was a concern but it was not a point that could spoil the deal.

Carl called his sons and asked them to come over. Chalk discussed the deal with them and they were not really looking for more cattle. Their current herds were already about all the land could carry. Chalk understood and thanked them for coming by.

Wanda and Charlie had a lot of female type discussions. One of the topics was Chalk being away a lot. In the past Carl had been away a lot of time when he was running wagon trains. Charlie told Wanda that she needed to find some activity, other than children, to keep her occupied when Chalk was gone. She told her it would make her time go by faster and easier. It would also make her a better, more self-sufficient person if anything ever happened to Chalk. This was great advice.

Wednesday evening Charlie had her cook fix dinner for everyone. This was more of a party than just a meal. Everybody had a great time. The buggy trip back to the Goodwin One was fun and Chalk laughed a lot.

When they got home a phone call had come in for Chalk from General Allen. Chalk returned his call and the General told him that he was going to go to Fort Clark himself the following week and wanted to arrive there on Tuesday. He wanted to see Chalks ranch in route and he asked if Chalk would get him a place to stay on Monday night. He wanted Chalk to go with him and they would leave Bandera early on Tuesday. Chalk agreed and was pleased that General Allen wanted to see his ranch operations.

Early Wednesday morning Chalk called his Goodwin Two ranch foreman and told him about the upcoming visit. Sarge wanted to have the place looking really good. He told all of the men how to act and what to do, and not do, around a high-ranking Army Officer. His Fort Clark experience was valuable.

The fact that Chalk was going to Fort Clark fascinated him. Sarge had spent time there and knew most of the people who were there when he mustered out.

Chalk walked over to the Goodwin One foreman's office and told him about the upcoming visit and asked him to get everyone on the Goodwin One ready to meet the General.

Wanda was equally excited. She had never seen a General. She had the housekeeper fix the guest bedroom for him and give the ranch house an extra good cleaning.

Chalk had told General Allen where he would meet him in town and they would see the ranch office operation, have lunch and then go to the Goodwin Ranch.

At about 11 AM Chalk went to town and tied up his horse in front of the Ranch main office. Mrs. Brock was busy doing her normal job and when Chalk told he about the visit she was surprised that an Army General was coming to town. Before coming to Bandera she had lived in San Antonio near the Army base. She knew that Generals were always special people and it was almost automatic to respect and cater to them.

He was scheduled to arrive about 11 AM on Monday. Chalk wanted to take General Allen to the Main ranch office as the first stop. He asked Mrs. Brock to made a lunch reservation at the best Mexican restaurant in town. The General loved Mexican food and the friendly atmosphere that always seems to be present in a good Mexican restaurant. From there he would go to the Goodwin Two ranch and review the horse operations.

Chalk got a quick sandwich and ate it as he rode out to Mr. Watter's ranch where the additional cattle deal was to be discussed. He arrived right on schedule. Mr. Watters, was anxiously waiting and had all of the information about his cattle ready for Chalk to review. Mr. Watter's wife brought in two big glasses of iced tea and took it to the big table in the dining room. All of the paperwork concerning cattle paperwork was laid out.

The paperwork identified 107 cattle, all of which were for sale. There was a paper record on every animal and all of them were reported to be in good health. A veterinarian had examined every cow and he had signed the individual documentation for each animal. Chalk looked at the paperwork. Everything was in good shape and Chalk wanted to see the cattle. Mr. Watters was too ill to ride a horse so he had his ranch foreman bring a small buggy to the house. He and Chalk got into the wagon and went to a near by pasture area where all of the cattle had been collected.

Chalk inspected several of the cattle and they looked great. On the way back to the house Mr. Watters told Chalk that he had 4 good cowboys and a ranch foreman that would all need a job when the cattle were gone. Chalk understood and said he would consider some of these people.

Back at the ranch Mr. Watters said he would like to get $25 per head for the cattle. He added that if he took all of them he would only charge him for 100. This would cost Chalk $2,500 for the entire herd.

Chalk asked if he could have a couple of hours to consider all of the other costs that would be involved. Mr. Watters then said he would have his cowboys deliver all of the cattle and would also throw in all of the hay he had on hand. He had about 200 fresh cut bales and it was in good shape.

Chalk understood just how anxious Mr. Watters was to sell his cattle. He thought the price was a dollar or two above what he wanted to pay but he still could make a profit if he chose to sell them within the next 6 months. Chalk said, "We have a deal".

However, Chalk added, he needed to have about 20 head, the ones with the widest horns, delivered to the Goodwin One ranch as soon as possible. A very special guest was coming to visit. Mr. Watters agreed and said this was not a problem. Everybody was pleased with the outcome.

Chalk went home and went to the Goodwin One foreman's office. He told him that he had made the deal for the cattle. The quick delivery of a few head was also discussed. The foreman understood the impact that Chalk wanted for General Allen. Chalk told him that he needed to do interviews with the available cowboys and the decision to hire or not was in his hands.

Wanda saw a big change in Chalk as to how he was managing the ranches. For the first time he was letting the foremen have more control and was leading more than he was managing. The ranch office in Bandera was another story.

All of the ranch money and business activity was controlled from this office. Chalk was not ready to loosen any control on that area of the business. He trusted Mrs. Brock, she was excellent at money management and accounting but she did not know much about running a ranch.

Thursday was a rainy and gray day. Everything that needed considered for the General's visit had been covered. Chalk decided to look at his Army manuals and to try to become more confident about himself and Army protocol for the trip to Fort Clark. The books were easy enough to read but the messages they contained were outlined in pure military language. Over a short period he covered two manuals and wanted to digest what was inside. After all, he was just getting into the Military and this was all still a lot of new adjustment for him.

In the afternoon he rode out to the Goodwin Two ranch and had a good chat with Sarge. He told him about his upcoming trip to Fort Clark and picked his brain to see what he might know.

Sarge had a lot of good suggestions and he also warned him that one of the men who had been assigned to the horse stable detail at Fort Clark was a drunk. He thought others with the same habits were also in the ranks. Sarge had personally had to take him home from Uvalde a couple of times to keep him from being thrown in jail. His name was Jerry Keck. Chalk wrote his name on a piece of paper and put it in his pocket.

Sarge told him a lot about how some troops at Fort Clark had previously been stationed to Fort Stockton. Fort Stockton was located further north and west Texas. This base had been a problem for the Army as many of the men who were stationed there had criminal records. This criminal history carried over to the time when they were in the Army. Fort Stockton was another one of the Army's original "Buffalo Soldier" outposts and dated back to the 1850's.

Many of the troops were uneducated and this deficiency contributed to a lack of discipline and a lot of problems in building a good band of men. This problem was obvious when the Officers would assign groups of men together for long patrols. In the 1860's the base was abandoned.

Then a few years later it was re-opened and a new set of officers were in command. Many men were from the southern United States and they had little to no respect for black men. Many of the problem troops were either mustered out or transported to Fort Clark.

Some corrected their habits and became good soldiers and some were just not capable of doing better in the military. A few of the better troops became career men and had stayed at Fort Clark. Several of these men were instrumental in helping new recruits get a better grip on military life. However, some were still problems and required a lot of the Officer's time

Friday was another busy day. Chalk wanted to do a walk through inspection on both ranches before the General arrived. Both ranches looked good but the men all looked like they just got back from a long and bad weekend. They all needed haircuts. They also needed clean, less ragged clothes. They reminded Chalk of a band of a bunch of poor dirt land farmers he had seen back in Kentucky. Everyone needed to shape up before they were going to be seen by the General. This included Sarge.

Chalk sent to town for the local barber and had him come out to the ranch and cut every man on the payroll's hair. He hired a local Mexican lady that did laundry. Her personally told her to spend all weekend if necessary, cleaning up the usable dirty clothes.

He told everyone if they did not have a respectable set of clothes to wear, go buy some. He paid the local clothing store to put new clothes on over 70% of the men and Chalk also paid for new boots and items like shaving supplies and soap. His ranch was not going to look like a bunch of ragtag outlaw bandits. This was a new side of Chalk's attitudes and everyone was a little surprised at his new approach on dress. They were also impressed as to how good they all looked when they were cleaned up and dressed better.

Saturday was an enforced scrub and clean day. The entire list of employees was aware that they were expected to look good and the ranches facilities were to look good on Monday. About 5 PM Chalk went out to the Goodwin Two and made his presence well known. He saw a new bunch of clean and respectable looking men and he was happy. He also saw a clean barn area and a lot of new paint in places that were showing age and wear. He was beginning to feel pleased.

Before he left he told Sarge that he wanted to see this standard of dress and housekeeping to become an expected part of working at his ranches. He also experienced the same good feeling at the Goodwin One.

Sunday was a family day and he and his "Girls" as he called them, spent the entire day together. They were all learning that time spent together was now more valuable than ever.

Chapter Two
Rank and Respect for His Men

Monday morning began with what could only be describes as a glorious sunrise. The clouds in the east were colored with reds, yellows and golden colored formations. Streams of brilliant sunlight were poking holes in the clouds and the blue sky beyond the clouds was a brilliant sight to behold. A warm front had passed through during the hours before sunrise and all of the remaining clouds were moving toward the eastern horizon. This day just had to be a success with a start so magnificent as this.

The ranch house was awake long before sunrise. Wanda had spent a lot of time and care on polishing the home's sparkling condition. The windows were all washed and the floors were spotless. The kitchen was full of the smell of fresh baked cookies, fresh cut wildflowers and baking bread. Wanda knew that the smell of good food and fresh flowers was always a sure way to impress a man. She wanted to make her home as welcome for General Allen as she could. She had never met him but was anxious to have him come and to enjoy the comforts of her home. The flower boxes along the path to the ranch house were all trimmed and blooming with many colors and sweet smells.

Lieutenant Goodwin got up, bathed, and put on his freshly pressed Army uniform. Wanda had seen him wear it before but none of the ranch people had ever seem him wearing it. After breakfast he had his horse saddled, mounted up and rode out to the Goodwin Two. When he arrived everyone was impressed as how crisp he looked and how much difference in appearance a uniform can make. They always respected him as the boss but now his stature as an Army Officer had just forced their level of respect go up several notches.

He looked the ranch over, he reacted with the cowboys and made comments about both good and few inferior conditions. His style was much like an Officer who was reviewing a soldier when he stands inspection.

Chalk called everyone together for a general "all hands" meeting. He thanked them as a group and told them just to be themselves when the General arrived. Chalk discussed what the General was coming to see. He added, and under all of his rank, stature and under all of the charisma, he was still a man. Chalk told the men he personally liked the General and he was really an OK guy. He told them to answer any question he may have. He stressed; the best answer to any of his questions was always the truth. He said don't tell half of the answer or stretch the answer to make it sound better, just be honest. He then rode off toward Bandera.

In Bandera the Ranch office was all dressed up with two flags, one American and one a Texas flag. They were mounted on the posts that held up the front porch roof. Inside the wood floors were shiny and all of the desks and chairs were clean and freshly wiped down with a special furniture polish from San Antonio. The chairs in the meeting room were setting in neat rows. Mrs. Brock had used a string to line everything up and had personally done most of the work herself. She also had been to a hairdresser and had a special hair cut and she looked very nice.

General Allen was scheduled to arrive shortly and his timing was normally accurate. Chalk walked out to the mailbox and dropped in a couple of letters. His next-door business neighbor saw him. He came over and wanted to make sure it was Chalk. His uniform had confused him as to who is this man?

Right on schedule, at 10:30, a snappy black buggy with a driver in the front seat and General Allen in the back pulled up to the front of the Goodwin Ranch office. A small star with a gold fringe flag was on the driver's side of the buggy. Chalk saw him arrive and immediately went outside to welcome him.

He greeted the driver and recognized him as one of his assigned enlisted men. The driver and Chalk opened the buggy side door and helped the General get out. Chalk personally greeted the General. They exchanged a few words and Chalk and took him into the office. His first business was to introduce him to Mrs. Brock and her small staff.

Mrs. Brock has a big pitcher of ice-cold tea and a tray of snacks setting on a small table by the door as you entered the office. When everyone was inside she offered refreshments and suggested that everyone take a few minutes to have a cold glass of tea and a snack and relax from the trip.

The iced tea was most welcome and the most of the snacks were consumed quickly. When everyone was finished Chalk stood up in front of the room and hung a map of the area on the wall. The map was specially marked to show the main buildings in the town and the locations of the two Goodwin Ranches.

Bandera County was not very large and the map was drawn to a fairly accurate scale. He stressed that south central Texas was a great place to live and the fact that the Army had selected the Goodwin Ranches to supply horses was a real economic positive for everyone in the community.

Chalk reviewed the history of his ranching operation and he stressed that many areas of help he had been provided by Judge Carl Harmony. He went to the map and pointed out Carl's ranch and the County Courthouse where Carl had his offices. The General was appreciative for the information and asked if he could stop by the courthouse and meet Judge Harmony.

Chalk asked Mrs. Brock to step over to the courthouse, which was only a few hundred feet away, and see if the Judge was available. Mrs. Brock returned shortly and said Judge Harmony would be coming over to the ranch office shortly. He had a trial in about an hour and would rather come to the office than confuse his staff with an unscheduled and somewhat different visitor just then.

While Carl was in route Chalk discussed the ranch's financial status. Chalk told the General that he had never liked dealing with banks, but he had given in to the economic system.

He also indicated that he had a substantial surplus of cash on deposit. The entire operation was financially stable and had adequate assets to do what ever was required to meet the customer's requirements. He was especially proud that his entire operation was debt free and he was able to stay current every month on all of the ranch's obligations. He thanked the Army for much of his success.

Judge Harmony came in and Chalk introduced him to General Allen. The General told Carl he was going to move his family to Texas soon and was considering the Bandera area as a possible place to call home. He was planning to retire from the Army in about 3 to 5 years and had always heard about the good people in Texas and how friendly they were.

He also told Carl how thankful he was for the vision and help he had been to Chalk. His words were sincere. The Judge thanked him for his kind words and told him he was always welcome in Bandera and if he could help him find a place, just let him know. The Judge shook the General's hand and said he was on a tight schedule and had to go. The meeting with Carl was an unplanned but eye-opening super success. General Allen used kind and sincere words to show his appreciation of the people who were hosting him. He reflected the attitudes of an honest and sincere individual. Carl respected him for his kind words.

At 11:30 Chalk took the General, his aid that was driving the buggy and Mrs. Brock and her staff to lunch. They walked to the restaurant, which was only a short block away. The General's uniform with a star on each shoulder was a real point of interest to everyone in the restaurant. Everyone looked but nobody was bold enough to ask Chalk any questions in front of the lunch party. The restaurant owner had set up a special table just for this visit and it was decorated with flowers and a special set of tableware. It was impressive.

The meal was Mexican style chicken with all the trimmings. Everyone enjoyed the meal and each other's company. After the meal they went back to the Goodwin Ranch office. The General thanked Mrs. Brock for her hospitality and then He and Chalk got in the buggy to go to the Goodwin Two ranch. Chalk tied his horse to the rear of the buggy and rode inside where he could talk with the General.

The road out to the Goodwin Two was dusty and the noontime sun was warming things up quickly. In about 25 minutes they arrived. The air was full of the aroma of cedar trees and the freshness they always add to the atmosphere. Purple sage was blooming by the side of the road and honeybees were swarming in the blooms gathering nectar.

Sarge understood Army protocol and had a large American flag hanging on a pole next to the front gate. This was a surprise to Chalk and a real delight for the General. The wagon pulled up to the ranch house where "Sarge" greeted everyone. The greetings were warm and friendly.

Sarge saluted and told the General he was once a soldier and saluting a General was an honor and a veteran's residual civic duty. Everyone then went into the house where a large room was set up for a small welcoming event.

Sarge stood up in front of the room, welcomed General Allen, and introduced a few key people from the ranch. He then went over the ranches status in a short but very meaningful summary. After the initial presentation, Sarge told General Allen that he had once been assigned to Fort Clark and that he had a lot of knowledge of the way things were being done there.

He then invited the General to go on a short walking tour to see the horse barns and observe some of the horses that were in training. Sarge wanted him to meet the working cowboys. They all went out the side door and started the tour.

Chalk let Sarge run the tour and only made comments when General Allen asked him direct questions. He wanted to let his men do their jobs and demonstrate that they were on top of the operation. The ranch foreman pointed out an area where they were building additional horse barns and where the new horse training facility was being built. This impressed General Allen. He told Sarge that this was a first class Military Army horse supplier operation. He added that the Army was proud of the ranch's ability to provide quality horses. He said the Army wanted to build on this standard for developing other quality military horses.

The General knew that the best information was always found within the people that were doing the work, not the owner. He often spoke with the cowboys and asked questions. They were quick to answer. The tour lasted for about 90 minutes and was well received by everyone. The men all looked clean and well qualified to do their jobs. The General paid compliments to many of the men and to the way they were developing the ranch.

It was obvious to Chalk that there had been a lot of cleanup work done since even his last inspection. The ranch really looked impressive. It was now mid afternoon and General Allen wanted to go to see the cattle operation before the day was over. General Allen thanked everyone for their efforts and commented that this was a first class operation. They then left, in the General's buggy, for the Goodwin One ranch.

The trip to the Goodwin One was a great opportunity for General Allen and Chalk to talk in the buggy. The conversation centered on the horse ranch.

The General then changed the subject and went into a discussion about Fort Clark. General Allen had received confidential information that troop moral there was very poor and the Officers in charge were not doing anything positive to help the situation. He also had been told that this Fort was going to become a center for several special operations that supported the political objectives of the Nation's President.

The constant negative reporting was a major concern to him so he had decided to go see for himself. He told Chalk that he would be his assistant for this trip. He also told Chalk that their arrival would be a surprise, he had not informed anyone that he was also coming.

Chalk told the General that he had made a room ready for him and his aid at his ranch house. General Allen was very pleased.

The buggy arrived at the Goodwin One ranch and the ranch foreman was waiting just inside the front gate. Another American flag was displayed at the entrance to the ranch. Chalk asked the driver to go to the front of the ranch house and park. Upon arrival Chalk invited the General to first come into his home and meet his family. Wanda was waiting. Baby Barbara was beside her. Barbara was dressed up in a green and white dress with white stitched flowers on the front.

General Allen greeted everyone and then reached down and picked up Barbara. He told her she looked a lot like his daughter who was now 10 years old and was still living in Kentucky. Chalk had never really seen this side of General Allen and was impressed that he was a solid family man. Wanda had the maid show the aide where to put everyone's travel bags.

Chalk took General Allen out to reconnect with the ranch foreman. Everyone went into the cowboy's lunchroom where a very special reception had been planned. There was an American flag hanging on the wall in the north end of the room. There was also a large collection of snacks and drinks to be enjoyed by everyone.

The ranch foreman had drawn a map of the cattle ranch that had the basic buildings and pasture areas identified. He explained that there were really three breeds of cattle being raised. The Herefords and Charlois had been the initial focus. These breeds ware good beef producers and were in good demand by the meat packinghouses. The recent addition of the Goodwin Two ranch was going to increase the heard size by over 100 Texas Longhorns. They were good meat producers but they had a lot of special focus in Texas. The entire cattle population was now nearing 800 head.

There was a small blacksmith shop that had been set up next to the main barn when there were horses. Plans were to move it to the Goodwin Two as soon a new building for ranch services was constructed.

The foreman then asked the General if he wanted to see the cattle. He responded that he was very interested and especially wanted to see the Longhorns. A cowboy pulled a specially outfitted ranch wagon up to the building. The wagon had three wide seats and a driver's seat up front. Everyone got on board and the foreman drove the wagon. Chalk told the General that this wagon had once been the supply wagon on the wagon train that he was part of when he came to Texas. He loved this old wagon and the memories that were with it.

He drove the wagon through several of the buildings and explained what was done in each. The General was very interested with the activities on the ranch. He recognized that raising cattle was much different than raising horses. One of his comments was that cattle don't need "shoes". This was obvious to the cowboys but a new realization of sorts to the General. He had never been around cattle before coming to Texas.

Chalk had planned a ranch dinner in the ranch lunchroom where all of the cowboys, his family and the guests were able to mix with each other. The ranch cook was a man who once cooked in a New Orleans restaurant. He could make simple food taste like wonderful and delicious restaurant dishes.

The meal was bar-b-qued beef, candied sweet chicken and spicy cabrito. The side dishes were refried beans with diced onions, a green garden salad with avocado slices and wild gulf brown rice. Flour torte's and cornbread were the breads for the meal. A big container of iced tea was at then end of the serving line. A special bar area was set up on a table at a different location in the room. Everyone was told, by Chalk, that after dinner, that the whiskey and beer was on the house and everyone was welcome to partake. One of the cowboys had a special nack for mixing Marguerites. This was a common dinner drink for a hot and thirsty Texan.

The meal was served in a "serve your-self" style. Prior to anyone going down the food line, Chalk asked one of the cowboys to deliver a blessing. The prayer was short but strong on thanking the Lord for all of the blessing that were at hand.

General Allen and then Chalk and his family led the group to the food line. Chalk had asked Wanda and Barbara to join them at the head table for the meal. She was right on time. Barbara followed her Dad down the line. General Allen had never had cabrito before and was anxious to taste the tasty meat. He knew it was goat meat but had never seen it served as a meal main course.

Everyone sat at the long tables where the cowboys normally ate their meals. Chalk had asked everyone to stay in the room after eating until he had an opportunity to speak to the group. The eating was hardy, as the food was plentiful and delicious.

When everyone finished eating a couple of cowboys collected all of the dirty dishes and wiped down the tables. Chalk stood up and introduced General Allen. He recognized him as the one individual who had been responsible for the recent ranch expansion. He received a large hand and he heard a lot of cowboy hoots and hollers. The stage was sat for the General to have a few words to everyone.

General Allen stood up, smiled, and looked around the room for about two minutes. He said nothing but looked at the crowd and saw the interest that was building as to what he was about to say. His presence was overwhelming to many and he knew he was going to be heard with intense interest. He then began to speak.

His voice was clear, strong and easy to understand. His style was to talk slow and let his words soak in as he delivered his comments. He thanked everyone for the fine hospitality and then went into a short discussion about his respect for cowboys.

He said his "all time military hero' was President Teddy Roosevelt. He then told a story about Roosevelt's role in collecting troops in San Antonio to support the United States Army in the Mexican-American war. He said that Teddy had gone into the old Manger Hotel in San Antonio, bought a round or two of drinks, and then told everybody whom he was. He said he was looking for a few good men who were not afraid to fight for what they believed in. Everyone knew that there was going to be a war with the Mexicans and their memory of past events were more than enough to convince them that this was a must win situation.

Teddy then asked if he could get any volunteers to go fight with him. Almost all of the men in the bar were cowboys and most of them proudly stood up and said they were ready. The result was the famous military detachment known as the "Rough Riders" that went on to become world famous.

General Allen closed the discussion by saying how important the "American Cowboy" image had become back in Washington DC. Their reputation was known all across the country and recognized as a breed and spirited group of men who stood for the best in America's entire western area. He then told them that their ranch was a showplace and they should be proud to be working there. Their horses and ranch reputation was well known in many high places in the military.

The meeting broke up and everybody went to the bar area and got a cool drink. Everyone mixed and talked with each other for about a half hour. Finally, the party broke up. Chalk and General Allen shook every cowboy's hand with a big thanks. They then went on their normal way. General Allen sought out the ranch foreman and personally thanked him for the tour and the excellent meal. Chalk told General Allen that his cowboys all called him by his first name unless he was in uniform. Then they often got confused as how to address him. They both laughed and said it was not the worst problem that a man can have.

Chalk and Wanda led General Allen back to the ranch house. Chalk showed the General his room for the night and where his bathroom was located. The bed was turned down and his clothes had been hung in the closet. His aide was shown the same level of hospitality.

General Allen took a bottle of prime Kentucky whiskey from his luggage and went to the large central room where Wanda, Barbara and Chalk were seated. It was cool outside, as winter was not yet completely over. A warm fire was burning in the stone fireplace and the smell of wood smoke had flavored the air in the room. Chalk asked to have the General's aide to join them. He came quickly and was pleased to be a part of the group. This was a special moment for Chalk and Wanda as it was the first time they were able to be a family and show off their home to an Army General.

The General sat the bottle on a small table next to his chair. The housekeeper noticed the bottle and quickly brought in several clean glasses and a bowel full of ice.

The General invited Chalk to join him for a nightcap drink. He asked Wanda if she minded him drinking whiskey. There was no problem and he opened the bottle, put some ice in three glasses and poured himself, his aide and Chalk a small glass of whiskey. The ice had been chipped from a large block and the whiskey, with the light from the fireplace made the glass sparkle with livid colors.

General Allen thanked Wanda for having a nice room for him and for his aide. He then said he wanted to get up early and get a quick start for the rest of the trip. Wanda set with them for a short time and went to the housekeeper and told her to have breakfast ready to match the General's schedule.

Barbara was still a 6 year old little girl and her attention span was gone in a very few minutes. Her presence was welcome but she was soon looking for other interests. Wanda excused herself and Barbara and they went to Barbara's bedroom where she was put to bed.

Wanda then went to her room so the men could talk in private. The first glass of whiskey was gone in a short time and the General poured Chalk, himself and his aid a second. He them took off his boots and began to relax. He said it was good to be in a home where there was a family and the smell of "home" was everywhere. He missed his family and the evening had brought back many memories of his family in Kentucky.

He told Chalk about his family. General Allen had a wife and two wonderful children, a small girl, age 8 and a 12-year-old son. They were living in military quarters at Fort Knox back in Kentucky. They were waiting for him to come and get them and take them to a new Texas home. The day had impressed General Allen and he told Chalk the whole day had been very special for him.

Chalk told him that he was glad he had come to visit his ranch and Wanda was glad to have been able to meet him. The General thanked him again. Then he started discussing the trip to Fort Clark. He told Chalk he would have a lot of things to discuss when they were riding in the wagon the next day. He told Chalk to bring two saddled horses, as they could need them when they reached Fort Clark. Everyone was yawning and the decision to go to bed was almost automatic. The day was over.

Chapter 3
The Trip To Fort Clark

The next morning the alarm clock went off in Chalks bedroom. He got up and went down the hall to see if General Allen was awake. He was a sound sleeper and had to be awakened. There were two separate bathrooms and both men went to clean up and get ready for the day. Both dressed in casual clothes and General Allen suggested they wear them rather than wearing military uniforms. When they finished their baths and got dressed the housekeeper had a big breakfast ready in the dining room. The General's aide had been invited to eat with them. The meal included scrambled Mexican style eggs, red eye gravy, biscuits, venison sausage, grits and plenty of hot coffee. The men ate a big breakfast and just as they were finishing Wanda came into the room. She had a cup of coffee and a biscuit with jelly. They were ready to leave and the General went to his room and got the last of his luggage. Chalk took Wanda into a private area, kissed her, and told her goodbye. He walked by Barbara's bed and she was sound asleep. He kissed her and made sure she was not awakened. He told Wanda he would be home soon and would call, as his schedule became clear.

The buggy was already tied up in front of the house. Two saddled horses were tied to the rear. The housekeeper had prepared a small box of cookies and fried fruit pies. They were already placed in the General's riding area. The two passengers came out from the house, waived goodbye and got in. Chalks had asked the ranch foreman to check the buggy and make sure everything was in good condition for the trip. The aide got in the drivers seat and Chalk told him the best route to follow to get on the right trails to the west.

The sun was just coming up in the east and the shadows were still long and dark. The driver got directions from Chalk about a shortcut to go to Hondo, which is located directly south. The trails were not marked in the open country areas and local people knew the best way to get to most places. From there they would travel west to Uvalde and on to Brackettville and then on to Fort Clark. The trip would take the whole day and the weather was fine for travel.

When the buggy reached Hondo everyone, and the horses, needed a rest. The driver saw a small restaurant so they pulled over and went in. The aide had an Army canteen and he had filled it with water at the ranch. On the road most of the water had been drank and it needed a refill. The horses needed a rest and also needed some water. A small livery stable was on the same street and the driver took the buggy to the water trough. He had the owner give the horses some oats and got a small bag of oats to take with them on the road.

The men got fresh coffee and some Mexican pastries and came back to the wagon. General Allen bought his aide a giant sized taco.

They then traveled west toward Uvalde. Chalk and the General talked about several upcoming issues, most of which were centered on the transfer of the balance of the horse unit from Kentucky. He also talked a lot about his family and how much they were looking forward to coming to Texas. The conversation then changed to issues about Fort Clark.

Fort Clark had been a key western Army base for several years. Originally the area was a campground for several local Indian tribes. There was plentiful water at the base that came from a local natural springs. The first construction was started when the Confederate Army set up a base to support the Civil War. From there it became a U.S. Army base that charged its focus to keep local Indians and bandits in the area under control.

Several famous Generals had served there and having both Black and Indian soldiers had help create the Army legacy of the "Buffalo Soldiers".

The Army wanted to increase the size of the base and use it to train soldiers for potential deployment should we need to fight a war in Europe. The President had been convinced that Fort Clark was a perfect place to do training because it was so remote. The railroad had just laid track near the base and transportation for troops would be much easier if rapid deployment became a requirement.

Over the past three years stories had circulated that the base was becoming soft and that corruption was everywhere. Getting accurate reports from this base was a growing concern at Fort Sam Houston. The reports that did arrive were not specific and were often obvious re-writes from former reports.

General Allen had spent time in Washington and had learned first hand a lot about west Texas. He had made friends with Representative John Nance Garner who was from Uvalde, Texas. He had been a Judge in Uvalde and told stories about how local county Judges in Texas were almost little local kings. They would not only judge the law, they often took the liberty of warping the law to meet personal opinions or to line their pockets.

He said remote military bases were sometimes guilty of similar attitudes if the people in Command were allowed to serve in one base assignment too long. The current command officers at Fort Clark were approaching 4 years in one place. Military life over this period had been relatively easy.

The buggy pulled into Uvalde about 2 PM. A found a small restaurant on the town squares and they parked the wagon in a small space nearby. The driver saw a water trough and took the horses over and let them drink. He used a bucket from the buggy and gave them the oats he had bought in Hondo. The officers went into the restaurant and ate a quick light lunch. They kept the stop time to a minimum and drove on. They still had about 30 dusty miles to go. General Allen wanted the men to wear civilian clothes so the local people near the base did not recognize them as soldiers. Their buggy was all black and had no obvious military marking. The General's flag was not on display and was stored inside the buggy. The disguise was working.

The trail was level for most of the remaining way. The railroad had recently built tracks next to the trail. About 5 miles from Uvalde a freight train passed them heading west. The train's engine was puffing smoke and chugging loudly as it passed the buggy. The engineer sounded his whistle to say hello and everyone waved back. The horses did not appreciate the noise and reared up a little. Horses were never comfortable with unplanned loud noises.

The afternoon was passing quickly as there was much to talk about. Chalk noticed that the General had on his Masonic ring and commented that it was just like the one that was worn by Mr. Reynolds, back in Kentucky, had been wearing. General Allen appreciated Chalk's observation and said he was also a mason. He asked Chalk what he knew about Masons? Chalk replied that he knew very little and repeated the story that Mr. Reynolds had told him about the Declaration of Independence. The General agreed that this story was true and he went on to tell how the Masonic Order was actually started back in the Roman Empire. It started when the slave labor stonemasons were fed up with not having any freedom and when they were seen as out of line with the masters, they were fed to the lions. It was no accident that all of these early men were of the Christian faith. He added that the order had survived over the decades and was still active in seeking a better life, freedom and love between all men.

Chalk asked the General how he became a Mason? He replied that he had asked to be admitted to the order and his petition was approved. Chalk asked him if he could become a mason? The General stuttered and stopped talking for a minute and was obviously in deep thought as how to answer this question. He turned and looked Chalk straight in the eye and said, "You are as qualified to become a mason as is any man but I must tell you something that pains me. Your skin is dark and in the social circles of the order, dark skinned men are not accepted. This is wrong and I am sorry to have to tell you this but reality is what it is." Chalk was quiet. He knew he was dark skinned and that the world was still a place where skin color was important but it still hurt him inside to face this reality.

The General spoke up and said that Lincoln had taken the first step in freeing the slaves but added this is only the first step of many steps yet to come that will someday make skin color a not so important part of how we judge each other. You just need to keep this in mind and remain dedicated to the things in life that you know to be worth your best efforts. The conversation ended and the two men were silent for a long time.

Chapter 4
Fort Clark Inspections

About 5:30 PM the buggy was near the final trail to Fort Clark. The aide pulled the buggy over to the side of the road. He went to the storage boot and took out a small flag with a single blue star sewn into the center of a white banner. He placed it into a special socket on the front of the wagon and drove on. This flag indicated that an Army General was on board and his stature was to be recognized at the gate to the Fort. This was normal military protocol.

In 20 minutes they reached the entrance to the Fort. A beautiful pond was directly in front of the front gate and there were several water birds feeding in the clear water. Two soldiers who were on guard duty saw the buggy pull up. They were confused. The buggy had a star flying on the front that indicated that a General was onboard. But, the men were not in uniform and were not familiar. The gate guards asked to see identification and The General and Chalk provided proper military identification.

The guards then snapped to attention and gave a snappy salute to the buggy. After all, there were two commissioned officers on board. General Allen requested to be directed to the Base Commander's office. One of the guards went to a small building next to the gate where he got a 2nd Lieutenant to come over. The Lieutenant said that he would lead them to the proper location. He mounted a horse and asked the buggy driver to follow him. The guards had no immediate way to get word to the Base Commander that there was a special party of Officers on the way to see him.

The buggy followed the officer, who was riding just ahead to the Base Commander's office. The office was in his home and the Lieutenant went to the door to announce the arrivals. General Allen made a comment to the greeting Lieutenant that they were not in uniform, as they did not want to wear military clothes for traveling on the dusty Texas trails.

There was an aide inside the front door He quickly welcomed both men into the entry and asked them to have a seat while he found the Commander. The Commander was still in his office and he was surprised to have visitors. He came out to the entry area and invited them into his office. He had his aid get a pot of fresh coffee and closed the door.

The Base Commander was also a One Star General and he was much older than General Allen. His name was general Warren Puckett.

He welcomed them, tried to put everyone at ease and asked what was the purpose for their visit? General Allen took out a document that he had brought from the Fort Sam Houston Commander. Fort Clark was responsible, in the local chain of command, to report to the Fort in San Antonio and The Commander immediately recognized that this was not a routine visit. There is an undocumented code of ethics between Army Officers that they always conduct themselves as gentlemen, even when they are in an uncomfortable situation. Both Generals were doing their best to follow this pattern of behavior. It was not easy, but it was working.

He let the Base Commander read the document and it authorized General Allen to do a complete base review beginning the next morning. The Base Commander was surprised and told General Allen he was not happy about not having any prior warning, but, in good military style, he would do what ever was required. General Allen thanked him for his support and requested that they be shown to the visiting Officers Quarters.

As the visitors were ready to leave his office, General Puckett summoned his aide and instructed him to furnish quarters and what ever else the visiting officers might need or want. They got back in the buggy and were escorted to the visiting Officer's quarters building.

General Allen and Chalk took their luggage into the quarters building and asked the aide to take care of the horses and buggy. After they got settled in, with the help of a soldier who was outside, they found the Officers Mess and had a late small dinner.

In the same period the Base Commander had called his entire base staff into an emergency meeting. He showed them the order from San Antonio and told them to do what ever they could to stand a quality inspection. The atmosphere was almost a panic but everyone recognized this was an extremely important visit. The lights were on late into the night and the activity in the several Officers' offices went far into the night.

General Allen and Lieutenant Goodwin went to bed, got a good night's sleep and woke up in time to hear the morning bugler sound his horn. The General's aide also shared a small room in the same living quarter's area. They were anxious and eager to get on with the base review.

At about 8:30 AM they walked over to the Base Commanders office. It was only about 1500 feet from their quarters. The Base Commander had fresh hot coffee and a snack ready for everyone. The Commander already had his staff of Officers assembled. They were waiting in a large meeting room. He escorted the visitors into the room and everyone stood up and saluted the two visiting officers.

Introductions were made and the floor was turned over to General Allen. He stood up, looked around and smiled at everyone. He was almost embarrassed and a little uncomfortable to be the focal point for this meeting.

He then said that he wanted to conduct an in-depth base review and he would appreciate everybody giving his or her best efforts to allow this review to proceed with accuracy and with reasonable speed. His purpose was not to embarrass or to find fault with any one individual or organization but to find out about reported problems and if possible, assist in corrective activities.

He asked if everyone had read or been told about the messages in his inspection orders? Everyone indicated that they had. He reflected the concern for San Antonio about moral and base discipline issues and assured them that the base would be given a fair fitness review.

He reflected that the Army was undergoing several major changes as a result of a potential involvement in the European war. He requested the Base Commander to identify if there were any problems in any base area that might interfere with this inspection? The Base Commander looked at ever officer in the room, one at a time, and as if to allow them to speak. Nobody said a word. The Commander said there were none. General Allen then asked General Puckett to give them an open authorization to the various areas to be reviewed. General Allen reflected that the Commanding Generals in San Antonio needed to know the realistic condition of every base within his command; Fort Clark was not an exception.

General Allen requested that the inspection begin with a base tour. He wanted to become better familiar with the physical base layout and then learn more about the troops and the operations within the entire facility. He wanted the Officers in command of actual areas to be included, when specific areas were being reviewed, and to take part in the actual inspection.

A special Officers wagon was waiting in the front of the office. General Allen, Lieutenant Goodwin and an older Colonel named Jerry White all boarded. The driver was obviously instructed by the Colonial as the route to take. Colonel White was a senior military person and had been stationed at Fort Clark for several years. He knew the base well and he knew most of the people who were serving there on a first name basis.

The first stop was the parade ground. Several groups were drilling and training horses in the center of the area. The horse show was obviously a last minute plan. It looked a lot like a circus act, not a military display. Everyone smiled, saluted and went about their business. General Allen told Chalk that a horse show does not tell me much about the troop's morale level.

From there they went to the stable area and General Allen asked to get out and review the horse barns. Chalk had a note pad and he was recording a lot of information. They went inside. The stalls were not clean and the entire area needed a good clean up. There were several horses in stalls. The front area stalls were in generally good shape. There were several other stalls, in the next barn, that were not clean and had manure piled against the outside walls. The tack room was next to the stable and the saddles and other items were not organized. Several saddles were on the floor and some had dried horse manure on them.

They got back on the tour wagon and went to the enlisted men's mess hall. The Officers all went in and the smell of cooking food was everywhere. The men doing the cooking were all Black. There were several other men who had high cheekbones like Chalk and he immediately recognized them as men who were part Indians. These were the Buffalo Soldiers that everyone had talked about. Many of the soldiers that had been seen on the parade ground were also Black and Indians.

The eating area was open and had large windows on every side to help keep it cool in the summer. Flies were a common problem and swatting was a standard way to protect one's self. The mess Sergeant offered the men coffee, which they gladly accepted. He was a big pleasant natured Sargeant and he was proud of his food. His food smelled great and the coffee was strong like everyone liked it. He was honestly proud of his operation but some of his words were obviously the result of very recent coaching.

While they drank their coffee Chalk took the opportunity to talk with some of the Indian troops who were also in the area. They bonded to Chalk quickly and General Allen almost had to drag Chalk away from the group that formed around him. The men were eager to talk to him. Seeing an

Indian as an Officer was unheard of at this base and Chalk really stood out.

The tour group then went to a small stone office where the Fort's military police had their office. The base brig was located in the back. A small covered walk connected the two buildings. The Duty Officer was cordial and took them a short but hurried tour. The cells were almost empty and the building was cold and uninviting. Two men who were in the cells were supposedly there for fighting. The Duty officer gave them a short verbal review of base discipline status and told them that the Colonel who was in charge of the Military Police operation was currently on travel.

The next stop was a training area where men were seen cleaning and polishing cannons and ammunition wagons. This was another quick show for the visitors. It was obvious as the corrosion on the brass and an iron part was still dark and red.

The soldiers living quarter's area were then reviewed. They did not appear to be clean from an outside view. Weeds on the lawns and trash in the area were commonly observed. The same condition was also present at several other key base buildings. There were men out policing the area for trash but the effort was too little and too late to do a proper job. The inspection party did not go into many buildings but observed them from the wagon in a narrated drive-by.

The inspection party then returned to the Base Commander's office.

General Puckett greeted them and gave them a list of his key officers and suggested an order that each might be contacted. It was almost noon and the Base Commander took all of the Officers mess for a special lunch. The lunch was supported by excellent food but the atmosphere in the room was tense and guarded. After the lunch the base Commander addressed the group and reinforced the need to be co-operative to General Allen.

After lunch General Allen asked Colonel White, who happened to be also an old acquaintance of General Allen, to set down for private man-to-man discussion. He had struck up a good relationship with him that morning and wanted to have a frank discussion about base matters. He knew that anyone else from the base being present might flavor the discussion. General Allen and Colonel White took a walk out into an area next to the parade ground. His honesty and openness were surprising and bore out many of General Allen's concerns. In about 30 minutes they returned.

General Allen told Chalk that he did not want to get into a specific review with each area Commander. They obviously had all been coached and any meeting would not be meaningful. Rather, he wanted to do a random audit and talk with a few of the troops face to face. To have a Superior Officer present for such an interview would not allow the individuals being interviewed to give honest and non-opinionated answers. Chalk understood completely.

At 2:00 PM General Allen and Chalk invited General Puckett to have a private talk. They all walked down to the Base front gate and found a pair of comfortable benches next to the small lake that were in the shade. General Allen asked the Base Commander for his opinion concerning the current moral in his men. General Allen was open with him that reports had been filtering back to San Antonio that there were a lot of suspected problems.

The Commander was honest and open and admitted that many of the men were not happy but he had not found any one good reason for their poor attitudes. General Allen asked him if he had personally talked to the troops and listened to their issues? He said that the area Commanders on the base left all communications and moral matters up to the Sergeants who were talking to the troops daily. He added, these men have more to do with the troops than anyone else so they are the real driving force for morale. General Puckett bragged that his staff was made up from soldiers who had been in the Army a long time and were all great combat hardened leaders.

General Puckett indicated that he had not personally had local community feedback that pointed to anything being wrong with the base or base personnel. General Allen asked him about his Sergeants attitudes and how well the men respected them. The Commander said that the base had a good staff of NCO's and the men all followed their lead as far as he knew. The Commissioned Officers always took the Sergeant's word for what was really happening. With hesitation, he admitted that some of the NCO's were not the always the best "people skilled" individuals. He admitted, several had risen to their rank by having time in the military and had been known to be drunks.

It was obvious that there was little open communication up and down the chain of command. General Allen asked if he could do interviews with both the NCO's and some of their men. The General had no choice but to agree. General Allen said he would like to pick the men to interview. He asked General Puckett if this was acceptable? He got a very quiet reply of "yes". General Allen realized that the Commander was potentially opening himself up to problems when he agreed to this request. However, he almost had no choice in this matter. General Allen shook General Puckett's hand and thanked him for his time and assistance. The men parted as gentlemen but both knew that things were not well on the base.

General Allen and Chalk went back to the stable area to find the Officer who was in charge. This Officer, Captain Armstrong, was a direct report to General Allen and he wanted Chalk to form an opinion as to what was happening. He was trusted, but only to a point. He knew a second opinion would help him confirm his value of this potentially marginal man.

Chalk was also conducting a review of all horse-related operations and wanted to learn how things were being managed. The Officer was unaware that Lieutenant Goodwin could soon be his senior officer.

The stable area was still not well kept. Thick matted manure still laced with bedding straw was common in every stall. The area had a strong odor on urine. The facility was well built but obviously poorly maintained. Fresh hay and oats were available but were in short supply. The few horses in the area were healthy looking but they all of them were dirty and needed to be washed and combed.

The blacksmith shop was adequate in size but the Corporal running it had almost no experience. He was trying to do his job but had never been given any quality training. When Lieutenant Goodwin entered he was attempting to put a new shoe on a horses front leg.

It was obvious to Chalk that the young man was struggling. Chalk smiled at him, took of his coat, borrowed an apron and showed the young man some helpful pointers. Chalk finished the installation and pointed out what a well-shod horse needed to look like. The Corporal was an Indian like Chalk and he appreciated the help he had just been given. The Captain just watched. He had no idea as to what was happening and lacked any skill with horse care.

Chalk asked the Captain how horses were issued to the men and what system was being used to keep track of each animal. He got a blank look and told him that there was a good system in use and the Sergeants were responsible for making it work.

It was obvious to Chalk why General Allen was concerned about this Officer. He was completely useless. In a side discussion he revealed that he was a brother to one of the other Officers who was stationed at Fort Clark. His brother was in charge of the Base maintenance efforts.

General Allen and Chalk to the officer's mess and had a quick private meal. General Allen wanted to visit the base Provost Marshal's office and review the status of base security.

He took Chalk with him and they were given an audience by a group of men, all who were members of the base security and legal staff. General Allen asked how many men were stationed at the base and wanted to see records about anybody that was a consistent troublemaker. That data should included soldiers currently in camp and those currently on patrols. He immediately saw that this was going to be a problem.

Nobody could agree as to where the men were assigned and a total was given as an estimate. There was a wide spread in the data and it was clear, the records were not accurate. Meaningful records on other issues were also non-existent and the confusion as how to answer every question was easily spotted.

He asked how many men had deserted over the past year and again the crowd was silent. Finally the Captain in charge said he would get a number and get back with them. One of the Sergeants in the group spoke up and asked about a Corporal named Franks. He said that this man went AWOL often and had been a troublemaker in the town of Uvalde. The Captain said that he was currently listed as on patrol but couldn't remember which patrol and when it was to return.

General Allen thanked the men and he and Chalk left. From there they went to the stable and each got their saddle horses. General Allen and Chalk rode out the front gate and found a spot near the pond that was quiet and somewhat isolated. They stopped, dismounted and General Allen asked Chalk what he had discovered. Chalk told him about the problems he saw and how poorly the horse stable area was being managed. General Allen told him that his reviews were similar in other areas. General Allen told Chalk that he had seen enough to form an opinion, and he was ready to go home. It was now Thursday evening and General Allen told Chalk to pack up immediately and get ready to ride.

General Allen stopped by the Base Commander's quarters and went in. He asked to see General Puckett. He was told the Commander had gone to town and was unavailable. General Allen told the aide to tell him they were done with the inspection and were leaving shortly. He told the aide to thank the General for his co-operation during their visit. He gave General Puckett's aide a bottle of good whiskey and asked that he give it to the General with his best regards.

They left the base at about 6 PM and the aide drove their buggy to the town of Brackettville. They stopped and got rooms in a local hotel for the night. They changed into non-military clothes and found a small restaurant where they had an outstanding steak and potatoes dinner.

Brackettville was the town closest to Fort Clark. The next morning General Allen went to the Brackettville Sheriff's office. The General identified himself and Chalk and requested some private time with him. He was a tall thin man with a big pistol on his left side. His voice was deep for such a thin man but it carried a lot of authority. He was obviously one of the natives and was considered a tough man to cross. He had heard of Chalk's work in Bandera when he had been the Sheriff and this was a good door opener that started the conversation.

Then General asked him if Fort Clark personnel were any problem in his town? He welcomed the question, sat back, smiled and slowly began to talk. He said I could write you a book about the local soldiers and the problems they have caused. He told them that many of the men were heavy drinkers and were constantly causing problems. The local women had told him to keep the soldiers out of town as they were preying on their young daughters.

He pointed out that he had got real tough on the troublesome soldiers about two years ago and now the really bad ones were not coming back; they were going to the next town, which is Uvalde. He was also quick to mention that several Officers were in the group of consistent troublemakers. Chalk asked for a list of names and what trouble they had caused. The Sheriff agreed to have his jailer put together a list and mail it to him the next day. The General thanked him and said he was sorry that Army personnel had caused problems but he would investigate the issues and try to see that these problems did not come back again.

On Friday morning they rode east to Uvalde where the General and Chalk again went to see the local Sheriff. The Sheriff was equally unhappy with the Army's personnel. He pointed out that he had 4 men in jail at the current time who had wrecked a bar the week before. To the General's surprise, one of them was a Corporal with the last name of Franks.

From there the General went to see the County Judge. He questioned him about past problems and discovered that the past two years were full of incidents where Army personnel were causing problems. The Judge knew Representative Nance Garner who was also a personal contact and friend to General Allen when he had been stationed in Washington.

One bit of information that upset General Allen was sad to hear was that Army saddles and weapons were commonly seen in local pawnshops. The soldiers would come to town, drink, go broke, pawn their saddles, side arms and other military items, drink some more and finally, sober up in jail. Then they would be kicked out of town and somehow get back to the base. This pattern was not uncommon. Several of the local citizens could be seen riding horses with Army saddles on their backs.

The Officers went to their buggy and started for home. When they reached Hondo the General instructed Chalk to go to his home in Bandera, document what he had seen and he would call him early next week from San Antonio. The men parted ways and both hit the trail to home.

Chapter 5
A Time To Count and Sort

Chalk arrived at the Goodwin One about 9 PM. It was a clear night and the moon made the trail easy to see. He went into the ranch house and Wanda was thrilled and surprised to see him. He did not have on his uniform but he was dusty and dirty from the trip. He took off his dirty clothes, took a bath and put on more comfortable things. He was hungry and soon there was great food on the table. Barbara was already in bed and Chalk just looked at her and told Wanda to let her sleep. He was glad to be home. He took a while to start writing his report and soon it was midnight. He wanted to write down his data before it was forgotten.

The next morning He and Wanda and Barbara had a big breakfast. Then they all sat down in the big room and relaxed. Wanda was nervous. She sat close to him and with a slow voice and a big smile on her face told Chalk that the Doctor had told her they were going to be parents again. Chalk smiled and started to understand what her words were meaning and what they were pointing toward. All of a sudden reality hit him and he grabbed her and gave her a big hug. What he had on his mind from the trip was forgotten and the entire conversation turned to talk about another baby.

The next day was spent between checking with the ranch operations, writing his report and just enjoying being home. Bedtime came early and Chalk was so tired that he fell asleep as soon as he laid his head on the pillow. Wanda had a glass of cold milk and followed him to bed.

Sunday morning came way too soon. The warm feeling of the quilt cover on the bed was wonderful. Getting out of bed this morning was not a planned event, it was a chore. Chalk had hung his dirty uniform on a hall tree and the housekeeper knew that it was time to get the washing started. Jeans and work boots were the choice of the day.

The alarm clock struck 9 AM and Chalk awoke like he was about to go to war. Baby Barbara was already up and had the housekeeper involved with a big plate of buttermilk pancakes.

Chalk got a hot cup of coffee and went outside. He sat down on his porch swing and enjoyed the smell of an approaching spring. Cedar trees were all around the porch and the aroma was intense. Wanda came out and brought her hot coffee. They sat and talked for almost an hour. Chalk told her that the trip was a real eye opening experience and General Allen was certainly going to report an Army base that was not doing well. He had to finish his report by the end of the day and somehow get the highlights of the trip to the General. He was hoping he could read key parts and mail the final version and making save a trip to San Antonio.

The report was going to contain information that was considered as confidential so he knew he might be going to San Antonio to deliver it. The housekeeper brought some fresh baked Mexican pastries to them and they were gone in a quick Texas moment. Wanda suggested that they not go to church that day as there was just too much to do at home and she was so glad to see him. He agreed.

Chalk then walked out to the cowboy bunkhouse and chatted with the guys for a while. This was an opportunity to relax and to report that the General's visit had pleased him a great deal.

The cattle were doing well and they were getting 40 head ready to go to the sale barn later in the week. The longhorn cows had delivered an amazing total of 12 new calves during the past week and 7 were male. This was good as strong males were worth more when they were sold.

After lunch Chalk sat down and finished a three-page report about his findings at Fort Clark. The comments were focused on responses he had received from the horse operation, his discussions covered with several enlisted men and his contact with several senior base officers. He also made comments about all of the staged activity that was generated just to impress them. It had impressed him for sure, in a negative way.

He reflected poor troop morale within every level of the base. He also identified a base commanding staff that had no apparent grasp for effective military leadership. His biggest concern was the Commanding Officers lack of knowledge as to troop status and the problems being reported from the local community.

Base Commanding officers had delegated almost every basic commanding control to the Sergeant level of operations. They had isolated themselves from most of the daily operational issues and in the process had allowed the troops to become less than professional military. An equally upsetting issue was the Senior Officer's responsibility for building a good positive image for the base in the surrounding community. All of these areas received failing scores.

There was one finding that really got to Chalk. The availability of Government property in local hockshops identified an equipment management system that was not functioning. Chalk knew the value of a good saddle and the obvious high value of an Army rifle or pistol. These items were actually more valuable than money. They were the working tools of the west. In the wrong hands a pistol could kill people, including soldiers.

There had to be much more wrong to allow to these problems to occur and the entire base system was in need of serious and immediate investigation.

When he finished the document and called the General. General Allen had him read it to him and told him to put it in the mail. He finished the conversation, folded the document and put it in an envelope. The next trip to town the envelope went into the mail.

Chapter 6
A Time Calling For Hard Decisions

Monday morning Chalk put on his ranch clothes. He Called General Allen in San Antonio and told him he had mailed his report. The General asked for a few additional comments and told him to relax a few days and to make sure that the next horse delivery was on schedule. His needs were not immediate and he knew that Chalk needed to be home for a short while.

Chalk then rode out to the Goodwin Two ranch. He wanted to see what was happening in the construction area and also give his men feedback from the Generals visit. When he arrived he saw a new pole barn structure taking shape. This barn would be where hay and grain would be stored. Next to it was a shop for a fulltime blacksmith operation. There were staked driven into the soil to identify the placement for poles for a new stable. Things were moving well and were actually ahead of the planned schedule.

Most of the morning was spent with Sarge. He and Chalk had a lot of things to go over and they needed this time to work out plans for the near future. One concern came up several times. There were several new colts being born every month. The ranch foreman wanted to have a qualified veterinarian on call to assure that the mare and the colt were in good health. There were also other times when a specialist was needed. Chalk had heard the same story from the cattle operation. The frequency of the requests was enough to identify this as a real problem.

Chalk told the Sarge to contact several Veterinarian schools and see if there was a bright young Vet graduating who would like work on his ranches. Chalk knew this person would be expensive but it was the right thing to do.

The noon lunch hour came and Chalk ate lunch with the men in the cowboy lunch area. When most of the cowboys were in the area he stood up and filled them in on the General's responses with the ranch's operation. He thanked them for their work and told them that more visits were probably be coming in the near future. Everyone was happy and encouraged from his words. He also told them to keep their hair cut and maintain themselves to the same standards that they had done for the visit. Everybody smiled and agreed.

After lunch Chalk went to Bandera and spent time with Mrs. Brock. He again thanked her and her staffs of two for making the past weeks visit a success. They went over the financial status for each ranch and Chalk agreed to purchase several items that had been requested.

Mrs. Brock has organized the books so each ranch had a separate accounting base. The two young ladies each had the responsibility for one ranch's records. Mrs. Brock strictly managed the over view for bank accounts and the total operation.

The "bottom line", as Chalk called it, was it was always easy to justify spending money if the procured item would make substantially more money than it cost. He was a sharp critic on the term cost. What was paid initially was only the first element of cost. He wanted to see all of the operating and maintenance costs also included. If the purchase still was a moneymaker it was probably the right thing to acquire. He also knew that it is better to do without sometimes. Making things too easy or too fancy tended to made people get lazy. Chalk absolutely could not stand lazy people.

Chalk was becoming a wealthy man and his businesses were all making a good profit. Another facet of his personality was becoming obvious. Over the life of the ranch Chalk had encouraged the hiring of young men who were willing to learn and wanted to make a better life for themselves. He often told the story of his friend in the coal mine who made a job available for him. This opportunity allowed him to learn some skills and become a productive person. He wanted to keep this memory alive and actively encouraged his men to seek out underprivileged youngsters who were going to be given a chance. He often said, " everyone is a person who wants to do better, what they need is a chance".

Another approach to his operation was that he kept all of his personal money and private assets separate from those involving the ranches. He had Mrs. Brock set up his ranch house at the Goodwin One as a separate asset. He wanted to let the ranch support itself and the cost of his home was his responsibility, not the ranch foreman's. Chalk and Wanda considered their personal finances as a very private matter. The only person who knew what they were was Mrs. Brock.

He still had his farm in Missouri and had purchased a tract of land in Hondo where he someday wanted to start a ranching equipment business. The railroad was just down the street and ranchers would be coming there often. Having ranch equipment to sell would be a great business.

He had the vision to see that someday machines would probably replace horses and ranching and farming power would be mechanical. His vision was to someday get into the motorized equipment business.

At about 3PM Chalk mounted his horse and started home. As he was leaving town he was approached by one of his former Deputy Sheriffs who hailed him. They exchanged greeting and Chalk asked how things were going. He said fine but there was one problem. Chalk asked what was wrong.

He replied that the new Sheriff had hired a female deputy. Chalk smiled. He knew that the Sheriffs area had always been considered an all man's world and could only imagine what was going on. He asked the deputy what duties she was assigned to. He said she was a jailer and had replaced a deputy who had left. Chalk asked him if she was doing her job? The deputy said, "I guess so". Chalk wished the Deputy a good day and rode on toward home.

When he reached home he went in and Wanda told him that the General had called and wanted to talk to him as soon as possible. Chalk went into his office and called. The General answered and was in a good mood. He had just left a meeting with the Fort Sam Garrison Commander and given him a first person account of his trip to Fort Clark.

The Commander, a two star General, was glad to get his preliminary report but very upset with what was going on at Fort Clark. He was recalling General Puckett and wanted him to be in his office in San Antonio the following Monday. General Allen wanted to have Chalk come to San Antonio on Thursday and participate in a closed-door review with the Senior Base Officers on Friday.

Chalk told General Allen that he needed to come over Wednesday afternoon and be available the first thing on Thursday. This plan was agreed upon.

Chalk then told General Allen that He and Wanda were going to be parents again. He told Chalk, "You are spending way too much time at home", then he laughed. This news surprised him but he was happy for them.

Chalk spent all day Tuesday with Wanda and Barbara. They told Barbara that she was going to have a new baby in the house and she would have someone at home to play with. She was happy and wanted to know when. Wanda told her to be patient as the date was still being determined.

Wednesday it was raining and the storm was full of wind and lightning. About noon Chalk decided to start for San Antonio. He wore a raincoat and put on clothes that were certainly going to get muddy and wet. It took much longer than usual to ride the trail but he arrived about 6 PM. He went to his assigned room and got out of his muddy rain soaked clothes. His men from the horse stable took care of his horse and brought him some hot coffee. All of his dress clothes and personal papers were dry and safe in his suitcase.

He dressed in his casual military clothes and went to the Officers Mess for dinner. General Allen was there and he hailed him down. They ate together and discussed the upcoming day. General Allen brought up the report Chalk had authored and made several comments. Chalk agreed with some of the General's comments and after finishing their meal they went back to Chalk's room.

Chalk reviewed a report that the General had written and saw that they were both in agreement on almost every issue. General Allen commented that the Base Commander from Fort Clark was going to be replaced and the entire staff of Officers was also going to be reviewed. He wanted Chalk to be considering going to the base for about 6 months to help with the "cleanup operation".

However, first the General wanted Chalk to go to Kentucky and move the men and horses still located at Fort Knox to Fort Sam Houston. He also asked Chalk to help grease the skids to get the General's family moved to Texas. He had been assigned a nice home in the base housing area and was longing to see them. Moving families was not a priority in some people's mind. The whole process and military paperwork were all taking far too long.

Thursday morning Chalk went to the General's office and greeted him with a smile. The two reports had been turned into a much larger document that was going to be presented to the Garrison Commander. General Allen gave it to him and allowed him to read it. They went through each line, one at a time, and checked the contents between themselves for accuracy. The General used a much more traditional military language than Chalk but that was understandable. The meanings and messages were the same.

General Allen had drafted a recommendation section at the end of the document. It had four key subjects. They were;

- Recall the Base Commander and replace him with a younger, more capable Officer.
- Evaluate, and if necessary, and replace every Senior Officer who had served under the current Base Commander.
- Evaluate the enlisted men's status, including Sergeants, and develop a program to build, quality and self-esteem within them and for the military.
- Have the new Base Staff work with local public officials to rebuild respect for the military and for he local base.

There was a strong side note that all government property records needed to be reviewed. If any property was found to be missing a full investigation as to where it may be needed to be undertaken. The General suggested that there were potential cases of intentional stealing and if proven the people involved needed to be prosecuted and serve jail time.

There was another reference to local pawnshops that would buy property that was clearly marked as Government Property. These merchants needed to be prosecuted by the local authorities and their operations shut down.

Chalk was in full agreement with every point. General Allen asked him to go with him and be seated next to him in the meeting. They had spent most of the day reviewing the document and it was now near dark. They had completely missed lunch and were hungry. They went off base to a local Mexican restaurant and had a big meal.

After dinner they went for a walk around the base and talked about Chalk's horse operation. It was soon clear to Chalk that the General was envious of his horse operation and would love to be in his shoes. Under all of his outside formal military self, there was a hidden rancher. They parted company, went to bed and got a good night's sleep.

Early the next morning another storm roared through the area. Water was standing everywhere and the local streams were all out of their banks. Chalk woke up at 5 AM and could not go back to sleep for the noise and sounds of wind and thunder. Lightning was making hits at places nearby and it was a real concern that everyone and all of the horses were inside. He got up, dressed and put on a raincoat and walked down to the stable area.

Everything was fine. Two soldiers had spent the night with the horses and they were all calm but a little nervous. Chalk then went for the short walk that took him past another horse barn and on to get breakfast. General Allen came into the mess hall shortly after Chalk. They had a hardy meal and went back to Chalks room.

Chalk had his men get a small covered buggy out from the stable so they could ride to the Garrison Command office without getting wet. The trip was slow and but them there about 5 minutes early.

An aide took them to a large room where several Officers had begun to assemble. They entered and were greeted with salutes and proper military respect. Everyone had an assigned seat and in about 10 minutes the Garrison Commander entered. Everyone stood up came to a snappy salute and remained standing until the Senior Officer said "be at ease" and they all sat down. There was no doubt, the Base Commander had to be respected.

The Senior Officer's last name was General Ken Cole. He opened the meeting and asked everyone to use first names in addressing each other as he wanted to make this meeting very open, somewhat casual and most of all, meaningful. He then said "my first name is Ken, please use it".

From there he made an opening statement that the Army had evidence that several situations at Fort Clark were out of control and this group was convened to develop a plan for corrective actions. He also told the group that General Raymond Allen had personally visited this Fort and had seen first-hand the real time conditions of the Fort. He then asked for General Allen's report.

Kenneth Orr

General Allen handed his report to the Commander and he reviewed it for about 10 minutes and asked General Allen to address the group going over every point in his document. General Allen stood up and introduced himself to everyone. He then asked Chalk to stand up and he introduced him as his assistant in this investigation. Everyone but General Allen sat down and he was ready to deliver the report.

The Commander broke in and asked each individual in attendance to ask any questions they felt were important when the report was completed and to identify themselves so everybody else knew whom they were working with.

Each person then stood up and told everyone what area they were representing. The group was a premium group of Colonels and Generals who had all been in the Army for many years. Several were from Fort Knox and two were from Washington Army Headquarters. Both General Allen and Chalk was impressed.

General Allen went through his complete report. When he finished he asked Chalk to add his comments on areas where he had gathered information. Everyone was taking notes and listening intently. When they finished the presentation the Commander asked that they take a short break. Everyone got coffee and snacks and returned to their seat. Commander Cole said he had every reason to believe this report was accurate and wanted to get a plan together today to resolve every issue. He asked if anyone in the room disagreed? There was no response.

The first person to respond was a Two Star General who was a senior troop Commander from Fort Knox. He recommended that a young General in his Command back in Kentucky be considered as a new Base Commander. He outlined the candidate General's record for being a combat troop leader and a man that was very much a hands on leader. The suggestion was recorded and the meeting went forward.

Another General was very concerned about the condition of base records and accountability. He stressed the need

252

to know how many men were on duty and where they were currently deployed. He offered to go to Fort Clark and fix the problems.

The Commander pointed to Chalk and asked him to point out what he thought would turn this base around the fastest and where it needed to begin. Chalk thought about his answer for a few seconds, stood up, looked everyone straight in the eye and slowly began speaking.

He said, "Gentlemen, the current Base Command structure needs to be replaced as soon as possible. Then a group of new, sincere, and trained military leaders need to sit down with every soldier and let them vent their problems. The troops need to see a clear, long term plan for consistent improvement and stability. He added, troop management begins with first line troop leadership. Changing by adding more Senior Officers and more regulations to follow will not correct this situation, it will only prolong the problems an in the long run hurt any corrective work that is undertaken. This base needs to be rebuilt from the ground up. The soldiers I saw there are basically good troops and they need to have the bad ones weeded out and let the dedication and honesty they have to be good soldiers come forward."

Chalk continued, "a positive plan with a stated and focused set of objectives can rebuild this base into the first class organization it needs to be. This problem is not one sided. Firm and fair leadership must absolutely be put in place. All levels of base command need to examined and structured to provide a clear and accurate channel for basic information flow.

Most of all, a command structure that recognizes the needs, concerns, needs and ability of these troops has to be established. Soldiers are people. Our troops want to be respected and they will return respect by being good soldiers."

"Then the local community needs to be told and shown that there are changes underway and they will improve things for everyone. Local support is vital to the success of this base. Right now it is not present. In fact, the local people would like to see this base go away."

Chalk then sat down.

The Commander thanked him for his advice and asked every other man in the room to answer this same question on paper and be back in two hours.

General Allen and Chalk were asked to come to General Cole's private quarters. They followed him into his office. He thanked each of them for their efforts and pointed out that he had been having serious doubts about the current base staff and their report was hard data for confirmation. He asked General Allen if he would consider being an interim Base Commander until they could decide whom to put in Command. General Allen replied that he was less than four years from retirement and did not want to stay in the military beyond that time, but if this assignment was part of his future he would be honored.

General Cole then turned to Chalk and told him he immediately needed more rank and told him he would immediately submit his name for approval as a Major. The Commander told Chalk that his background was just right to allow him to quickly become an effective Officer at Fort Clark. He also told him that his future was up to him and if he wanted to be a career military Officer, it was his choice.

In two hours everyone returned. Each had a paper summary of his opinions and they placed the on the table. The Commander again returned and the meeting came to order. Each person was directed to pass his or her report one person to the right and to read the document. After this was done the commander told them to repeat this shuffle
.

This continued until everyone had read the suggestions from every other person. The Commander read every recommendation and made comments.

The Commander finished the review then said that he had made some decisions. He asserted, the decision as to how to correct this situation is clearly on my shoulders. The advice all of you have shared with me has been invaluable. Thank you for your inputs and help. He added that the comments for the assembled officers had confirmed his decisions. He said the following plan would be implemented within the next 15 days;

- General Allen will be assigned as the temporary Base Commander and will serve until a permanent Base Commander was named. There was no schedule for this second event other than it was not to be longer than three to four years.
- General Allen will have access to any support he needs from Fort Sam Houston to investigate and, if necessary, prosecute anyone who is guilty of criminal activity.
- The Provost Marshall from Fort Sam Houston will send a high level detail to Fort Clark to work with troop discipline issues, both on base and off base related. His people would visit with local authorities to understand their issues and improve community relationships.
- Lieutenant Goodwin would immediately be promoted to the Commissioned rank of Major and would take command of all horse and horse management issues at both Fort Sam Houston and Fort Clark. He would continue to have his command located in San Antonio and would also be expected to occasionally work from his home in Bandera while in this assignment.
- General Allen will be promoted and given a second star

Everyone in the room was told to support General Allen's outlined program and to respond when requested from General Allen. The meeting was ended and everyone

went away with a set of clear concise responsibilities to guide them.

General Allen and Chalk went to the officer's club and ordered a light lunch. General Allen congratulated Major Goodwin on his new rank and reminded him that he had told him he would experience rapid promotion. Chalk told the General that he wished him well in his new assignment and additional rank and how much he was impressed with his leadership skills and approaches. He thanked him for his support and advice. They had a stiff drink of premium Kentucky whiskey and enjoyed a small celebration unto themselves.

General Allen then asked Chalk to catch the train at about 3 AM the next morning and go to Fort Knox to oversee the final move of the horse soldier operation. He agreed to go. General Allen gave his wife's name and contact information to Chalk and told him she was going to move to San Antonio as soon as the movers could finalize the paperwork and load her personal things onto a train. He asked Chalk to make sure that everything was going well.

Chalk called Wanda and told her all of the news. She was both happy for Chalk and concerned that he might be getting into the Army so deeply that it would take him away form home a lot more.

Chalk boarded the passenger train headed north early the next morning. The train was a combination passenger and freight hauling all types of cars in its mixture. The weather was warm and the sound of nighttime bugs and bullfrogs were everywhere.

The train was routed to go to Memphis, Tennessee where Chalk changed trains at about two hours past noon. The second train went to St. Louis, Missouri. Again he changed trains and headed for Louisville, Kentucky. In Louisville he met a special military train that was headed for Fort Knox and got on. It was now late Sunday afternoon. Sleep was not a luxury of train travel. You slept if you could, when you could.

When Chalk arrived on the base he found a military policeman that escorted him to base quarters for the night. The next morning he found the Major who was responsible to support the Fort Knox part of the Horse and troop transfer. The Major had everyone and everything ready to load onto train cars on Wednesday morning. Chalk reviewed everything and found that there was an excellent plan in place.

Chalk asked the Major if he knew where to get in touch with General Allen's wife. He said he knew her and the children and knew where she was living. The Major took him over to her quarters and introduced him. She was glad to see him and she introduced him to her children. She was still working with base personnel for moving arrangements and she was becoming frustrated.

Chalk asked the Major how much room was available on the train he had planned for the horse group moves. He told Chalk that there were four train cars for horses and three for personnel and one car for freight. One of the passenger cars had sleeping compartments and was much nicer than the coach cars. The major was sure that the General's wife and family along with their household goods could be added to the moving list with no problems.

She would need to get her household items packed and moved to the railroad siding as soon as possible. The Major immediately assigned 6 men to go to her home and pack her things that night. Regular moving boxes were not available so the found a supply of used ammunition cases and began packing. It was not the fanciest packing job ever done but it was what had to be done to keep on the schedule for the train. Mrs. Allen and her children moved into an overnight quarters room at the base guest officer's quarters.

Chalk then went to the stable area where the troops and horses were all located. The group was mostly senior men and most were anxious to go to Texas. The arrival of Major

Goodwin was a welcome event. His presence was the official event that signaled the moving date was at hand.

On Tuesday night the railroad cars were pulled onto a siding next to the horse stables. The soldiers immediately began to load the freight and horse feed for the animals. The relocating soldier's personal items and Mrs. Allen's home furnishings were also loaded onto the freight car. The next morning before dawn the horses were given a good meal and loaded. The horse cars had plenty of hay and water and they were not crowded. There were 44 animals in the group. Several of the troops had bought several bottles of whiskey to take to Texas. They had heard that good Kentucky whiskey was scarce and expensive in San Antonio.

At 8:30 AM all of the people and their travel items were asked to board. Chalk took personal command of getting Mrs. Allen on board and made sure she and the children had one of the sleeping compartments. Promptly at 8:45 a small switching engine hooked up to the cars and hooked up. Chalk made a last minute walk through to make sure everything was in order and told the engineer in the locomotive they were ready to go. The engine pulled the section of cars out of the base onto a siding next to the main line rail tracks. There the smaller engine remained coupled and the cars waited for the train that was going to pull the special army cars to arrive. The wait was not long.

At 9:35AM a freight train heading south pulled up next to the siding. The switching engine pulled the military cars onto the main track and attached it to the rear of the train. The engineer waived goodbye and sounded his whistle as he pulled away. When they were hooked up, the engine sounded its whistle to signal everything was ready to roll. The train pulled out and was headed for Nashville, Tennessee.

By late afternoon the train rolled into the Nashville rail yard where a second train heading to Memphis, Tennessee and then to Dallas, Texas was already waiting. The switch from one train to the other went quickly and they were finally headed west.

The train rolled on throughout the night. It made several stops to take on water and coal. When they reached Memphis, Tennessee the train stopped to allow several cars just ahead of the Army cars to be removed. The Army cars were then reattached and the train went across a new bridge over the Mississippi river and chugged on toward Dallas, Texas. That leg of the trip took about 24 hours and was highlighted by several refueling stops and a train crew change in Arkansas.

In Dallas a group of local soldiers, who had been alerted by telegraph as to when the train would arrive, met the train and brought several baskets of fresh food on board. They also had ice-cold "Lone Star" beer and a fresh supply of Jack Daniels whiskey. Army regulations were not set up to buy whiskey and beer but simply calling it food covered this procurement roadblock. The Kentucky troops soon saw that good whiskey was available and plentiful in Texas.

The military cars were switched to another train that was going south to San Antonio. It was a combination passenger and freight train and stops were frequent and often for a long time.

The "food" was very welcome and it had arrived just in time to allow the train to be relocated to the next train. The horses were riding well. The troops were in good spirits. The trip going south was slower than the first part of the trip as the train had several cars of freight that was being dropped of in local train stations along the route. By now everyone was getting tired and the ride was becoming less comfortable. In Hillsboro, Texas the freight cars in the middle of the train had to be pulled out and the train re-connected before it left the station yard. Several of the soldiers used buckets and got some fresh water to keep the horses supply filled.

The General's wife was riding in a passenger compartment car where she and her children were next door to Major Goodwin. Everyone was taking turns sleeping on seats that folded down to make a bed. The children were the best travelers. They were having an adventure and nothing was going to make them unhappy. They liked the sound of the whistle blowing and the Texas scenery was all a new adventure to behold.

At 7 AM on Saturday morning the train rolled past Fort Sam Houston and stopped. A small engine pulled up to the rear of the train and attached onto the Army cars segment. The cars were removed and pushed onto a siding just inside the base. When the train stopped all of the troops let out a big yell and started to get off at every available door. General Allen was standing on the siding and was looking for Major Goodwin. He had kept track of the train over the telegraph and knew that it was running on a predictable schedule.

Major Goodwin saw him immediately and went outside to meet him. He saluted, shook his hand and told the General that he had a surprise for him. He took him into the train compartment where his family was riding and everyone was happy beyond words. He was not aware they were on the train. He and his wife both burst into tears at the joy of the reunion. The children grabbed him and would not let go.

It was a great day for everyone and the local troops helped unload the horses and freight. In good Army fashion all of the empty cars were cleaned and made ready for the next assignment.

Chalk was tired and he went to his quarters. There was a note pinned on the door that had "urgent" hand written on the front. Inside it read, "call home as soon as you get this message, Wanda". He went into his front room and dialed the number. The phone rang several times and the housekeeper finally answered. He asked if Wanda was home. He told her that the message said he had an urgent concern at home. The housekeeper said that there was bad news. Judge Harmony had died on Thursday morning and his funeral was going on at that very moment. Wanda was at the funeral. Chalk broke down and cried his heart out. He told the housekeeper to tell Wanda he would be home as soon as he could get there.

She said the Judge had been in his quarters at the county courthouse and the bailiff was waiting for him to come to the bench for a trial. He did not come out. The bailiff went to see why and he found him lying on the floor. He had suffered a massive heart attack and was dead.

Chalk went to General Allen's quarters and knocked on the door. The General answered. Chalk was in tears and told him that he had to go home immediately, Carl had died. The General comforted him as best as he could. He told Chalk to set down for a minute and have some coffee. Chalk came in and sat at a small table. The General's wife brought him some hot black coffee and a handkerchief. The General sent for his personal carriage. When it arrived he told Chalk that he was in no condition to ride a horse that far and his carriage was at his disposal as long as he needed it. Chalk thanked him and got in the back of the carriage.

They drove by his quarters and he got some clean clothes. The driver was the same aide that had taken them to Fort Clark and he was already a good friend to Chalk. They started for Bandera and drove at a brisk pace.

The aide already knew the way to the Goodwin ranch and went straight to the ranch house. Upon arrival he pulled up to the front of the house and the housekeeper came out. She said that Wanda and Barbara were at the Harmony ranch comforting Charlie and her sons. He asked the driver to take him there. It was now near dark and the dirt road seemed to be much longer that it had ever been before.

When they arrived he went in the front door and there was a somber and deep sense of sorrow everywhere. Charlie was setting on the living room couch with her oldest son. Wanda and Barbara were in the dining room with friends and the whole house was contained in an atmosphere of grief. Wanda saw Chalk and immediately came to his side. The held each other and openly cried. Carl had been like their Father and they were not going to let go easily. Chalk then went to Charlie's side and hugged her. John and Jim, Carl's sons, came over and hugged Chalk. He was special people to the entire Harmony family and they were all in deep mourning.

Wanda told Chalk that Carl had been buried in a small plot next to the Medina River and a great many people had attended the funeral. The Sheriff's department led the procession from the Lutheran Church in Bandera to the gravesite. She told Chalk, it was now a time to remember all of the good things about Carl and to gather the strength to go on.

As the sun went Chalk, Wanda and Barbara got into the military carriage and slowly rode home. The Goodwin One ranch foreman and a few of the ranch cowboys who had been to the funeral and slowly followed them home. When they arrived they went into the house and took a few minutes to just let their emotions go. Everyone was in tears and the moment was full of pain. Chalk asked the housekeeper to fix a room for the Army aide and make sure everyone was well fed. He and Wanda went for a walk in the dark and talked about a lot of old memories. When they came back their bed was pulled down. Wanda had not noticed that Chalk was wearing the insignia of a Major and when she saw his Army coat was different she was completely surprised.

Chapter 7
Duty and Responsibility

Chalk stayed home for three full days. He Called General Allen on Monday and told him he would be back on Wednesday about noon. General Allen told him that his schedule was fine. He said to have the aide and the carriage stay in Bandera until he was ready to come back.

Wanda was beginning to add obvious weight and was making plans for the new baby. Chalk went with her to the doctor's office and he said everything was going fine. The date was now August 30th and she was going to deliver, if on time, in late December.

Wanda and Chalk spent some time with Charlie and tried to share and help her with her grief. Chalk and Wanda went to see Carl's grave and was saddened at the sight. They took a spray of roses, which were Carl's favorite flower, and placed it on the grave. He knew that his life was greatly the result of Carl's help and would have been a lot different without the continuing sponsorship and support from Carl.

Flowers were still heaped on the unsettled soil on the grave. It was a beautiful gravesite but a place where a quiet and lonesome sadness also was present. Giant cypress trees surrounded the whole area and the many varieties of songbirds were making their many sounds of nature.

Carl was the one individual that Chalk had learned he could always trust when he needed advice. When Chalk had something special to enjoy, he had always made sure that Carl was involved. From here on his decisions were strictly his own and his joy from sharing with Carl was ended.

Monday and Tuesday Chalk visited with his ranch personnel and made sure that everything was going well. The construction at the Goodwin Two was moving along and the buildings were starting to take final shape. The summer heat was intense and the hay fields were getting dry. Rain was needed but the skies were blue and crystal clear. River flowage was way down but there was still plenty water in the "tanks" for all of the livestock.

Wednesday morning Chalk got up and put on his uniform. He had breakfast with Wanda and Barbara and told them he would soon be going to Fort Clark for a few of weeks, possibly longer.

General Allen had asked him to go there and stand in for him for a few days. He knew that the work to be done there was going to be difficult and might take more time. Wanda understood and asked him to call home when he could. Army life was taking away much of his family time and he knew it was not going to be any different for some time to come.

Chalk went out front and the aide had the carriage ready to go. He got in the back and was soon on the road back to Fort Sam Houston. Barbara cried when her Daddy was leaving. The Army aide was a friendly and considerate man and had been a real help in helping the Goodwin family in this most difficult time.

The buggy arrived at Fort Sam and Chalk went to clean up in his quarters.

It was lunchtime and Chalk went to the Officers mess where he ran into General Allen. General Allen told him he had moved his family into an Officer's quarter's house located on the base. Everyone was glad to be back together as a family. He asked Chalk about his family and if there was anything he could do to help? Chalk thanked him for his concern and said everybody was doing as well as could be expected. Then, he brought up the matter of fixing problems at Fort Clark.

The current Fort Clark Base Commander had been recalled to Fort Sam Houston and diplomatically relieved of his command. He had been given an Honorable discharge and told he could go home to Pennsylvania at the Army's expense.

The Garrison Commander had sent a message to Fort Clark putting a Colonel White in the position of "Temporary- Post Commander". This Officer was a man who he knew and he could hold things together until General Allen arrived. General Allen wanted to be on the base by the first of November and was putting a plan together to "recondition" the entire base command. Chalks presence would help this transition and he was a vital part of the plan. General wanted stability, firmness and leadership that had the big picture and future in his vision. Chalk fit this description.

He wanted Chalk to be there for several weeks and support him as he put his plan into effect. The General also knew that Wanda had a new child due in December. He asked Chalk to read his initial restructuring plan and to comment on his approach. He gave him a copy to read and mark up as he saw fit.

The General also had drafted an announcement that was to be posted on the base as soon as Chalk Arrived. It was intended to let every soldier on the base know that the new command would be different and make this Army Post a better operation.

US Army
Fort Clark, Texas

Effective November 1, the following conditions and Post Regulations Are Imposed:

- General Allen will assume command and be there for approximately 24 months, possibly longer. He is the designated Fort Clark Commander and may become the permanent Base Commander.
- The entire post would be closed immediately to everyone except assigned base personnel for the next full month. All personnel coming and going onto or out of the post would require written orders from Senior Commanders and would be strictly monitored by the main gate guards.
- Any soldier who had a current patrol scheduled would be allowed to serve this assignment, but all patrols in the future would be a maximum of 21 days.
- A complete physical inventory of military hardware and supplies would be undertaken. Each man is responsible for having and providing all equipment that was assigned to him. Any missing items must be paid for from the soldier's salary. All enlisted men and Officers are responsible to meet these requirements.
- A fitness review would be performed on every soldier, both enlisted men and officers. Those that are judged to be not qualified for their current assigned duties would be either reassigned to an area where they can meet requirements or will be discharged.
- The Base Military police would visit local communities and assist the help of local police to go to every pawnshop and recover every item that is identifiable as Army property. Any merchant that refuses to surrender these materials and the records as to how he obtained the items will be taken to Civil Court and charged with soliciting and receiving stolen government property. Any involved military personnel will be reported to the base Military Police.
- Any soldiers who had been AWOL or away from the base without clear information as to where he was located

could potentially stand court-marshal. If found guilty they would be given a Dishonorable Discharge.

- All soldiers would be allowed to discuss matters where they have problems with openly with Senior Officers. All subjects were open to discussion and rank was not to be a restriction to not allowing these discussions to be open and frank.

Chalk looked at the document and saw a tightening up of everything. He was in agreement with everything and put a few notes on the edge of the documents.

Chalk wanted to take a blacksmith from Fort Sam Houston to Fort Clark to teach the person assigned to that job to be trained properly. He also wanted to locate a Veterinarian on the base full time to care for the horses.

A serious concern was the lack of respect between the many of the White officers and the Black and Indian troops. Chalk wanted to start programs that were designed to diminish and quickly overcome the worst of these conditions. The first step would be common eating and housing areas. Beyond this the officer ranks needed to include several Black and Indian officers. This would require time but it had to get started or it would never happen.

Chalk went to meet with all his assigned troops and see how the new troops from Fort Knox were fitting in. To his delight everyone was happy and glad to be in Texas. The horses from Kentucky were all in good shape and the train ride had not caused them any problems. The troops were enjoying Mexican food and Texas bar-b-que. They also found adequate places to buy good Kentucky whiskey. Most of the men were southerners and they had little problem with the Texas heat. They liked the local food and especially the nightlife.

General Allen took Chalks notes and read them. He saw a leadership side of Chalk that he had not seen before. He was sincerely looking out for the men. He took the list, with Chalks suggestions attached, and forwarded it on to the Garrison Commander for his review and approval. He was instructed to post the notice in prominent locations so every soldier had access to the information. Chalk left the next morning and was in Fort Clark by nightfall.

General Allen had told Major Goodwin to spend time at home whenever he could between then and October 25th. In simple language, Chalk knew that his presence at Fort Clark was very important and he represented change. General Allen wanted to leave for Fort Clark on that date and needed the time until then to get ready.

Chalk made his presence known on the Fort Clark Post and went home over a weekend to make plans for being gone until it was time for Wanda to deliver the new baby.

Wanda made similar plans to have people with her to care for her normal household chores until the baby came. Her second child was a blessing to her but the experience from having Barbara had given her a lot of background as to what she needed to be expecting.

Chapter 8
A Time of Change

September came and went. October was a month when Wanda was nearing childbirth and Chalk's foremen had his affairs at the ranches in good order. Mrs. Brock was doing a great job of keeping the money moving and the bills paid. Bandera was not a concern for Chalk and he was thankful.

The people who were renting the farm in Missouri contacted Chalk through the bank and asked if he would consider selling. He knew that he was never going to have a need or desire to live there. He had really never become involved with anything concerning the property other than getting the ownership clear and keeping it rented. Mrs. Brock had suggested that the renters pay the rent to the local Bank in Bandera as there would be a better record of the account should he need to take an eviction action. The current renters were over a year overdue on the rent payments. Mrs. Brock and the bank had sent them letters concerning the rent but they had never responded.

Chalk sent them a letter stating that they needed to get the rent current and then make him an offer. They wrote back and said that they had built several buildings, to which they had deducted the cost from the rent, and were responsible for several substantial improvements. They wanted Chalk to give them some consideration for these expenses in the place of rent. Chalk understood the offer but still could not get past the fact that they were way overdue. In his mind he felt that it might be reasonable to consider some adjustment, but not to agree until he had more information.

He called them and had a frank discussion about a price. They offered him $100,000 cash. He asked them to get an appraisal before he gave them an answer. Chalk was willing to pay for the appraisal. When the appraisal came back it was over $300,000. The local community had nearly surrounded much of the property and values were way above what they were just a year ago. Chalk called them and asked them to justify the difference in value from the current offer in price. The land was obviously in a prime location that was growing rapidly. The renter's offer was way to low to be considered as fair. Nothing happened for a week. About a week later he got a phone call from a Real Estate company that had been involved with the Appraisal Company. They told him the appraisal was doctored by a crooked real estate company who really wanted to make a big profit and was not accurate.

They said the property was really worth substantially more that the estimated value and wanted to buy it immediately for $500,000. Chalk called his renters and told them what was happening. They said that they could not afford any more and would be moving to a new farm they could afford. Chalk called the Real Estate Company and said, send me a check. The deal was closed.

General Allen and Chalk talked on the phone frequently and both were glad to have some limited time with their families. Fort Clark problems were commonly being discussed. The upcoming changes were constantly being reviewed and discussed as to the expected impacts. They both agreed that they were going to see resistance. However, the current situation had to be corrected.

On October 22nd Chalk had gone home for a weekend and he planned to stop at "Fort Sam" on the way back to Fort Clark. He was home overnight and he left the next morning for San Antonio. When he arrived he saw that there were several wagons setting in the area where railroad cars were normally loaded. They were marked FORT CLARK MATERIALS. He went to see General Allen and caught up on the plans for the next 30 days. General Allen told him the Chalk's report concerning the level of many supplies at Fort Clark was being answered. The current supply of food, medical supplies and spare uniforms were major concerns.

The wagons had replenishments on board and were going to be loaded onto rail cars the next morning. Chalk and General Allen were going to travel on a train with the supplies and show up on the post as a team. General Allen wanted Chalk and himself to be comprehended as Officers that were concerned for the well being of the troops.

The next morning several flat bed rail cars and two boxcars pulled into the base siding. The wagons were loaded onto flat cars and strapped down. There was a complete blacksmith shop on one of the wagons and two qualified, seasoned, "horsemen" were going to Fort Clark to assist in rebuilding the blacksmith operation. Additional horses, hay and horse feed were loaded onto the boxcars.

At dawn an engine pulled into the rail yard and hooked onto the cars. Everyone boarded and the train pulled out. The locomotive was going all the way to Fort Clark and never slowed down. The train arrived in 3 hours. The cars were pulled onto a siding on the base and the local troops quickly unloaded the wagons. Horses were attached to the wagons for the final leg of the journey. Each wagon had been given an assigned destination on the base.

General Allen went to the temporary Commander's office and was warmly received. Chalk was by his side. A full base muster was scheduled for the next morning and a special detail was assigned to rope off the main parade ground. Everyone had a good meal and went to bed.

The next morning the entire base was up early. The new food supplies were already in the mess halls and the soldiers were all offered a great breakfast with fresh bacon and eggs. There was plenty and everyone was told to eat all they wanted. A full base muster was scheduled for 9 AM. The base carpenters had setup a makeshift stage on flat bed Army wagons to hold the people who were scheduled to speak. Every platoon was asked to bring their duty flags and was assigned a location on the parade ground. Everyone showed up on the announced schedule and took their position.

At about 10 minutes after 9 the Army speakers and senior officers arrived on horseback. The Mayor from Uvalde was also on the stage. A large new American Flag was flying on the parade ground flagpole. The dignitaries went ushered onto the stage and everyone was waiting in silence for the program to begin. The Base Band was attempting to play the National Anthem. The music was symbolic but way off key. The Temporary Commander opened the event with a sincere welcome to everyone. He them asked the Base Chaplain to deliver, A Catholic priest named Dominick to deliver a prayer. He preyed in both English and in Spanish.

The Chaplin finished his prayer and sat down. The temporary Commander then stood up and spoke to everyone. He informed them the Army command at Fort Sam Houston had assigned a new Base Commander to take his place and this meeting was an official change of base command. He thanked all of them for the support they had give him and for the improved image that the base was beginning to develop. He then introduced General Allen as the new base Commanding officer.

General Allen took the podium and his first words were to recognize the service that the outgoing temporary Commander had given. Then the mood of his speaking changed.

General Allen told the troops that the Command in Fort Sam Houston had major plans for this base and from past reports they had determined that Fort Clark was not ready to accept this new responsibility. He said his job was to correct any problems that were present and to bring the standard of Army Post disciplines up to the level that the Army requires to successfully meet new programs.

He then went into several base issues that were going to be addressed. He said that troop conduct, both on the base and off the base was a current concern.

He then told everyone that less than expected performance, as a soldier, both on base and off base, would not be tolerated. He informed everyone that every soldier on the base was going to be evaluated for fitness. He added that leaving and entering the base was going to be controlled, effectively immediately.

He added, "I am aware that several of you men have dogs that occasionally like to have them ride with you. I am also aware that prior rules were not focused on taking care of your personal animals. I personally find this disgusting. He added, I personally like dogs and I am ordering the post cooks to make any leftover food that is healthy for dogs, available on a first come, first served basis. A dog is man's best friend and when serving your nation a dog is a wonderful companion."

To further soften the impact of his statements he added that every good soldier was going to be respected and had nothing to fear. He then added a strong and pointed statement that the Officers and NCO's on the base were all going to be evaluated first. The troops were all quiet.

General Allen added that every man had a right to good food, respect and good equipment. He brought up the concern that there was missing government property showing up in local pawnshops and anyone responsible for this situation was going to be prosecuted.

From there, he recognized the contributions of the Army Calvary in controlling the many problems in the western frontier. He said the Army was proud of their record and this base was expected to carry this tradition forward. He addressed the special contributions made by "Buffalo Soldiers".

He discussed the war that was going on in Europe and said this base was going to be involved if our country has to get involved. He justified his new Base management program based on this impending situation.

Before he closed the ceremony he introduced the visitingmayor and asked him to say a few words. He gladly accepted the invitation. His words were simple. He wanted the Army soldiers to feel welcome in his town and past problems would be overlooked so long as they were not repeated. He also told the troops that General Allen had told him to contact him personally should any problems occur.

General Allen then closed the ceremony and asked everyone to consider what they could do to support this program and to stand ready for whatever situations and needs might come. He said the new rules document would remain posted in key locations and told everyone that they were now subject to meeting these requirements. He added, these rules are fair and designed to make this Post and You a better part of the Army.

The speech was finished. The change of command was now completed. All of the personnel on the stage left the area on horses. The parade ground cleared slowly and everyone knew that change was at hand.

At noon General Allen met with a delegation of local area Judges and Law Officers who had been invited to a special base luncheon. The luncheon was held in the Officer's mess area. He addressed them as friends and called them his partners in building and improving the quality of life in the local community.

He told them that a detachment of Army Military Police would be coming to each near-by town to recover any Army property that may be in the hands of the pawnshops or other unauthorized people. He also told them that any soldier that was in trouble in a local community would probably stand a military trial, on base, for the crimes and conduct problems they caused off base. He softened his stand a little and added.

Let's got the old habits and problems put out of our minds, forget past issues and find new ground where we can and move forward together. He promised that any new problems would be brought to his attention. He assured them that

Military Justice would be applied and each problem would be dealt with immediately.

This meeting was a positive start to fixing the image on the base within the community. The response from the community leaders was very open and positive. In early December the base did a review of incidents reported from the community and the number was zero.

General Allen was considered a hardnosed Commander by some and his respect for the military image, both outside and inside the base was being rebuilt.

Major Goodwin was working behind the scenes to assist with the implementation of changes. He took the new blacksmiths to the stable and introduced them to the Corporal blacksmith he had talked with before. The young man was still struggling. They sat up a side operation to help reduce the backlog of work. The new equipment made a great improvement in the operation and everybody was pleased. Major Goodwin got the Corporal to the side and told him he would receive training to better enable him to become better at his job. His words were most welcome.

Chalk was put in charge of all base housing and food services. The mess hall had been segregated both physically and in spirit by not allowing Black and Indian soldiers to eat in the same area of the room as white soldiers. They also had a separate, poorly supplied, food serving line. The Officers mess was way overstocked and food was spoiling before it could be used. Both situations were corrected immediately.

This "Buffalo Line" food serving line had never been supplied with the same quality or supply of food as were other serving lines. Chalk ordered all food services to be supplied to all enlisted soldiers on one equal basis using one mixed personnel serving line. Food quality and serving amounts were to be adjusted to allow everyone all they wanted to eat.

He had one of the older enlisted men's barracks evacuated, torn down and rebuilt. It had holes in the roof and was leaking like a young river. The men were forced to use an outdoor outhouse located far from the barracks and bathe in an outdoor shower area. The floor was dirt as the original wood floor had rotted away and was never replaced.

Major Goodwin hired several local contractors to do the work and everyone soon had running water, both hot and cold. He also added new heating and a recreation and lounge area to the building. After the first unit was completed he had the base housing office assign a platoon to live there that was made up of Black, White and Indian troops. The NCO's in charge were also assigned to live in these same general quarters.

Other base housing units were in similar conditions. Chalk immediately scheduled most of these structures to be either torn down or re-conditioned. The troops saw this as a real positive move and did a lot of the work to get the housing units ready for rebuilding. Completely new facilities were also being added to get ready for an influx of new troops. The base troop count was scheduled to grow quickly. Unfit soldiers within the current ranks were being identified they were quickly being removed from the Army.

New base policies and personnel reviews went on for several days and the impact was significant. General Allen was a man the troops had initially considered as a negative man. Over a few days the general attitude started to change. The base started to look better and the personnel, both enlisted and commissioned, were recognizing that this was an Army post, not a place to get a free ride on society. A time of real change was at hand.

Chapter 9
Changes and Results

In early December General Allen had all Senior Officers report to his office to discuss the status for their responsible organizations. Over 50% of the old staff was gone and the new Senior officers were composed of men who were previously serving in lesser roles or had been brought in from other bases. The new commanding officers all had positive fitness reviews were all upscale and positive. The respect for every soldier and for the Army military reputation was starting to show. General Allen congratulated them for giving their support and gave them recognition for being involved with the improvements that were being made.

Like clockwork, the General requested that he be shown the new living situations. He also requested that he be put into situations where he could make his presence known as a General that knows his troops.

About a week later The General called all of the Officers and NCO's into a special meeting and had a real informal meeting to discuss Post psychology for the future. He said he had been watching and listening to the officers and he was concerned that team morale building in many of the operational base areas was going far too slow.

In the next few words he asked if anyone knew the difference between the words "I', "Me", and " "My"? He wanted them to see that all of these words were normally associated with people who were self centered and normally not good team builders. He just looked at everyone for about two minutes and said that he wanted everyone to think about how they talked to subordinates and how they viewed their troops in general.

He added, "I have been listening to all of you since I arrived and we are not all of the same attitudes, yet, but we will be soon." He stated that he had personally witnessed several

officers using these positive words often as they spoke with the troops. Then he added, some of us have not been gone beyond this level of communication.

In about five more minutes he put up a big chart that had the words "We", "Our", and "Us" printed on the first section. In a few minutes he asked the men to think about how these words were different but transmitted a better, more powerful message.

His next topic was team building and Military Leadership. He cautioned everyone to listen and to think about the past month and how they were addressing their troops. A few men were asked to discuss this topic and to not be ashamed if they were not doing the best job. That was considered excusable at this time. The message was very clear; the topic of troop team building and respect was going to be a major theme in General Allen's base overhaul.

He then went on to remark that an Officer should not ask a soldier to do something that he himself would not do. He told them in a stern and strong voice, "These same men you teach to march and ride may be asked to fight to the death by your words". They deserve your respect and consideration for them as American soldiers. The meeting ended with a positive tone. Everyone applauded the General.

Chalk had been talking to Wanda back home and it was obvious that her time was close and she was missing him. On December 16th he went into see the General and told him that he needed to go home. The new baby was near and his family needed him right now. General Allen immediately agreed with Chalk's request. He also told him that his efforts in the base repair program were working and the troops appreciated what he was doing. The troops had quickly grown to respect Chalk as a man of character and an Officer that understood how to handle troops. General Allen was also anxious to go home and see his family but his wife was not pregnant.

Chalk checked out a good Army horse from the stable and rode home on Saturday morning. When he got there his whole organization of people was anxious to see him. The happiest was Wanda. Barbara had been growing and was ready for the arrival of a new baby. She was also eagerly anticipating the coming of Santa Clause. The ranch house had been decorated for Christmas and had never looked so good.

Chalk put Barbara on the front of his saddle and rode into Bandera. They went to see Mrs. Brock and then to see Charlie. Wanda was too far-gone into the baby-bearing event to ride that far. They were all glad to see him and had missed his ever-present smile. Barbara was all excited and had a list of things for Santa to bring. Chalk was proud of her and took her all over his ranches from his horse. The Goodwin ranches were all very busy. The cowboys were looking forward to a little time off at Christmas. The year was about over and the profits were good.

On the evening of December 24th Wanda told Chalk it was time and he sent for the Doctor. The Doctor arrived and within an hour there was a new "Male" Goodwin on the ranch. Chalk was happy to have a son and Wanda had gone through the birth with no problems. They had already decided to name a son "Carl" in respect for their relationship with Carl Harmony. Little Carl was healthy and soon was asleep in his crib.

The word of Carl's arrival spread quickly. The happiest to hear of the new arrival and the name selected was Charlie. On Christmas afternoon she had her sons take her to the Goodwin ranch house to see Carl. Jim and John had one son each but had never named any of them after their Dad.

Charlie was growing weak from a sickness that was unknown to the local doctors. She was not able to ride in a buggy for very long and had to have a person with her most of the time. Her sons made sure she was always well cared for and as comfortable as possible. Old age, poor health and a failing body were all working on her physical condition and she knew that her time was short. Charlie passed away in the following spring and was buried by Carl. Her funeral was as large as Carl's and had just as many flowers.

Chalk called General Allen who had gone home to San Antonio for Christmas and told him the news. He was happy for Chalk and told him that the news would be passed on to his men.

In January Chalk had to go back to Fort Clark. He rode back on the Army horse that he had ridden home and arrived on the evening of January 5th. The weather was raw and a wind from the north was blowing a light snow shower over the trail. He was pleased to see the new attitude and the new tighter passage procedures at the front gate. When he got to his quarters his troops had built a fire in the stove and the room was warm. There was a large box of baby gifts from the enlisted men for his new son. This was not a standard practice in the past. Officers and enlisted men had seen each other as living in a different zone of life. Chalk went to the enlisted men's barracks and thanked all of the men for their thoughtfulness. They all thanked him for his efforts in fixing the barracks and having good heat stoves installed. They were all much more happy than they were the preceding January.

Major Goodwin was excited about the progress and recognized that the new changes in personnel management were working. General Allen arrived back the next day and saw the same positive changes.

Over the holidays the local Sheriffs and a detachment of Military Police had visited every pawnshop in Brackettville and in Uvalde. They recovered 17 saddles, 12 Army pistols and a large amount of other Army owned items. One pawnshop merchant was not willing to surrender the items he was taken into custody. The Sheriff arrested him on the spot and visibly put him in jail. He was charged with accepting stolen Military owned goods and scheduled to be put on trial.

The new troop quarters were taking shape and the troops were getting acclimated to living with mixed races. The food facilities were quickly and quietly adjusting to a non-segregation facility. The troops were not complaining. They were eating better and were not being placed into class structures and sleeping on dirt floors.

General Allen requested a status on troop fitness reviews. He was seeing a change in attitude and he wanted to see the underlying changes in the troop structure profiles. He saw that several of the old guard Officers were gone, they had voluntarily resigned or taken early retirement. Several key openings existed in the base staff organization chart.

Enlisted men were also being removed from the ranks. The drunks were the first to go then the men who were simply not qualified to be soldiers. The remaining troops were basically loyal and qualified to serve. They just needed training and leadership to point them in the right direction. All of these changes were positive and a new and better base attitude was growing.

Chalk was proud to have been a part of this change. He believed he had made a difference. He was also comfortable that the Army was going to be ready to accept additional troops and to provide an Army ready to meet any new demands.

For the next three years Chalk was spending time at home, at Fort Clark and at Fort Sam Houston. His life was settling down to a routine and he was happy. General Allen was considered a hero and was retained as the base commander at Fort Clark for a little over 3 years. He took retirement in 1910 and moved to a small home that he had bought in Boerne, Texas. His wife had moved there 2 years earlier and was raising their children in that community. He had bought 20 head of longhorn cattle from Chalk and started a small cattle ranch. He also bought several good horses, just to ride and play with.

Chalk was still assisting with the daily business of troop food service, base housing, basic recruit training. He never wanted to give up running the horse section of the operation and this part of his job kept him interested in staying in the Army. His methods and approaches were seen as a model for other Army bases and soon he was being sent to give speeches at military installations all over the western United States. His reputation was good and his stature was growing. Chalk was requested to come speak to several graduating classes at various colleges. He saw this a recruiting duty assignment and encouraged young men to consider military careers as a future. His efforts were productive and after every graduation there were always several young men lined up to become soldiers.

Another part of his duties was doing base inspections and fitness reviews. His insight into the inner working of a military base were respected and sought after by the top Generals in Washington. He always wrote reports that were clear, very honest about the situation and constructive for adding improvements. His leadership and keen ability to seek out the real status quickly were rare.

The military was not the only element that had participated in causing trouble in the community. Shortly after the change of command was over a young lady showed up at the main gate wanting to see a soldier named Homer Moore. Homer was an enlisted man who was currently on patrol and he was not available. The lady was pregnant and told the gate guard that Homer Moore was the baby's father and she wanted him to pay for her medical expenses. She was about to have the baby and refused to leave until she got satisfaction from someone.

The guard knew that he had to do something but he did not know what. He called the security office and had an Officer come over and talk with the lady. The Officer questioned her and she claimed that Homer had been her close friend about a year prior and he and her were planning to get married. She claimed that the baby was the result of their close relationship.

The Officer took all of the information and told her that the base would check into the matter and let her know. She was told to leave an address where she could be reached. She refused to leave and insisted that she be given a place to stay immediately. The Officer took her to the security office and called his superior. It was cold outside and a lady that was near term full pregnancy was not someone to argue with.

The Officer in charge of all base security called the platoon office where Corporal Moore was assigned. He confirmed that he was on a patrol and would not be back for over two weeks. He also found out that this was his first patrol and he had only been stationed at this base for about 2 months. Prior to that he was in Kentucky and had never been to Texas prior to this assignment. The Officer knew immediately that this was a scheme to get the military to pay for someone's baby being born. There was no way this soldier could have fathered this child.

He escorted her back to the gate and told the lady that there was no way this scheme was going to work. He told her to leave the base immediately or he would have the County Sheriff come get her. She left at once.

The Senior Security Officer started checking back into the hospital history and learned that young pregnant women from the local community had pulled this scheme several time before. They would get a soldier's name for someone and wait until it was about time to deliver the child and show up at the front gate. In the past the gate guard would send the lady to the base hospital and she would stay there until the baby was born. The soldier in question would deny any responsibility but that was a useless discussion after the birth was over with. This never happened again.

In 1911 Chalk saw a rapid change happening in the Military. The new approach for moving troops and fighting war was rapidly changing from using horses toward gasoline-powered trucks, tanks and a new flying machine called an airplane.

The historic practice of using horses as the primary source for Army field service was now beginning to fade away.

The orders for horses from the Goodwin Ranch were becoming less and the ranch was becoming over staffed. Chalk tried to adjust by increasing the number of cattle and putting them on the horse ranch. He also was offering prime quality horses to the local cowboys at bargain prices. It was clear to Chalk, his time as a major horse supplier was about over.

In 1912 Chalk went to see the Commander at Fort Sam Houston and told him he had given the military his best efforts and the time had come when he wanted to resign his commission, leave his military career and go home. He was now an old man and his time to rest was near. His request was understood but the General asked him to wait a week for approving his decision. Chalk agreed. The Commander knew that Chalk was looking forward to going back to his ranch and to his family.

He had no reason to deny his request. What he wanted was some time to put together a fitting final tribute and thank you to Major Goodwin from the Military. On March 1st, 1912 Chalk was requested to report to the Base Commanders office for a formal, honorary Military Discharge ceremony. He was told he should bring his family. This was not going to be a normal discharge event.

The day arrived and Chalks entire family had spent the night before on the base. They went to the Commander's office where they were greeted and taken to a large meeting hall that was located on the base. Chalk was asked to sit on a stage with the Base Commanding Staff. The Brigade Commander, who was a 3 star General, stood up and welcomed everyone.

He then took out a proclamation signed personally by President Woodrow Wilson awarding Chalk the Honor of a Special Congressional Medal for his efforts and support in developing the current Horse Calvary system.

He was also awarded a lifetime commission as a Full Colonial in the Army.

All of the troops in attendance cheered Chalk. Many of them knew him personally and many had made the trip from Fort Clark just to be at this event.

Colonel Goodwin's family was invited to join him on the stage. They were also applauded. The Base Commander then looked to his right and now retired General Allen came onto the stage with a large bouquet of flowers for Wanda. Chalk's children were both given a smaller bouquet of flowers.

The General asked Chalk if has anything to say? He stood up, looked at all of the people in the area and tears came into his eyes. He regained his composure and said from his heart," My Army experience has been a major highlight in my life. It has also been a point of pride for my Family and for my people back at the Goodwin ranches and the troops at Fort Clark. We all gave it our best efforts and these efforts have been returned many times over in every way that could be imagined".

He directed a special thank you to General Allen for his support and for the opportunities and friendship he had allowed him to enjoy. He closed by saying, "Thank you" from the bottom of my heart and God Bless the Army and this Country."

The meeting was closed and a party was held in Chalks honor. Everyone had a good time and the party was closed at 1000: PM when the Fort Sam Houston Military band played of the Battle Hymn of The Republic. A special horse drawn carriage was made available to take Chalk and his family back to a guesthouse on the base.

The next morning Wanda, Chalk and their children were given a ride home to Bandera in the Commanders personal carriage. They were welcomed by all of the cowboys and people who worked at the Goodwin ranches. When the carriage pulled away from the ranch Chalk recognized that his days as a soldier were now behind him for good. He was more than a little saddened by the thought.

The housekeeper and the ranch cook had put a big party together for Chalk and his family. They had a full afternoon of greetings old friends and party activities. Chalk was home to stay and he was now a famous person. He had served his country and was proud of his contributions.

The next day Chalk took his family to visit Carl and Charlie's graves. They brought flowers and a small oak tree that was planted just above the gravesites. This visit made everyone remember what they had lost and what they had gained.

Chalk had always had a special spot in his heart for the old wagon that once served as the supply wagon for the wagon train he worked on when he and Wanda came to Texas. This wagon had been his most prized memory from that experience and it still was stored on his ranch. When he came home he saw that the ranch cowboys had moved it to the gate by his ranch and planted purple sage along side of the front and back. Chalk was happy to see this old "schooner" in such an important place. Over the years there had been new wheels, new sideboards and a new tongue added. But, it was still the same old wagon to him

He took a long look at it as he drove into the ranch and knew that it was a symbol of Texas and the western economy that he had helped build.

Chapter 10
The Best Part of Life

The next few years were spent in managing the ranches and in adjusting to the changes that came with a constantly declining demand for horses. Wanda and Chalk took advantage of the new passenger trains that were now running all the way across the country. The traveled west and enjoyed the warmer California coastal weather in the winter months. The second year they went traveled to California, Chalk and Wanda bought a second home, for vacations in the hills near San Diego. They also traveled to Washington DC to see the nation's capital and to meet several old military friends.

In 1912, while Chalk and Wanda were in California Becky Brock had a heart attack in Bandera. She never recovered and was dead the next day. Her funeral was simple. She was buried in the Harmony family burial plot. Jim had sent a telegraph to Chalk about her passing but it was not delivered for almost a week. Wanda and Chalk were deeply saddened.

The War in Europe was destined to draw the United States Army into the conflict. Our country was still posturing itself to be ready when the time came. The Army was learning how to use the new mechanical approaches to fielding an Army. The "old reliable element", horses, were still the backbone of the Army. Many of the Calvary's horses were wearing the branded numbers from the Goodwin Ranch. The efforts the Goodwin Ranch had made to provide these horses were bearing fruit. Chalks efforts in the Army to train men and to assure that the men were available when needed had been very successful. Chalk and his Family were all proud.

In 1920 Chalk took stock of his holdings and decided the time to adjust things for the future was at hand. He wrote a will that left most of his personal wealth to his immediate family. He also left a generous portion to those that had been his faithful employees for many years.

The Goodwin Two ranch property was cut into smaller parcels and several of his management level employees were given land to use as they saw fit. These gifts were made with one binding stipulation. None of it was to ever be given, sold or traded to people who were not willing to serve in the military of our country. Fathers were encouraged not sell the land but to leave the land to their children. Chalk and Wanda wanted the tradition of being a Texas cowboy to go on and not be lost into history.

Barbara Goodwin had entered The University of Texas and was about to graduate with a degree in teaching. She wanted to travel to Cincinnati, Ohio and do graduate work at the school where her mother had attended. Carl was not impressed with being a cowboy but wanted to be a businessman. He had was still to young to do a man's work and worked with the local bank sweeping floors keeping the place tidy. This job was not much to brag about but he was meeting people and learning how to be a young man.

Carl was interested in a career in some similar field. He respected his father's career and liked the idea of travel and excitement that a soldier can experience. He also was very interested in the Army's opportunities. The advent of the airplane and the activity at San Antonio in developing a pilot training base really got under his skin. It was obvious that both children were not going to be dedicated to maintaining the ranch in the future. Carl and Wanda understood each of them and were not going to pressure either of them toward a career they had not wanted.

Chalk sold most of the ranch cattle to Jim and John Harmony for very reasonable prices. The ranch equipment was also sold. Chalk kept his home and a few barns and the garden plot. He had a surveyor cut the largest portions of the ranch into smaller marketable size areas. The plots were sold to local cowboys. Cowboys who had worked on the ranch got first buying priority status at reduced prices.

Chalk and Wanda had not discussed the wagon trip to Texas very much after they got married. Chalk always knew that Wanda was deeply in love with her first husband and that she had a strong memory of the times they had enjoyed in Ohio. That part of her life was long past, but the closure was never really complete. Walter Anderson had been buried by the trail in north Texas and Wanda had never completely forgotten him.

On a cool Sunday evening, Chalk took Wanda for a walk in the cemetery where Carl had been buried. He brought up the fact that her first husband, Walter Anderson, was buried by the trail in a grave that was marked by a stack of stones. Chalk also recalled the funeral for his Mom where Digger Maggard had put her coffin in the ground behind the old home place.

He asked Wanda if she would like to go find Walter's gravesite and have a permanent stone with his name carved into it placed there? He said that this was only fitting for a man who had been so much a part of her life many years ago. Wanda was surprised at this offer but quickly recognized that this was a real part of her life she had enjoyed and wanted to keep in her memory.

About a week later Chalk and Wanda got out their best traveling clothes, hooked up the buggy and went north toward Waco. The old wagon trail was hardly there any longer but after searching for a couple of days the discovered Walter's grave. It still had the stones on top of the dirt and the wooden sign was there, but was not readable any longer. It had fallen to the ground a long time ago and the wood was deteriorating.

Weeds and cactus were growing in between the rocks and a few small yellow wildflowers had grown up next to the grave. They stood in silence when then realized they had found the grave and both of them cried a little. Chalk took Wanda in his arms and comforted her. In about 20 minutes they decided to go into Waco and have a rock cutter make a proper headstone for the grave. They wanted to see it installed prior to going back home to Bandera. They got a hotel room for three days while the stone was made ready.

When the stone was finished Wanda went to the local Lutheran Church and asked the preacher to go with them and say a few words over the grave. Walter and Wanda had been married in a Lutheran Church and her former husband was a religious man. A minister had never been involved with the funeral. When Walter died Carl Harmony had asked the wagon train members to prey with him and then they all moved on. Wanda wanted to bring a Christian closure as a last act of respect.

The headstone was loaded onto the stonecutter's wagon and the Goodwin carriage followed it to the church. At the church the preacher got on the front seat of the stonecutter's wagon and they proceeded to the grave. The trip took almost two hours. There was really no trail to the grave's location and the wagon had to cut across several fields to get there. A new trail had been built about 200 yards away and the old one was mostly grown up with weeds. Upon arrival the stonecutter, Chalk and the Preacher took turns digging a suitable hole in the hard earth to locate the headstone. They also cleared a few cactus plants to outline the top of the grave. The headstone was then placed into the hole and neatly backfilled with the earth that had been removed.

The preacher said a few Christian words and asked the Lord to watch over this spot and the soul that had departed the body that was there. In about 10 minutes it was all over. Chalk gave the preacher a generous amount of money for his time. Everyone got back into their buggy and wagon and started for home. Wanda was now at peace about Walter's passage and ready to add closure to this part of her life. Chalk was happy for her.

Their children, Barbara and Carl were each given plots of land on the Goodwin One ranch and ownership of several business properties that Chalk had accumulated. They were also to be provided with large amounts of money that they would be free for them to use as they chose.

Carl and Wanda set up a scholarship program at the University of Texas to assist students who were in need and were studying to become teachers. They remained anonymous as to the donors. They also donated money to the Texas Peace Officer's Association to help provide for the families of fallen Officers.

In the spring of 1922 Chalk came down with pneumonia and passed away quickly. He passed away in his bedroom at the Goodwin Ranch. His funeral, at his request, was simple and at Wanda's request only the family was in attendance. She did contact General Allen and told him Chalk had often talked about having a military funeral. General Allen saw to the matter and had a small platoon on men dispatched to the ranch to do the services. Chalk's casket was a common wood military issue item. Wanda did not want to have a large group of people to deal with as she was growing frail and had a hard time walking. Jim and John Harmony asked Wanda to consider burying Chalk next to their parents in the Harmony family cemetery. Wanda was honored and accepted the offer.

Wanda followed him in death about 8 months later. She had contracted an internal sickness and it was not clear as to the exact cause. The doctors thought it was failing kidneys. Her funeral was equally simple and private.

Chalk and Wanda had come a long way from Ohio and Kentucky to Texas. They were both resting next to Carl and Charlie in the small cemetery next to the Medina river riverbank. They had been the best of friends in life and would rest close to each other in ground that was permanently a part of both of their family heritages. There had been a lot of stops along the way and every one of them had been an exciting experience. Each one was a special part of the spirit and force that was working toward building the character of the American West.

This story is dedicated to the memories of the Men, Women and Children that were all so vital in the development of the American pioneering image in the West. Times change, people are replaced by new generations and still, time goes on. However, we all have roots in people just like all of these hardy folks. We need to appreciate what we have today from their efforts that were so freely given by our ancestors. People like Chalk and Wanda taught the rest of us how to live, and in the end how to die and leave the world a better place than it was when we entered life.

We all also need to keep contributing to the wholesome things in life that will be the hand me down legacy to the Country we live in. These will be the real and most lasting gifts we can ever leave to our children and grandchildren.

LaVergne, TN USA
03 November 2009
162828LV00003B/5/A

9 781425 934347